Death in the High City

A Butler and Bartorelli Mystery

Val Culley

East Wind Publishing

All the characters and events portrayed in this work are fictitious

Death in the High City

A Butler and Bartorelli Mystery

East Wind Publishing

ISBN: 978-0-9929443-1-5

For my mother, Alice Joan Sansome,
who loves Piazza Vecchia.

1

When you first arrive in a new place you are acutely aware of everything that is strange or different about it.

It was mild here, muggy even, compared to the crisp September morning Kate Butler had left behind her in England. There was a strange smell in the atmosphere outside the airport she couldn't identify. It was pleasant though, perhaps the scent of a bush, or some flowers that were unfamiliar to her.

The scenery was like no part of Italy she had ever been in before. Now she was on the bus she could see through the windows that the mountains in the distance had snow on the tops, and yet there were flowers growing at the side of the road and lush, green fields stretching out in every direction.

The neat houses reminded her of alpine chalets and did not look at all Italian. Soon they passed other houses grouped more closely together and interesting-looking shops and restaurants. She saw that they were running alongside the railway line and when the bus pulled up outside the station she joined the crowd getting off, lifted her case down on to the pavement and set off to wheel it to her hotel.

It was late afternoon and people were hurrying about their business, coming out of work, going shopping or meeting up with friends in bars. She had bought a map at the airport to help her find the hotel and was able to make her way purposefully down the main thoroughfare, feeling as though she was part of the rush hour.

Then she stopped abruptly in the middle of the pavement seeing the Città Alta ahead of her in the skyline for the first time. There was no mistaking

Bergamo's famous high city. The afternoon sun shone on towers and cupolas that seemed to float among the puffs of white cloud. It looked like something out of a fairytale, better than any of the pictures she had ever seen of it. She was sure she had seen it described somewhere as the most arresting view in all Italy.

She stared at the skyline with fascination, but also with a feeling of dread, because she knew that it was somewhere up there, in that beautiful city, that her cousin Sophie had died and soon she would have to go there herself to visit the place where it had happened.

Her Aunt Edna had been rendered incapable by grief at the loss of her daughter and was depending on her. She had begged Kate to go out to Bergamo as soon as possible to try to find something, anything at all, that would help her make sense of the tragedy.

Although it was September and the summer holidays were over, Kate had been unable to get a room in the small hotel in the Città Alta that her aunt had recommended. But she had booked the earliest available flight to Bergamo Caravaggio airport and had found a hotel near the railway station for the first night. She had arranged to move the next day to the Città Alta, to the hotel where Sophie had stayed when she first arrived in Bergamo.

When she had received the call from Adam Leighton, the manager of Aunt Edna's nursing home, to let her know Sophie had died, he had said her cousin had been found dead in bed by her landlady.

She knew Sophie had been staying in Bergamo while carrying out research for a book she was planning to write about the composer Gaetano Donizetti. She was not aware her cousin had been suffering any health problems and had therefore been stunned by the news.

Sophie's late father, Henry Westmullen, was Kate's uncle. He had also been a writer and a historian and had already been in his mid-forties when he married Edna, a wealthy and generous woman, who had happily funded the restoration of the somewhat run-down Hampton House, the Westmullen family home.

Kate's mother was Henry's younger sister, but had been the first to marry and have a child. Edna had adored Kate from the moment she was born. Sophie had come along, much to the delight of Henry and Edna, a few years later. But although Kate had tried, she had never been able to get close to her younger cousin. Precocious and strong-minded little Sophie had always seemed to keep her at arm's length.

Now Kate was about to start digging into her personal life. Ironically, she was going to get to know more about Sophie now she was dead than she had ever managed to do while she was alive.

She could see a sign for her hotel further along the street and soon recognised the exterior from its picture on the internet. As she wheeled her case into the immaculate reception area the air conditioning came as a relief, but she felt sticky and untidy as she checked in, against the backdrop of shining marble tiles and white statues.

After signing a form and leaving her passport with the man behind the desk, she took her case to her room and was glad to be able to have a quick shower and dress in lighter clothes before going out again.

Guided by her map she walked in the direction of

the station for the funicular railway that transported passengers up and down to the Città Alta. By now the street was full of people out for the *passeggiata*, the evening stroll popular with Italians before dinner, and Kate felt more cheerful in the lively atmosphere.

She had bought a bus ticket at the airport that entitled her to unlimited travel for the first three days and when she showed it to the driver standing by the barrier at the station, he waved her through to the small, orange-coloured train waiting next to the steps. She was quickly carried up the steep hillside to the Città Alta and only a few minutes later was following her fellow passengers out of the station into a small square.

It was as though she had travelled back in time compared with the more modern Città Bassa down below. Tall medieval buildings lined each side of the square and at street level there were quaint-looking shops and bars behind the stone porticoes.

Kate knew from the map that the street where Sophie had lived was off the square to the left and immediately began making her way up the hill towards the apartment building.

She could tell by the house numbers that she was getting close and soon found herself at the ornate, wrought iron gates of the old palazzo where Sophie had rented an apartment. She could see into the courtyard, where there were neatly trimmed shrubs in heavy terracotta pots and two old grey statues that appeared to be peering over the white marble balustrade at the Città Bassa, the lower town.

Kate looked at the names alongside the small brass call buttons next to the gates. She saw an Italian name and then surprisingly below it she saw that there was another English name as well as the one she was looking for, Westmullen. She reached out to press the button but then let her hand fall limply to her side again. There was no point, she thought sadly, because Sophie would not answer.

She looked at the list again, guessing that the Italian name must belong to the woman who looked after the building. She was a sort of concierge, her aunt had said. Maybe she should start by talking to her.

Kate stood on the pavement in front of the apartment building, suddenly aware that she was not prepared for any of what might be about to happen. In the rush there had been no time to plan what she was going to say or how she would gently pave the way towards asking the questions she needed answers for.

She had not had a moment to spare since receiving the bad news and the summons to the nursing home to see her aunt. But now she was here she felt uncertain about what to do next. If the concierge did not speak much English it was up to Kate to speak to her in Italian. But she might not welcome Kate asking her about things that presumably she had already been asked about by the police. Maybe it would be better to prepare what she was going to say in Italian before she went rushing in. After all, as a journalist, she would always plan her questions if she had to do an important interview.

At the end of the street there was a turning leading to Piazza Vecchia, which she knew was the main square in the Città Alta. She set off to walk in the direction of the square but stopped at the first bar she came to, sat down at a table outside and ordered a glass of wine.

Opening the notebook she always carried in her bag, she started to prepare some questions in Italian, knowing she would have to tread very carefully because she had no idea what had taken place in the apartment or whether the concierge might have played any part in it. But she was determined to make an attempt at interviewing the concierge for Aunt Edna's sake, to try to find out anything that might help her understand what had happened to her daughter.

She could picture Aunt Edna lying in her bed in the nursing home two days previously. The elegant, fashionably dressed woman she was used to seeing had been replaced by a frail old lady with a haggard face drained of colour. She had seemed smaller and less imposing than Kate remembered her.

Kate knew she was the only family member Edna had left still living in England and had dropped everything and rushed to Warwickshire to be by her aunt's bedside.

She thought back to her arrival at Hampton House, once her family's home, but now converted to provide luxury accommodation for the elderly. Adam Leighton, tall and slim in a smart, dark grey suit, had been in the large reception area talking to a member of his staff when she arrived. He had broken off his conversation immediately and advanced towards her with an outstretched hand.

'Thank you for coming, Mrs Butler. I'm so sorry to have had to summon you, but, I am glad that you are here now. Your aunt has been getting increasingly agitated over the last few hours, waiting to see you,' he said, shaking her hand formally.

Then he led the way to the heavy oak door on the left side of the reception area that Kate remembered well. It had once led to her uncle's study and had been out of bounds to her when she was a child.

Adam held open the door and she took a deep

breath to calm herself before she entered the room that was now her aunt's bedroom.

Aunt Edna lay propped up on two substantial-looking white pillows in her bed in the centre of the room opposite the enormous old fireplace.

She turned a tired face to look at Kate as she walked in and said: 'Oh Kate, my dear, at last. How glad I am to see you.'

'Aunty, I am so sorry,' Kate said, approaching the bed, feeling the words were inadequate.

Her aunt's normally bright grey eyes were red rimmed and her face looked thinner.

'Oh, my poor Aunt Edna,' Kate said softly and a tear rolled down her aunt's pale cheek.

'Don't! Don't be nice to me, I couldn't bear it. I've asked you to come here to talk about Sophie.'

'I was so sorry to hear the news. I just can't believe what has happened.'

'Don't say anything yet. Just get yourself a chair and listen to me, please, because I urgently need your help. According to my solicitor, the Italian police aren't sure what happened to her.

'At first they thought she had been…" her aunt faltered, unable to say the word. Then she cleared her throat and said determinedly: 'They thought she had been murdered!'

Kate was too shocked to speak for a moment. Her aunt looked straight at her and said: 'Well, she was young and fit, she led a healthy lifestyle, so why would she suddenly die? I suppose it makes some kind of horrible sense, doesn't it?'

'But it is terrible to think someone might have killed her,' Kate protested, sitting down next to the bed.

'Yes, well, the Italian police seem to share your view because now they are saying she may have died as a result of natural causes after all.

'I don't know what to think. But I am not satisfied with being told what might have happened. I want to know all the facts. I feel so helpless just lying in this bed when I should be out there trying to find out what has happened to Sophie. I have to know the truth.'

Kate said: 'But what are your solicitors doing?'

'Oh, they are making enquiries through the official channels on my behalf, but I'm not expecting much to come of that. The main thing they can do for me is to arrange to have her brought home. She is my darling girl. I want to be able to bury her here in Hampton. I can't bear the thought of her lying dead out there in some hospital in Italy all on her own.

'I am sure Travis Brown will do their best, but they will only be able to find out what the police and the authorities tell them officially. I can't be satisfied with that. If someone has killed her, I want them to suffer, like I'm suffering now. I don't want them to get away with it because the Italian police don't investigate it properly, or do anything to try to catch them.'

She turned her head to look at Kate again: 'That's where you can help me. I want you to go out there and ask questions and confront the police and find out what they know, but are perhaps not admitting that they know.'

'But they are not likely to tell me anything because I would have no official status,' Kate protested.

'But you're a journalist, you're used to finding things out and you speak good Italian. Also you just happen to have a boyfriend who is a policeman,' Edna said, looking Kate directly in the eye.

Kate felt a pang of misery when Steve was mentioned. She said: 'He's very nearly a retired police officer and he's extremely busy at the moment so he wouldn't be able to come with me. I might struggle to get any information out of the Italian police. Even though I can speak the language reasonably well, they aren't going to tell me anything they don't want me to know.'

'But you know a lot about the police, you know how they operate. You are an attractive woman, I am sure the Italian officers will respond well to you. I can't believe you won't be able to do better than Travis Brown.

'You're all I've got now, Kate, and when I go everything I own will be yours. Please do this for me, I'm depending on you. Now you're retired I am sure you must have plenty of time on your hands.'

Kate chose her words carefully: 'Of course, I want to help you in any way I can, but just supposing I do go out to Bergamo, what exactly would you want me to do?'

'Oh, I don't know, just try to find out what you can for me. Anything would be better than not knowing what has happened. I'm sure I can rely on you to ask the right questions. Talk to the woman who found her, who owns the apartment block where she was living. Go to see the police and ask them why they changed their minds about the cause of her death. And ask the landlady who her friends were, who came to the apartment to see her. Try to find out whether she had been having any problems with anyone.'

With an effort, her aunt reached for a card she had placed ready on the bedside table. 'Take this. It is a card for the hotel where Sophie stayed when she first went out to Bergamo before she got the apartment. Book yourself a room there. Don't worry about the cost, I will pay for everything, of course.

'Travis Brown are instructing an Italian legal firm to represent me out there because I want to see the results of the post mortem examination and I want some proper answers. But they have said it could take quite some time and I don't know how long I've got. Once you have had one stroke you don't know when you are going to have another. I don't want to die without ever knowing what happened to Sophie.'

Aunt Edna started to sob, but made an effort to control herself and continued to speak in a determined way: 'I don't want things to drag on indefinitely so that I am never able to give Sophie a proper funeral. She was my only child and I want to bring her home and see her laid to rest properly before I die myself.'

Kate felt tears come into her eyes but wiped them away with the back of her hands hoping her aunt wouldn't notice.

Aunt Edna steadied herself again: 'I am sure you are the right person to send and that Steve will be able to help you unofficially. And in any case there isn't anyone else I can ask, is there?'

Kate knew she could not refuse to help her aunt, even though she had misgivings. She tried to pull herself together. 'All right, I will go. I will do my best for you, but don't be too disappointed if I don't get to know much more than your solicitors are able to find out for you.'

She could sense that her aunt relaxed a little then and seeing how tired she looked, decided it was time she left. She moved nearer to the bed and kissed Aunt Edna's soft cheek. Then she said: 'I will get a flight to Italy as soon as I can. Please try to rest and look after yourself while I am away. I will do my best to find out what happened to

Sophie, but whatever I do find out, we'll both have to accept it. We won't be able to change anything, I'm afraid.'

'Thank you, my darling Kate,' her aunt said, sleepily. Kate went towards the door. She turned back to look at her aunt before she left the room and saw that she had already settled back on to the pillows and closed her eyes.

Adam seemed to be waiting for her near the study door when she came out into the reception area.

'How do you think she seemed?' he asked anxiously.

'She was obviously very upset but she was composed and talked quite sensibly about it all,' Kate said.

'She has asked me to go out to Bergamo to try to find out more about what has happened to Sophie.'

He looked surprised: 'But I thought she had been on to her solicitors to get them to make the arrangements.'

'Yes, but she wants me to ask around and try to find out a bit more about the circumstances. It is worrying her that the police thought Sophie's death might have been suspicious but then changed their minds and said it was probably natural causes after all.'

'Well, they are not likely to tell you anything,' he said quickly. But then he seemed to check himself and made an effort to recover his usual poised manner. 'Anyway, thank you so much for coming down here. I hope that your trip to Italy goes well.'

As she sat outside the bar in the Città Alta, sipping her wine, she remembered the expression on Adam's face and wondered why, just for a few seconds, he had looked annoyed when she had told him she was going to Bergamo.

2

Kate shivered and her wine glass started to shake in her hand. She carefully placed her drink on the table in front of her as an unpleasant feeling welled up inside her. Every now and then she would realise Sophie was actually dead. She was not yet used to the idea and was experiencing the same symptoms of shock each time she remembered.

She was not in Bergamo for a holiday, she was there on Aunt Edna's behalf to find out more about the circumstances of Sophie's death. She had become lost in her thoughts but now she had to pull herself together and focus on what she had to do next. Suddenly filled with resolve, she picked up her pen and started to write some questions in Italian in her notebook.

A few minutes later she was back at the palazzo and pressing the brass button next to the Italian name, Mattozzi.

After a while a weary voice responded through the intercom at the side of the brass buttons: '*Si?*'

Kate, speaking in Italian, explained who she was and a few minutes later a small, thin woman with short, dark hair appeared at the iron gates and looked at her warily through them. She was wearing a short sleeved, black cotton dress that looked far too big for her and flat sandals with black leather straps that fastened with a buckle over her bare feet.

Kate introduced herself again, trying to pronounce the words to the best of her ability, and the woman stared at her for a few seconds before seeming to come to a decision. Reluctantly, she opened the gates and ushered Kate through an old wooden door into a small, dark room to the left of the inner courtyard.

Unopened letters and magazines in plastic wrappers lay on a dark wood table with a scratched surface just inside the doorway. There were two hard, wooden chairs and Signora Mattozzi indicated that Kate should sit in one while she took the other. It seemed to be an anteroom to the main building from where the tenants collected their mail.

Kate spoke slowly, occasionally having to search for the right word.

'Sophie's death has come as a great shock to both me and my aunt.'

Signora Mattozzi looked at her without changing the stern expression on her weather-beaten, lined face. She didn't bother with any words of sympathy.

Kate continued: 'My aunt is not well and could not make the journey herself so she has asked me to come to Bergamo to make some enquiries on her behalf.'

'What kind of enquiries? What are you trying to find out?' Signora Matozzi demanded.

Kate was surprised by her aggressive tone. She said: 'Sophie was still a young woman and has always been very healthy. Naturally we are shocked that she has died so suddenly and we are trying to find an explanation for the cause of her death.'

Signora Mattozzi shrugged her shoulders and held her hands out, palms upwards. 'I cannot help you with that, Signora, you will need to speak to the police.'

'I am planning to go and see them tomorrow, but I wanted to introduce myself to you as soon as possible. I understand that it was you who discovered Sophie, dead in bed.'

Signora Mattozzi shook her head: 'No, it was Luisa, the maid.'

'Oh, right. Well, when did she find her?' Kate asked, surprised by this new information.

'It was first thing in the morning when she arrived for work. She let herself in with her key as usual thinking the Signorina had already gone out. When she went into the bedroom she found that she was still in bed. Then she realised she was not moving or breathing so she came out on to the landing and screamed for help and I rushed upstairs to see what had happened. But it was Luisa who went into the room first.'

'What happened when you got upstairs?'

'On the way I passed the other lady's door. Signorina Anderson must also have heard Luisa scream and she came out into the corridor and followed me up the stairs. When we got up to the apartment we saw what had happened.'

She stopped speaking, as if she felt she had said enough. Kate leant forward and prompted her to continue: 'What did you actually see?'

'Luisa was waiting for us in the doorway of the apartment. She looked terrified. We all went into the bedroom and I saw the Signorina was still in bed. She wasn't moving and seemed to be dead, but I telephoned for an ambulance anyway. They came quite quickly but said they could do nothing for her.'

Again Kate had to encourage her to continue speaking. She said: 'Well, what happened after that?'

Signora Mattozzi shrugged her shoulders again. 'I suppose the ambulance people must have told the police about it because some officers came and looked round the apartment later. There were a few of them, coming and going throughout the day. I can't remember everything that happened exactly.

But later that day they took her away. The next day one of the policemen came back and asked me some more questions. Afterwards he told me not to go into the apartment again and so I have kept it locked up and haven't been in there since. I have not heard anything more from him.'

She sat back in her chair seeming satisfied she had said everything she was going to say.

Kate said: 'Did they give you any idea at all as to how Sophie died?'

'No, Signora.'

'Do you have the name of the policeman who came to see you?'

'Yes, it was the Commissario, Signor Esposito. You can contact him at the Commissariato in Via Roncalli.'

Signora Mattozzi stood up then as though indicating that the interview was at an end and Kate had no alternative but to allow herself to be ushered back out into the courtyard.

Disappointed not to have been able to ask anything else, Kate left the courtyard. As she walked further up the steep street she heard the sound of the iron gates clanging together as Signora Mattozzi closed them behind her.

She emerged into what she realised must be Piazza Vecchia, the main square of the Città Alta. She had read about it in the travel guide she had brought with her. There was a dark medieval palace at one end of the square and an elegant white marble building at the other. There were still plenty of people sitting at the tables outside the two bars on opposite corners of the piazza, enjoying the early evening atmosphere.

Kate took a seat outside the bar next to the grey stone Palazzo della Ragione and ordered herself another glass of wine.

She felt suddenly overcome with the sadness of it all. Sophie had been living in this beautiful city, Sophie, the woman with everything anyone could ever want. She was pretty, she was clever and she always had plenty of money. But now she was dead and gone forever.

Aunt Edna, who Kate had always loved so much, would probably never recover from the shock and might not live much longer herself.

Also, at the back of her mind were nagging worries about Steve. How would finishing work affect him? Would things ever go back to being the same between them?

She could not help thinking how much more exciting it would have been if Steve had been with her and they had been about to start a holiday together.

She thought of him back at home, spending his last few days working as a police officer. There had been no question of him coming to Bergamo with her because he was about to leave the police force he had served for nearly 30 years. Although his leaving date had been decided for him because the force had to make spending cuts, his sense of duty hadn't changed and he was working round the clock to try to tie up an outstanding case.

Recently, he had seemed to have very little time to spend with her and she had begun to feel as though he regarded their relationship almost as an inconvenience to him. Still struggling to come to terms with her own redundancy, she had felt lonely and unsettled.

Her job and her relationship with Steve had been the main things in her life. They were both divorced and had grown-up children. Although they had never formally decided they would live together, they had spent most of their time at either her house or his. Now, suddenly spending days and nights on her own and with no job to go to, her existence had begun to seem purposeless. They had talked about having a holiday later in the autumn but Steve had said he couldn't even begin to think about it until he had finished work.

It didn't help that Piazza Vecchia seemed full of people out together having an enjoyable evening. She felt as though she was an outsider, watching the romantic couples and families on holiday having a good time, but not part of things.

But this was no time for self-pity. You're going to have to pull yourself together, she told herself sternly, you're not here to enjoy yourself, you've got work to do. She took out her notebook again and made a list of the people she needed to talk to: The Commissario, Sophie's neighbour, who was someone called Anderson, and the maid, Luisa.

She took a sip of wine and then jotted down a plan of action: Check Sophie's mobile phone and diary for the names and numbers of her friends, she wrote. Try to reconstruct the last few days of her life and find out who she was spending time with.

She would think of more questions to put to Signora Mattozzi in Italian and then go to see her again. She was disappointed with the way the interview had gone. It was typical of me to go blundering in without thinking in advance of how to handle things properly, she thought, annoyed with herself. But she would do better with Signora Mattozzi next time.

Having finished her wine, she was beginning to feel cold sitting outside the bar and was ready for something to eat. She handed a ten euro note to the waitress as she went past and while she waited for her change she took out her phone and texted Aunt Edna: 'Arrived safely. Seen Sophie's landlady. Try to rest. I will do my best for you. xxx.'

Walking down Via Gombito back towards the funicular station, she passed a restaurant advertising Bergamo specialities and went inside to ask for a table. Once seated, she made up her mind quickly and ordered *casoncelli alla bergamasca,* the local stuffed pasta, served with butter, pancetta and sage. She chose braised beef with polenta as a main course and asked for a small carafe of the local white wine.

An hour later, feeling uncomfortably full, but happier, she walked the rest of the way down the street to the funicular station. She sat in a carriage with two young couples holding hands. As they descended toward the Città Bassa, with its glittering lights set out before them, she wanted to share the moment with Steve and tell him what she had been doing since she arrived. But she did not know where he would be or what he would be doing and fear of disturbing him stopped her from getting her phone out of her bag. She decided to wait a while, but by the time she had walked back along the main street to her hotel and collected her key and passport from reception, the moment had passed. After all, she had texted him to say she had landed safely and all she wanted to do now was climb into the comfortable-looking bed, pull the crisp white sheet over herself and lose herself in sleep.

When Kate opened the shutters and looked out of the window the next morning the sky was an intense deep blue without even a wisp of cloud and she could tell it was going to be a hot day. She looked down at the busy street and saw there was a bus stop opposite the hotel. It might be easier to go up to the Città Alta by bus than wheel her case to the funicular station in the heat, she thought.

After breakfast and checking out she was soon being transported up the hill away from the Città Bassa. The bus passed through one of the gates in the massive stone walls that she had read had been built by the Venetians in the 16th century when they had ruled Bergamo. It went along a tree-lined avenue overlooking the Città Bassa and stopped in a square where tourists were crowding around the wall at one side taking photographs of the lower town.

Kate did not stop to look at the view. Having already checked her map she went straight under the archway into Piazza Cittadella and walked, pulling her case, along a narrow, cobbled street until she found the turning into the small square where the Albergo Milano was situated. The hotel looked small, but the entrance lobby was stylishly furnished with pieces of highly-polished antique furniture and an old leather settee. It was very Sophie. Nothing flashy or touristy, but probably rather expensive, she thought. She noticed that its restaurant was open to the public and had an entrance door that opened on to a street at the side. She looked at the menu on display in the reception area, thinking it might be handy to eat there on some of the nights.

A tall man with dark, wavy hair and a long, thin tanned face with remarkably high cheekbones stood behind the reception desk. Kate explained to him in Italian that she had booked a room for a week but may need to stay for longer, depending on how her business affairs went. The man studied a leather bound book for details of her reservation and then carried her case up a flight of stairs and showed her into a pretty room. The walls were painted pale green and a pretty silk cover in the same shade was draped over the double bed. The furniture was all made from light wood and the tiles on the floor were of pale, grey marble. The effect was light and spacious and there was a good sized window through which Kate could see into a courtyard garden. She was pleased with the room and made an effort to unpack properly and set her things out.

Having had a good night's sleep she felt fresh and ready for her visit to the police station. But to give herself an excuse for talking to the man on reception she took her map out of her bag, went downstairs and stood by the desk while she waited for him to finish a phone call.

'Could you show me the street where the Commissariato is located?' she asked, handing him her map when he had put the receiver down.

The man pointed out the route to Via Roncalli, which she already knew was perfectly straightforward, but then politely asked if there was a problem that he could assist with.

Kate said: 'My cousin stayed at this hotel some time ago, before she found an apartment to rent in Bergamo. I wondered if you might remember her. Her name was Sophie Westmullen.'

The change that came over his handsome features was remarkable. His eyes at first looked startled but then became wary. He looked down at the desk and seemed to consider his next words carefully. Eventually he said: 'Of course, I remember her well, Signora. I was very sorry to hear about her death. It was so sudden. I am so sorry for your loss.'

Kate thanked him and then explained she had come to Bergamo to sort out Sophie's affairs.

He introduced himself as Roberto Mariotto, the manager of the Albergo Milano. He said: 'Your cousin was a very charming lady. Please accept my sincere condolences and don't hesitate to call on me if I can be of any help to you while you are here in Bergamo.'

Kate thanked him and stepped out into the sunny square, ready to walk through the streets to the Commissariato. She wondered why the hotel manager had seemed so guarded when she had mentioned Sophie. Clearly, he had already heard about her death. He had said all the right things in the end, but there had been a brief hesitation before he had been able to bring himself to speak to her about her cousin.

3

Of course, when she thought about it later, she realised that police officers were never just sitting around in the police station waiting to see casual callers.

She had found the Commissariato easily enough using her map. It was tucked away in the corner of a quiet square at the end of Via Roncalli, made obvious by the number of police cars parked outside.

The officer on duty in the reception area had been behind a single panel of glass, showing a remarkably casual approach to security by the *Polizia dello Stato*, she thought, although in sharp contrast he had been wearing a gun in a holster. Despite the ringing phones and the procession of people coming in and out, a large German shepherd dog lay fast asleep on the floor near the entrance. He had obviously had a hard morning.

When Kate finally had chance to make her enquiry, the officer told her that Commissario Esposito was out of the station at that moment but suggested she called back at midday, by which time he was expected to have returned. She left her name and told him what her visit was in connection with, hoping it would help gain her an interview with the Commissario when she went back.

With time to kill she wandered through the streets of the Città Alta exploring until she came across a bookshop with a book about Donizetti on prominent display in the window. The cover naturally caught her eye, given Sophie's reason for being in

Bergamo. There was a poster next to it advertising a talk and book signing by the author but she realised she had missed it. The event had been on Wednesday evening, the night before she had arrived in Bergamo and the shop had obviously not got round to taking the poster down yet.

The writer, Edgar Wallenheimer, was described as an American expert on Italian opera. He was young and good looking if his photograph was anything to go by. Kate went inside and when she found the book on display in the shop, she picked it up eagerly. Kate liked opera but had had neither the time nor the money to see many performances over the years. She knew some of Donizetti's music but hardly anything about the life of the composer. Curious to find out more about the life of the man who was to have been the subject of Sophie's next biography, she decided to buy it.

After leaving the shop she continued to stroll along until she found a table free outside a bar. She sat down and ordered a cappuccino to drink while she looked through the book. Every now and then she glanced at her watch and when she saw it was time to return to the Commissariato, she made her way back along a different route, having already got to know the layout of the Città Alta.

At the Commissariato, the officer told her to take a seat in the reception area. She flicked through the book again and her attention was drawn to the pictures of Donizetti's birthplace in Borgo Canale just outside the Città Alta and the images of the memorial monument to the composer next to the red-brick Teatro Donizetti in the centre of the Città Bassa.

Then she became aware that a small, slightly built man with brown, curly hair wearing dark blue jeans and a pale blue, long sleeved shirt had come out into the reception area and was looking across at her.

'Signora Butler?' he enquired. Kate stood up and he came over to her and shook her hand. 'Please come with me,' he said in clear, confident English.

He led the way down a corridor off the waiting area, opened a door about halfway down and stood back to let her enter the room first. He pulled out a chair and put it in front of the desk and invited her to sit down. It was a small room and seemed to have far too much furniture in it. Two large filing cabinets on either side of the desk seemed to overshadow the small figure of the Commissario as he sat down opposite her.

'Allow me to offer you my condolences on the death of your relative,' he said politely. 'It is a sad reason for you to have come to Bergamo, for the task of collecting her property.'

'That's not really why I am here. I have come to try to establish exactly what happened to my cousin.'

The Commissario said: 'A formal report will be prepared about the cause of death and your family will be informed through your legal representatives here in Italy, who I can assure you, have already been in touch with us.'

Kate said: 'My cousin has an elderly mother who is not in a very good state of health. Naturally she is anxious to find out what happened as quickly as possible. She will want to get on with making the funeral arrangements but she is extremely agitated as a result of the conflicting information that has been relayed to her by her solicitors in England.'

The Commissario looked concerned. 'I am sorry to hear that she has been given additional worries at this tragic time. Can you explain exactly what you mean by this?'

Kate said: 'First she was told Sophie had been found dead in bed. Then she was told that the police here thought the death could be suspicious, which was obviously very upsetting for her. But then her solicitors contacted her again and said that the police here thought Sophie probably died from natural causes after all. So she is now frantic with worry and doesn't know what to think about it all.'

The Commissario frowned. 'It is very unfortunate that her solicitors told her that there was any possibility at all that the death might not be as a result of natural causes. We can't say anything for certain yet. I understand that a post mortem examination has been performed but I am still waiting for the official report.'

'Do you have any idea about what the report will say?'

'I am sorry, but I really can't speculate about it in advance.'

'But none of it makes any sense to us. Sophie was generally very healthy. Why would she suddenly die in her sleep?'

'These things do happen to healthy adults sometimes, sudden unexplained deaths.'

'Well, why then, did my aunt's solicitors receive information that there was a possibility that the death might be treated as suspicious?'

'I'm afraid I can't discuss that with you until I have received all the relevant information in the report.'

Kate decided to try another line of questioning. 'Do you think there is any chance at all that someone could have broken in and killed my cousin, perhaps while burgling the apartment?'

The Commissario said firmly: 'Look, I have

already told you that I can't sit here speculating about it with you. The cause of death will not be announced until the report on the post mortem examination is complete.'

Kate's heart sank because she could tell that she was not going to get any further with him. She felt that she had failed again, just like she had with Signora Mattozzi.

Her disappointment must have shown on her face because she was aware of the Commissario looking at her intently for a few seconds, after which he seemed to relent.

He said: 'I can promise you that I have looked into your cousin's death personally. I always make a point of reviewing the file when there is a sudden death in the Città Alta.'

Kate did not know what to say and while she thought about her next question he continued to look at her thoughtfully. Then he seemed to make his mind up. 'All right, what I will do for you is take you to have a look round the apartment so that you can see the situation for yourself. It is on the top floor of the building and the front door was locked when the maid arrived for work on the Monday morning with the poor Signorina already dead inside.'

He smiled pleasantly at her for the first time since they had met. 'I think you will be able to make your own mind up as to whether an attacker could have got into or out of the apartment after you have seen it for yourself.'

'So, the door was locked and no one could have got in without a key,' Steve said thoughtfully that night after she had recounted the details of her meeting with the Commissario over the phone to him.

'Yes, and he has offered to take me to the apartment tomorrow so I can see for myself that nobody could have got in and killed her or got out again afterwards. If that clears the matter up it will be a huge relief for Aunt Edna.'

'All the same, it is very strange, isn't it? Someone from the Italian police obviously jumped the gun by telling Edna's solicitors that it could be a suspicious death. There must have been a reason for that. But then the police there sound about as disorganised as our lot.'

'How is your work going at the moment?' Kate asked.

'Oh, it's hopeless. I only have a short time left and there is still a lot to deal with. I am afraid I will be walking out on the operation tomorrow leaving my work half finished. If they had just allowed me a bit more time I might have been able to get a result. But they are not prepared to let me go even one day past my specified retirement date,' he said bitterly.

'I'm so sorry,' Kate said, knowing as soon as she had said them that the words were inadequate

'Well, I'm just going to have to come to terms with it, aren't I? I can't expect anyone else to understand how I am feeling right now. I am being forced to walk out on an operation that I have put months of work and effort into without being able to see it through to the end and get a good result. And after I have tied up a few loose ends tomorrow, that's that. It will be the end of the job I have loved doing for the last 30 years.'

'Well, I think I probably understand more than most people,' Kate protested, stung by his words. 'It wasn't all that long ago that the same thing happened to me.'

'Yes, but it wasn't exactly the same.'

'No, if anything it was worse for me. At least no one has got it in for you personally. If you remember I was happy on the newspaper and people had always told me I did a good job. Then a little, fat bespectacled nonentity who hadn't held down a job as a journalist for years was brought in as a so-called consultant to make cuts.

'We let him see how we worked and gave him access to everything we were doing because he said he was going to come up with ideas for how the newspaper could be run more efficiently. But in reality he was gunning for everyone who was over 50.

'As you may remember, his email telling me that the newspaper no longer required my services contained five separate spelling and grammar errors.'

'I know, Kate, I know, I remember it all. I'm sorry for moaning. I haven't forgotten what a hard time you had."

There was a pause while neither of them spoke until Steve broke the silence. 'I am well aware that I am just wallowing in self-pity at the moment.'

'That's okay, you are perfectly entitled to wallow. I just wanted you to know that I can understand how you are feeling at the moment,' Kate replied more calmly.

'Thanks, but I promise you, I will buck my ideas up when this is all over. In fact, I tell you what I will do, when I have recovered from my leaving do, I will have a run down to Hampton to see Aunt Edna on Sunday.'

'Oh, thank you. It would be a big relief for me if you would check on her and let me know how she is afterwards,' Kate said, pleased that Steve was sounding much more like his old self.

They had talked to each other pleasantly for the rest of the phone call and Kate felt happier as she went for an evening stroll along Via Colleoni before dinner, looking in the shop windows at displays of local produce and examples of Bergamo's culinary specialities.

When she came to a restaurant she liked the look of, she went inside, was shown to a table and after a quick look at the menu, she ordered a pizza and some wine.

After visiting the apartment the next day she promised herself she would make an effort to track down some of Sophie's friends and arrange to meet up with them over the coming days. She would ask them for anecdotes about Sophie and take some photographs of them so she had something to show Aunt Edna and talk to her about when she got home. And after meeting Sophie's friends there really would be nothing else to keep her here, she thought with relief.

When she got back to the hotel Roberto was in the reception area and she thought she would make the most of the opportunity. 'Do you have a few minutes for a chat?' she asked.

'Of course, come through to the bar, it is empty at the moment.'

He went behind the counter of the small bar next to reception and produced a bottle of white wine from a fridge. 'Try some of our wonderful Valcalepio Bianco wine,' he said, pouring them both a glass. Kate sat on a stool at the bar and watched him put the bottle back into the fridge. '*Salute!*' he said, as they both raised their glasses.

She asked: 'Did you get to know Sophie well, while she was staying here?'

'Not really. We talked sometimes about places to see in Bergamo and about her work here, but that is all.'

'Do you know if she made any friends here?'

'Yes, I know for certain that she did. She was often with the same people, another Englishwoman, who lived in her apartment building, and two Americans. I would regularly see the four of them out together in different bars and restaurants around Bergamo.'

'Did she seem happy living here?'

He paused for a moment, seeming surprised by the question. 'It's difficult for me to say really. She seemed to like Bergamo, particularly the Città Alta. Bergamo is a very peaceful, friendly town. She gave me the impression she enjoyed her work, looking at the documents in the library in Piazza Vecchia and at the Donizetti museum in Via Arena to get ideas for her book.'

He was silent for a moment and then asked: 'Did you find out what you wanted to get to know on your visit to the Commissariato?'

Kate said: 'Not entirely, but tomorrow the Commissario is going to show me round Sophie's apartment and I will get the chance to talk to her landlady and the maid.'

Once again she saw his expression change and he became guarded. Then he said rather abruptly: 'Forgive me, but I realise that I haven't locked the outer door of the restaurant yet. I am neglecting my duties and so I am afraid that I must go. But please feel free to stay here as long as you like and enjoy the rest of your wine.'

4

Aldo Esposito was waiting for Kate in reception the next morning when she came out of the breakfast room.

'Buon giorno, Signora Butler,' he said to her in a friendly way. He was dressed casually in beige cotton trousers and an open neck, short sleeved, pale blue and white striped shirt.

'Good morning, Signor Esposito, I am sorry I am not ready. I will just go and get my bag,' Kate said, flustered.

'Call me Aldo, please,' he said at once. 'And how is your first name pronounced? It is Katerina in Italian, is it not?'

'Everyone calls me Kate,' she replied and then hurried upstairs.

She quickly got ready and after leaving the hotel they crossed Piazza Vecchia, which was being warmed by the early morning sunshine, and made their way down Via Gombito in the direction of Sophie's apartment. Kate had the uncomfortable feeling she was towering over the Commissario as they walked along together.

'Look at that, isn't it beautiful? It has been there since the 16th century,' Aldo said, gesturing towards an ornate, white marble fountain in the middle of a small square that they passed through.

'The Venetians had beautiful, decorative fountains designed for the people to drink from when they ruled the city. They wanted to show visitors who came here how wealthy and powerful they were so that they would let the rest of the world know.

'Now we Bergamaschi are able to live our daily lives surrounded by these artistic treasures.'

Signora Mattozzi came to let them into the courtyard of the palazzo in a rather reluctant manner as though they were putting her to a lot of trouble. Once inside the iron gates Aldo took charge of the situation immediately. 'You lock the gates to the courtyard every night, I believe, Signora.'

'Yes, after the ten o'clock bell I usually lock up for the night if both of the women are at home.'

'And what do you do then?'

'Well, then I watch television for a while, or read, before going to bed,' she said, seeming surprised by the question.

'What do you do the next morning?'

'In the morning I unlock the gates before anyone else is up and about and before Luisa arrives to do the cleaning.'

'And on the night before Signorina Westmullen was found dead, what exactly happened?'

Signora Mattozzi said: 'I remember seeing her during the evening. She came down to my apartment to talk to me. I knew that she was staying in for the rest of the evening and that Signorina Anderson was also in her apartment so I locked up just after ten o'clock as usual.

'The next morning I got up at half past six and I unlocked the gates ready for Luisa's arrival.'

Aldo said: 'So there is no way that anyone could have entered the building or left it during the night.'

'No, Commissario. I would have heard if anyone had come past my door and in any case I would have had to get up to unlock the gates for them.'

Kate said: 'Could I see Sophie's apartment, please?'

With no attempt to conceal her look of annoyance, Signora Mattozzi went through the doorway into her own apartment to collect her pass key and then led the way up a narrow flight of stone steps.

On the first landing they passed a closed door and Aldo said to Kate: 'That is the door to the apartment where the other English lady lives.'

They continued up the stairs to the next narrow landing and Signora Mattozzi went ahead to unlock the door at the end of it. She led the way into the main room of the apartment, which would have once been the principal *salone* of the palazzo. It was surprisingly light because of the full height windows that opened out on to a pretty stone balcony overlooking the street.

Kate was surprised how vast and empty the room looked. There were suitcases in the middle of the room as though someone had already packed up Sophie's possessions.

'Has someone been in to clear the apartment?' she asked.

'No, Signora. No one has been in here since the police asked me to keep it locked. This is just how it looked the morning we found her. Everything had already been packed up ready for her new furniture arriving.'

'New furniture?' Kate asked in surprise.

'Signorina Westmullen said she did not like the furniture that was in this room. She said it was too big and dark. She asked for it to be taken away and she chose modern pieces of furniture to replace it.'

Kate started to ask something else but Signora Mattozzi said dismissively: 'It is no good asking me. You will have to speak to Luisa about it because I wasn't involved with any of the arrangements.'

'I see. Well, could we see the bedroom, please?' Kate asked quickly, sensing that the subject of the new furniture was a source of irritation for Signora

Mattozzi.

The concierge opened one of the doors that led off the *salone* and stood back to allow Kate to see into a gloomy room with a double bed in the centre. It had been stripped of all its sheets and covers and there was a folded white duvet and two pillows lying on it. The bedroom was dark in contrast with the light airy main room because the shutters were closed across the small window at the side.

Kate swallowed hard to try to overcome the feeling of dread she had when she thought of pretty little Sophie lying dead in that bed.

'Has someone taken the covers off the bed?' the Commissario asked in surprise.

'I told Luisa to tidy up after they took her away. She will have washed the sheets, pillow cases and the covers, I expect,' said Signora Mattozzi in a matter of fact way.

Aldo threw up his hands in annoyance and said: 'But I asked you to leave everything exactly as it was.'

Signora Mattozzi simply shrugged her shoulders and gestured with her hands but did not bother to say anything in reply.

Aldo recovered his poise quickly and showed Kate the neat kitchen, which was equipped with smart cupboards and modern appliances and had room for a table and two chairs. He then opened the door so she could look into the bathroom which looked immaculate and appeared to have been recently installed and had a bath, separate shower, wash basin, toilet and bidet.

When they were back in the main sitting room he said: 'So, on Monday morning Luisa let herself in through that door with her pass key. But, as you can now understand, no one from outside the palazzo would have been able to do that during the night.

'If you look out of the window, you will see it is a sheer drop from the balcony to the road which is two floors below, and so no one could possibly have climbed up or down that way or got in or out through the bedroom window.'

Kate looked at Signora Mattozzi and said hopefully: 'Would it be possible for me to meet Luisa?'

Signora Mattozzi shrugged again and said dismissively: 'She will be somewhere outside I should think.' She led the way out of the apartment and stood back to let them pass her on the small landing before pulling the entrance door firmly shut behind her.

They found Luisa outside in the sunshine watering plants on the terrace at the back of the building, which overlooked the Città Bassa.

She was a young, slim, woman with dark hair pulled back into a pony tail and she was wearing a pale green, cotton maid's dress. Signora Mattozzi went up to her and said a few sharp words that Kate did not understand and thought must have been in *bergamasco* dialect. Luisa immediately looked across at them nervously.

Kate introduced herself in Italian pronouncing her words carefully and asked Luisa to tell her what had happened on the morning when she had found Sophie dead in bed.

Luisa looked at Signora Mattozzi for guidance but the older woman's face remained impassive. Luisa said timidly: 'I have already told the police about this.'

Aldo said pleasantly: 'Don't be afraid Luisa, we just want you to tell us again so the Signora can hear it directly from you.'

Luisa said: 'I let myself into the apartment thinking the Signorina had already gone to work. She often went out early and would have her breakfast later in a bar.

'I went into the kitchen and put my bag down and reheated the coffee left in the pot and then poured myself a cup.

'I started to wash up the dishes the Signorina had left to soak in the bowl but then I was surprised to hear the buzzer from the intercom. It turned out that the men had arrived much earlier than I expected to take away the furniture.

'I had a list of what was to be removed from the apartment and so I watched them to make sure they took the right things.

'When all the furniture had gone I cleaned off the marks where it had stood on the floor.

'But when I went into the bedroom to start to clean in there I found the Signorina was still lying in the bed. I knew immediately there was something wrong and so I called for help. Signora Mattozzi came to see what had happened. I must have woken up the Englishwoman from the apartment below because she came to see what had happened as well. It was still very early and she had obviously been asleep in bed because she was still wearing her night clothes. When we could not rouse the poor Signorina at all, Signora Mattozzi went to call for an ambulance.'

'Are you sure that the men who collected the furniture did not go into the bedroom?' Kate asked.

'I am sure they did not. I watched them all the time. All the furniture they were taking away was in the main *salone*.'

Kate turned to Signora Mattozzi again and asked: 'Is there any other way into the building apart from through the main entrance gate into the courtyard?'

Signora Mattozzi said: 'There is the door there that leads from this terrace into my apartment. But it is a sheer drop on to the rocks below. No one could have climbed up the rocks and on to the terrace. And even if they did they would have had to come through my apartment to get to the stairs to go up to the other two apartments, so I would have heard them.'

Kate said: 'I would still like to meet Signorina Anderson. I understand she and Sophie had become good friends.'

Signora Mattozzi said: 'I am afraid that she is out at work. She teaches students on a Saturday morning.'

Kate took out one of her business cards and wrote a message on the back asking Sophie's neighbour to contact her on her mobile. She handed it to an increasingly irritated-looking Signora Mattozzi and then thanked her with somewhat exaggerated politeness for being kind enough to spare the time to show her round the apartment.

Once they had been shown out through the iron gates again and were standing on the pavement, Aldo said: 'Let's go for a cup of coffee and have a talk.'

He led the way to the bottom of the street and they sat down at a table outside the bar opposite the funicular station.

When they had both ordered their coffee he said: 'So now you have seen the apartment, what are your impressions?'

Kate said: 'Well, I can see that no one could have got in through the iron gates between the times it was supposed to have been locked.'

Aldo said: 'And I don't think anyone would have

been able to climb up the sheer rock face and over the balustrade to get on to the terrace outside Signora Mattozzi's sitting room. Even if someone had tried to get in through the door from the terrace into her apartment, I am sure the Signora would have heard them.'

Kate said: 'So, the only people who had the opportunity to do any harm to Sophie while she slept were Signora Mattozzi, or the other tenant, Signorina Anderson?'

'But Signora Mattozzi and Luisa are the only people who actually had keys to the apartment. And you have to ask yourself why either of them would have wanted to harm your cousin. Signora Anna Mattozzi may not be *simpatica,* or as you say in English, very friendly, but she is well respected in Bergamo.'

'What about Luisa, or even the furniture removal men? Didn't they all have an opportunity to go into the bedroom while Sophie was still asleep that morning?'

'Luisa is positive the men did not go into the bedroom and she insists that she did not discover the Signorina dead until after they had gone. I have no reason to disbelieve her. Her version of events has remained entirely consistent.'

Their coffee arrived then and Aldo waited until the waitress was out of earshot before he said gently: 'In all probability the post mortem examination results will prove that Sophie died from natural causes.'

Tears suddenly came into Kate's eyes and she found it impossible to stop them. Aldo patted her hand. He said gently: 'I know you are going through a very difficult time right now and I am sorry for you. But I wish with all my heart that you are somehow able to find a way to enjoy the rest of your time in Bergamo. I would like you to take away some good memories of the city with you because I think it would help both you and your poor aunt to come to terms with your loss.'

5

Steve saw the familiar stone walls come into view at the side of the road and slowed down to turn into the entrance of what had once been Kate's family home. Although it didn't feel like it, he had managed to get a few hours sleep since the farewell party organised by his fellow officers the night before and now he was glad to be up and about and have somewhere to go to take his mind off things.

He had been preoccupied with thoughts about the operation he had been working on for most of the drive from his house in Yorkshire to the village in Warwickshire, but as he parked in one of the bays marked for visitors to the left of the central lawn and flower beds he made himself put all thoughts about work and his former colleagues to the back of his mind. He got out of his car, picked up the bunch of flowers he had placed on the back seat and walked across to the front door slowly, preparing himself for what might be to come.

Adam Leighton was standing behind the reception desk talking to another man of about the same height. Both of them were wearing a similar style of grey suit.

Why does he always insist on dressing as though he is about to attend a wedding, Steve wondered, watching Adam and the other man with amusement.

Adam broke off his conversation abruptly when he noticed Steve and hustled the other man in the smart suit into a small office off the reception area as though he wanted to get him out of the way. Then he advanced towards Steve with a welcoming smile.

'It's Mr Bartorelli, isn't it?'

Steve said: "It wasn't yesterday, but it is today.

Yesterday it was Detective Chief Inspector Bartorelli. How quickly things change."

Adam looked puzzled for a moment and then a nervous look came over his face. It was an expression Steve had seen many times before.

But the nursing home manager recovered quickly. "Well, it's nice of you to pay us a visit. Edna will be thrilled. But you should have let us know you were coming.' He led the way to Edna's room on the left of the reception area and knocked on the door. When Edna's voice invited him to come in, Adam held open the door for Steve, who braced himself before he entered the room.

He was pleasantly surprised to see Edna sitting wrapped in a fleecy dressing gown in an armchair in front of the fireplace, although it was too warm a day for the fire to be lit. She looked thinner than he remembered but he was pleased to see she was out of bed.

Edna looked up from the book she was reading and exclaimed: 'Steve! What a lovely surprise, how glad I am to see you.'

'What beautiful flowers, you're spoiling me,' she said, accepting the bouquet he held out to her. She sniffed the head of one of the blooms and a tear rolled down her cheek.

'I was so sorry to hear about Sophie. I would have come before if I hadn't had to work all week,' Steve said.

'What does it feel like to have finally retired?'

'Oh, let's not talk about that now. I want to know how you are. You've been through the mill since the last time I saw you, haven't you?'

Edna sighed and put the flowers down next to her chair on the carpet.

She said: 'It's been like a nightmare that I can't

wake up from. I still can't believe Sophie is dead and that she's not coming back from Italy.'

Steve pulled up a chair to sit close to her and said: 'Well, it was so unexpected, wasn't it? I never remember Sophie having so much as a day's illness.'

'That's why I can't get over what my solicitors told me right at the beginning, that the Italian police had said that she could have been murdered. Horrible though it is to think such a thing, I can't help but feel it is the only explanation for her death that makes any sense.'

'Tell me exactly what you were told right at the start.'

Edna sank back in her chair. 'I had a horrible feeling about things, even the day before. Funnily enough I had been a bit out of sorts, with a strange sensation in the pit of my stomach. It was almost as though I had some kind of presentiment that something terrible was going to happen.

'I remember going for a long soak in the bath to try to make myself feel better. But when I came back in here I had the feeling that someone had been in my room.'

She hesitated for a few seconds and then said: 'Anyway, you don't want to know about all that.'

Steve said: 'Yes I do, I want to know everything. Tell me what you remember about that day, anything at all.'

'Well, I could tell that some of the furniture had been moved about. It was the wrong time of day for the cleaners and, anyway, they never left the room looking like that. There was a steel measuring tape lying on the carpet in the middle of the floor. When Adam Leighton dropped in to see me later I showed it to him. He said one of the maintenance staff must have left it because he had asked them to test my radiator. The weather forecast predicted it was going to get colder and he thought we might have to start having the heating on.

'I said that I wouldn't have thought they would need to measure the radiator to make sure it worked, but he didn't really answer. He just gave me one of his little smiles.

'Anyway, during the evening Sophie rang from Italy to see how I was and she seemed absolutely fine. She sounded really happy and said that the work on her book was going well. After we had been chatting for quite a long time, she said she was going to get back to work and that she was planning to stay in for the rest of the evening and keep writing because she was making such good progress.

'I remember that I had a terrible night's sleep. It was very windy and some odd sounds came from the old chimney. I woke once or twice thinking I could hear someone calling for help and when I did fall asleep again I had some strange dreams.

'At one point I thought I saw Henry working at his desk on the other side of the room. I sat up in bed to have a look but then I realised there was no one at the desk. I told myself not to be so silly and turned over and tried to make myself go to sleep again.

'As a result of having such a restless night I woke up later than usual the next morning and did not ring for my tea until after ten o'clock.

'Adam brought my tray in himself. He looked immaculately turned out and was wearing a suit as always, but his usual smooth manner seemed to have deserted him.

'He mumbled a few words to me as though he was unsure of what to say and after he had poured the tea he went to open my curtains and stood looking out of the window while I took a few sips.

'Eventually he came and sat down in the chair next to the bed and took hold of my hand. He said that he was sorry but he had some extremely bad news for me. He had received a phone call from the police in Bergamo to inform him that Sophie had been found dead in her apartment.'

Emotion overcame her momentarily and she gave a little sob. 'I'm so sorry, Edna, this must be very hard for you,' Steve said.

'No, let me keep going, I want to tell you everything. I asked Adam to contact Travis Brown, my solicitors, to get them to liaise with the Italian police to try to find out what had happened and I asked him to let Kate know as soon as possible.

'First I got a call from my solicitors saying that the Italian police were treating it as a suspicious death. But then they rang back and said that their information had been wrong and the Italian police thought she had died of natural causes after all.

'If anything, it made the whole thing worse, not knowing what to believe. That's why I felt I couldn't rest until I had persuaded Kate to go to Bergamo on my behalf.'

Steve said: 'Well, Kate rang me last night, so let me bring you up to date on the progress she has been making out in Bergamo.'

'Are the Italian police still saying that Sophie died from natural causes?' Edna asked, getting straight to the point.

'Kate says they are still waiting for the official results of the post mortem examination but they seem to believe Sophie could have suffered some kind of adult sudden death experience because there is no evidence of anyone having got into the flat from outside.'

'That is a relief, I suppose,' Edna said, dabbing her eyes with a handkerchief. But then she suddenly sat up straight in her chair and said: 'But on the other hand it still leaves questions to be answered, doesn't it?'

Steve thought carefully about his next words before he spoke. 'Kate told me on the phone last night that it seems as though the only two people who could have got into the apartment while Sophie was asleep in bed are the landlady and some sort of maid that worked there. But the police think neither of them would have had any reason to harm Sophie.

'I am sure that everything will be resolved soon. Kate is going to try to meet up with some of Sophie's friends and ask them for anecdotes about her time in Bergamo and she says she hopes to bring back some pictures of them for you to look at.'

Edna said: 'You don't know what a relief it will be for me when we find out for certain how Sophie died. But until we know everything, I want Kate to continue to keep her eyes and ears open and find out what she can for me. I want to know about the sort of people Sophie was mixing with and whether she had any enemies.'

Steve felt uncomfortable. He would have been surprised if Sophie hadn't made an enemy or two while she was living out in Italy. But he could hardly say that to Edna.

'I must say, it has been a great comfort for me to get texts from Kate from time to time,' Edna commented.

'Texts!' Steve exclaimed.

'Don't sound so surprised. I may be over 80 now but I still have all my faculties and I am capable of texting people.'

'But I didn't know you had a mobile phone.'
'That's because I don't want people to know. It's my bit of security, Sophie got it for me. It keeps me in touch with people in the village. I ask them to bring things in for me from time to time when they visit. I don't want to have to rely on the people here too much.'
'Do you feel that you can't rely on them?'
'Oh no, most of them are fine, but I just like to have my little bit of independence,' Edna said evasively.
'Anyway, while you are here, you can do something for me. Open that drawer for me and programme your number into my phone,' she said indicating the bedside table.
Steve opened the top drawer in her bedside table and saw a fairly new-looking, mobile phone.
'Where's the charger?' he asked as he obediently programmed in his own number.
'In my make up bag in the next drawer down.'
'Why do you keep the phone in the drawer?'
'I've told you I don't want people to know it's there because I don't want it to disappear one day.'
'Why would it disappear?'
'Because they might suddenly make a rule that you can't have a mobile phone in here.'
'But, doesn't anyone ever hear it ring?'
'No, because I always keep the phone on silent and anyway, I only ever use it to text people.'
Steve wasn't happy that Edna felt she needed to keep her mobile hidden, but he didn't want to question her further about it because he was worried about tiring her out. She seemed to be holding up well, he thought, considering that she had received such devastating news and had been forced to cope with so much over the last few days but he could tell

she was getting weary. He changed the subject by asking Edna about the book she had been reading and they talked for a few more minutes.

When he got up to go, he said: 'Kate is hoping to meet up with the other English woman who lived in the same apartment block as Sophie and with two Americans that she has been told she went about with a lot in Bergamo.

'I will tell her how well you are looking when I next speak to her as I know it will be a huge relief for her to hear that you are all right.'

'You are an old flatterer, I know I look like a complete hag,' Edna said with a sigh, relaxing back in her chair again.

Steve went over to her and kissed her on the cheek. 'Ring or text me if you need anything, anything at all,' he said firmly.

'Don't worry, I will.'

He closed Edna's door gently behind him and then found Adam was waiting to speak to him in the reception area.

'How do you think she seemed?' he asked.

'She seems to be coming to terms with it all. She's a tough cookie, is Edna.'

'What did she have to say about things?' Adam asked casually.

'What sort of things?'

'About what Kate has been finding out in Bergamo.'

'She said she wants Kate to carry on digging until she is absolutely sure she has got to the bottom of everything out there. And just to let you know, I will be popping down here from time to time to keep my eye on her until Kate gets back from Italy.'

As Steve drove back to Yorkshire he worried about the effect the terrible news about Sophie would have on Edna's long term health and how Kate would cope with this.

But from time to time he also found himself remembering the expression on Adam's face and wondering why he had seem so concerned about what Kate might be finding out in Bergamo. Why did he have the feeling Adam couldn't be trusted?

6

While Steve was on his way to visit Aunt Edna in Warwickshire, Kate was having coffee with Jean Anderson, Sophie's neighbour, in her first floor apartment. She had received a call from Jean as she was finishing breakfast on the Sunday morning and had hurriedly got ready and made her way through the streets to the palazzo.

To her relief, she found talking to the English teacher about Sophie easy. She had struggled to find out the things she wanted to know during the awkward conversations she had been having with other people in Bergamo. It was also reassuring that Jean's reaction to Sophie's death was exactly what she would have expected.

Jean said she still could not quite believe what had happened and that the last week had seemed like a bad dream. She still could not get used to the idea that Sophie was dead and wouldn't be coming back to live in Palazzo Mattozzi. Kate thought it was odd that everyone else she had met in Bergamo up to that point had seemed to take Sophie's death in their stride.

Roberto at the hotel, Signora Mattozzi and Luisa had all seemed calm and matter of fact about her cousin dying so suddenly.

'She always seemed so full of energy, she was always on the go,' Jean said as she poured Kate a second cup of steaming, black coffee from the silver-coloured metal *Napoletana* she had heated on the stove.

Her sitting room was similar in size to the main room in Sophie's apartment but seemed a lot smaller. It was dominated by large pieces of dark furniture and every available surface was covered with piles of books and different objects. They were sitting at a cluttered dining table in the middle of the room and Kate noticed a vase containing wilting red roses and an empty champagne bottle in the middle of all the stacks of books and files of papers.

'I never ever heard her complain that she was feeling ill at any time. She was probably the last person in the world I would have expected to suddenly stop breathing. I still haven't really taken it in, you know,' Jean said shaking her head in disbelief. Her short blonde hair was cut in a neat bob with a fringe, but her nose was too big for her face and she had a very pink complexion.

She was probably younger than Sophie, but nowhere near as attractive, Kate thought.

'Had you become good friends?' she asked.

Jean seemed to think about it for a few seconds before she answered. 'Well, we had a lot in common, but we also kept ourselves to ourselves, if you know what I mean.

'We both liked the theatre and opera and we would go to performances at the Teatro Donizetti together sometimes. I am a member of an opera society and so I introduced Sophie to my friends in the group when she first moved in here. She got on particularly well with two American friends of mine, Edgar and Marge.'

'Yes, someone else told me that she had become close to two Americans,' Kate said.

'Edgar is a well-known writer and an expert on Donizetti. He has taken a house near the funicular railway station in the Città Bassa while he is doing his research here,' Jean explained.

'Is Marge his wife?' Kate asked.

'Goodness, no! They are just old friends,' Jean

said, and gave an embarrassed giggle. 'Marge's family have known Edgar's family for years. They live near each other back home in the States.

'Edgar has based himself in Bergamo while he is working on his next book. Marge came to look him up while she was travelling round Italy. She is 'doing Europe' as the Americans call it. But she has ended up staying on here quite a while. She has a suite at the Majestic, the big hotel immediately opposite the Città Bassa funicular station. No, they are definitely 'just good friends', nothing more.'

She seemed to think it was important to make this point, Kate thought.

'Do you think Sophie was happy living here?'

Jean considered the question and then said: 'Yes, I think so, on the whole. She seemed to enjoy her work. She said she liked Bergamo. She was always out and about somewhere doing things. Yes, I think you could say she was happy.'

'Do you remember her ever having problems with anyone?'

'No, not really. I mean, I suppose Signora Mattozzi isn't always the easiest person to get along with and they sometimes clashed a bit. Also, Marge has a very strong personality and Sophie did like to poke fun at her occasionally, which caused tension between them sometimes.

'I think she thought Marge was a bit trivial and only really interested in clothes and shopping. She sometimes said she thought Marge was just pretending to be interested in art and music. I suppose Marge wanted to look as though she was interested in Italian culture because it justified her being here for so long. However, on the whole I would say Sophie got on well with most of the people here.'

'So you never had problems with her?'

Jean went a deeper pink. 'No, not really.' Then she added: 'I'm not going to pretend we were close, she was quite difficult to get close to. She was extremely self-sufficient and liked doing things her own way.

'And, then we both had our work. I have to put the hours in teaching English in order to be able to afford to live here. Sophie didn't have that pressure, of course, but she was always off somewhere doing research for her book, or so she claimed. Like I said, we used to keep ourselves to ourselves but we would occasionally go out for a meal or to the theatre together.

'When she first moved in here she seemed to bond with Luisa the maid and for a while they seemed to be the best of friends. Of course, that was a bit odd when you come to think about it because Luisa was being paid to clean for her. But she certainly seemed to like Luisa to begin with and treated her more as a friend than a maid.

'Then something seemed to happen between them, I don't know what exactly, but they had a bit of a falling out, I think.'

Jean suddenly seemed to realise how much she was saying and looked at Kate with more interest. 'Why are you asking me all these questions, anyway?'

'I want to be able to go back to Sophie's mother, my aunt, and be able to tell her something about Sophie's life out here and who her friends were because I think it would give her some comfort. I would like to meet your American friends and take a picture of you all together to show her, if possible.'

Jean seemed to like that idea and said eagerly: 'I can arrange for us to get together if you like. I have the morning off tomorrow, so I will see if I can get them to come and meet us in Piazza Vecchia for a drink.

'You will like Edgar. He was very helpful to Sophie after I introduced her to him, showing her round the library and putting her in touch with valuable contacts in the area. I suppose it was a happy coincidence that she came to live in this building, really, because I had already become friends with Edgar and was able to introduce her to him.'

Was there a hint of resentment there, Kate wondered? Was she saying 'I saw him first, so hands off'?

She put Jean to the test by saying: 'I suppose they must have had a lot in common. Did they discuss their work much?'

Jean flushed and said, pointedly: 'Well, Edgar has already had one book published on Donizetti and is now working on a follow-up so I am sure that Sophie would have found all his knowledge of the subject quite valuable, but I'm not sure you could say they had a lot in common. I would say it was a lucky day for her when she came to live here because I already knew him and was able to introduce them. He is very much respected here in Bergamo. Sometimes when I have been out with him, people have recognised him and asked him for his autograph.'

Kate said: 'Funnily enough I bought a copy of Edgar's book on Donizetti from one of the book shops in the Città Alta a couple of days ago. Now that I have started to read it, I have begun to wonder about Sophie's book and what it would have been like.

'I would like to have a look in Sophie's apartment

to see if I can find her manuscript. I am sure when my aunt is feeling better she would be interested to read it.'

'Okay. If you like, I could ask Signora Mattozzi for the key and we could go and have a look now,' Jean offered.

Kate was pleased not to have to ask Signora Mattozzi herself as the woman had not seemed keen to have her in the building on their previous encounters.

She finished her coffee while Jean went down to the concierge's apartment to borrow her pass key. When Jean returned she was looking red in the face and flustered.

'Really, that woman is abominably rude to me sometimes. I mean, I do pay rent for living here, but she frequently makes me feel as though I am a terrible inconvenience to her.'

Kate followed Jean up the narrow staircase to the top floor flat and watched her struggle to open the door with the pass key.

'These old doors are all different. I suppose you develop the knack of opening your own in the end but this one seems terribly stiff.'

Kate took over and eventually managed to turn the key in the lock and get the door open so that they could go inside.

'I can't believe how big it looks without all that dark oak furniture,' Jean said when they went into the main room.

'This is the first time I have really seen it looking like this because when I was in here last Monday when we found her I didn't really notice…' she stopped herself, as she was clearly embarrassed.

'I'm so sorry, Kate.'

'It's okay, I knew what you meant,' Kate said. 'I

just want to find her writing things, any files, or notebooks or printed pages that I can take back with me.'

'Well, I know she used to use her laptop at the big dining table that stood in the middle of the room, but that's obviously been taken away with the rest of the furniture. I also remember sometimes seeing her writing in longhand in a notebook. You could try the small desk over there. That is one piece of the old furniture she obviously wanted to keep.'

Kate went over to the dainty antique desk in the corner and pulled open its five drawers one by one but all she found were envelopes, writing paper, new notebooks in different sizes and files containing bank statements.

She saw that there was a small CD player on top of the desk and when she pressed the play button the apartment was suddenly filled with the soft, sweet voice of Pavarotti singing the first few words of 'Com'è gentil' from Don Pasquale. It was one of her favourite pieces of music and she was amazed and touched to discover that Sophie must have liked it too. It was so beautiful that tears came into her eyes and she switched it off quickly and turned away to look round the room again.

'I suppose her writing things could be in one of the suitcases over there,' Jean said pointing to the stack of luggage in the middle of the floor.

Kate tried the first case and found that it wasn't locked, but all it contained were pretty dresses and skirts neatly packed with folded tissue paper.

'She always dressed very well,' Jean said sadly.

The other two cases also contained clothes as well as underwear and bags of toiletries.

'I would imagine the Commissario will have taken the laptop and her phone to examine them, but I can ask him if he also found any files or notebooks relating to the book,' said Kate, closing the final case.

They left the apartment and Kate, who was holding the key, pulled the door shut behind her. When they reached the door to Jean's apartment she said: 'I will call on Signora Mattozzi and give the key back to her on my way out.'

Jean was obviously relieved not to have to see the concierge again and promised to text her with the arrangements for meeting up the next day before going back inside her own apartment.

On her way out of the building Kate knocked on the door of Signora Mattozzi's apartment. After a few minutes the concierge came to the door with a grim look on her face and took the pass key back from her without saying a word.

'Signora Mattozzi, could I ask you something about Luisa? I have been told that my cousin had a disagreement with her recently.'

'I'm sorry, I don't know anything about that.'

'Was Luisa good at her work?'

'As good as any other young girl is these days.'

'Then why would my cousin have fallen out with her?'

'Perhaps she found that she couldn't trust her,' Signora Mattozzi said slyly.

'Can you tell me what you mean by that?'

'I suppose she has been gossiping to you about these things,' said the concierge gesturing in the direction of Jean's apartment.

'Well, she did say Sophie used to be close to Luisa but that they seemed to have fallen out recently.'

'Well, I wouldn't take too much notice of anything she says. The truth is she did not like your cousin very much.'

Kate asked: 'Do you know why?'

Signora Mattozzi gave an unpleasant little smile. 'Perhaps it was because all the men were interested in the pretty little Signorina and none of them took any notice of her less attractive friend.' She then quickly shut the door before Kate could ask her anything else.

7

'I wanna green salad and a diet coke, that's all!'

Kate turned slightly in her chair to see who was speaking and saw a waitress trying to hand a menu to the elderly man at the next table, who was refusing even to look at it.

He was wearing a white baseball cap and had obviously had too much sun as his face was a deep shade of pink and beginning to peel. He wore a T-shirt in a shade of pink that clashed horribly with his skin colour and grey shorts that revealed too much of his thin white legs, which were shod in white trainers and white ankle socks.

When Kate turned back to her own table she caught Edgar Wallenheimer's eye and they smiled at each other.

'I sometimes despair of my fellow countrymen and their obsession with the baseball cap when they are in Italy!'

'You do wear one yourself sometimes,' the woman sitting next to him pointed out.

'Marge, please, that's an outrageous slur,' Edgar said in mock indignation.

'Well you do! When we were out in the boat on that lake the other day you got one out of your pocket just like that, because you didn't want to get sunburn.'

'Was that when you went to Lago d'Iseo?' Jean asked, leaning forward eagerly.

'That's right!' Marge said. 'We were going across the lake to that cute little island and the sun was really beating down on us.'

'I must have worn it for all of ten minutes,' Edgar said smiling at her indulgently. 'I refuse to have it held against me.'

He was dressed more like an Italian than an American, Kate noticed, thinking that it must have been a conscious decision on his part. His cream linen jacket and navy blue shirt and trousers were stylish and looked expensive. His silver hair was cut short but left fashionably thick on the top and he was tanned as a result of months living in Italy. When he smiled across at her again she noticed what attractive brown eyes he had, although she thought he looked older and thinner than his publicity picture.

His friend Marge was a striking redhead with an air of self assurance about her. She was tall with a good figure and wore a white cotton open neck shirt and beige trousers. Her clothes looked really simple but Kate felt sure the outfit would have cost a great deal of money.

The two Americans had politely expressed their sadness at Sophie's death and pointed out that they had frequently had drinks with her sitting outside this bar.

'We were often at this very table with your cousin,' Edgar had said.

They had gone on to chat easily and confidently with Kate as though they had all been friends for ages and there had been no recent tragedy.

Kate had explained that she wanted to hear anecdotes about Sophie's life in Bergamo and take pictures of Sophie's friends so that she could show her aunt when she got back to Britain. Edgar and Marge had happily posed at the table together with Palazzo della Ragione in the background, making quips at each other's expense like some well-rehearsed double act. Stepping back a few feet, Kate had also taken a distance shot of the table to include

Jean on the opposite side.

'Sophie was such a sweet little thing. I took to her immediately. We loved to have our girly days out together in Milano,' Marge said, pronouncing the name of the city in a very American way, with an elongated middle syllable.

'You should have seen us on the Via Monte Napoleone. Boy, we did some serious shopping along there!'

'How did you first meet Sophie?' Kate asked.

'It was at the Donizetti theatre, I think,' Edgar said.

'That's right,' Marge joined in. 'Jean brought her along to an opening night and introduced her to us during the interval.'

'I met Jean when I first joined the opera lovers' group here,' Edgar said smiling across at her. Jean went a shade darker than her normal pink complexion.

'It's a great group. You get to go to previews and talks and meet the director, stuff like that,' said Marge. 'And of course Edgar liked Sophie immediately because she knew who he was and had read his book on Donizetti. He loves people to recognise him and it is even better if they have read his book,' she said with a grin.

'When I found out that Sophie was here to do her own research I was more than happy to show her round the Civic Library and the Donizetti museum and introduce her to a few useful people,' Edgar explained to Kate.

Marge chipped in: 'They would work together in the library all morning and afterwards we would all meet for a drink and then go for lunch at one of the cafes or restaurants around the square. We always got VIP treatment from the restaurant staff because we were with our local celebrity author here. We became known round here as the fabulous foursome.' She gave a sideways glance in Edgar's direction and pulled a humorous face at him.

'I still can't quite believe Sophie has gone for good. I just can't understand how someone so young and healthy could suddenly die like that,' Kate said, to steer the conversation back to her cousin.

'Oh no, it happens, believe you me,' Marge said. 'I had a cousin in LA who died in his sleep at the age of 57. His wife said she heard him take one last, really deep breath and then that was that.'

'The police have said they can't be sure exactly what happened until they get the results of the post mortem examination,' Kate pointed out.

'Oh, I wouldn't hold out much hope of that happening any time soon,' Marge said. 'I mean, I just love Italy and all that, but the police aren't exactly known for their efficiency, are they? A woman in my hotel had her bag snatched a few days ago by one of those immigrants who hang around outside the railway station. She reported it straight away but the police still haven't got back to her with any news about it.'

'To be fair, Marge, this is a bit more important,' Jean said timidly.

'Oh I know, dear, but I am just saying that they may not be able to tell Kate anything before she goes back home.'

'How long are you planning to stay here?' Edgar asked.

'I'm not sure, really. Probably a few more days and then I will need to get back home to see my aunt.'

'Well, be sure to tell her how sorry we all are,' Edgar said.

'Yes, of course I will.'

Kate took another sip of her wine and then asked casually: 'How did Sophie seem in the last few weeks? Did she ever complain of feeling unwell?'

'Not to me,' Marge said at once.

'Did she seem happy? Or, did anything seem to be bothering her?'

Edgar and Marge exchanged a look as though they both knew something that might be significant. 'She seemed very happy,' Marge said. 'She told me she had met a new man and he seemed to have made a big impression on her.'

'Did you ever meet this man?' Kate asked curiously

'No, she was a bit coy about it all, but you can take it from me there was definitely a new man in her life.'

'That's why she dumped poor Ernesto,' Edgar said.

'Who is Ernesto?'

'Ernesto is the darkly brooding manager of La Torre ristorante,' Edgar explained. 'We often dined there and Sophie had been having a bit of a fling with him. But she ended it when she met this new guy and Ernesto has made no secret of how badly he has taken it.'

Kate was just about to ask something else when there was the sound of glass breaking behind her. She turned round to look and saw a large pigeon had landed on a table nearby and was pecking at left over crisps and crumbs on a plate. His greedy activity had caused him to knock over a couple of wine glasses, which had rolled off the table and shattered into small pieces on the stone slabs.

The waitress came hurrying out of the bar to clear up the glass and Edgar signalled to her for the bill.

Jean said to Kate: 'You'll pass La Torre on your

way back to your hotel. I've got to go up to Largo Colle Aperto to get the bus to the Città Bassa because I'm teaching this afternoon so I can show you where it is on the way if you like.'

Edgar and Marge each kissed Kate on both cheeks when they said farewell and Marge took her mobile number. She wanted to arrange for Kate to have dinner with her in the rooftop restaurant at her hotel. 'You get the most fabulous view from there of the Città Alta lit up at night,' she explained.

Kate and Jean walked across Piazza Vecchia past the white marble fountain surrounded by lions and sphinxes in the middle and then turned up Via Colleoni.

'How did you get on with Signora Mattozzi when you took the key back?' Jean asked.

'Oh, she was all right. I asked her why Sophie had fallen out with Luisa and she implied that Sophie had found that she couldn't trust her.'

'Oh, that's really sad,' Jean said.

'Why do you think Sophie left the Albergo Milano to go and live in that particular apartment in the first place?' Kate asked.

'I think it was because Roberto Mariotto arranged it all. He made it really easy for her,' Jean answered. Seeing Kate's look of surprise she continued: 'Roberto has a financial interest in the Palazzo Mattozzi and when Sophie mentioned that she wouldn't mind having her own apartment he offered to rent the top floor to her. He had it decorated and furnished before she moved in so that it was really nice for her.

'It had been standing empty ever since I moved into my apartment, I don't really know why.

'I think that is one of the reasons Signora Mattozzi and Sophie fell out. The apartment contained some of the best pieces of antique furniture in the palazzo that had been in the Mattozzi family for generations. But Sophie said she didn't like them and wanted to buy some new things. She got Roberto to agree to them being put in store and Signora Mattozzi was furious about it.'

'That seems very odd. I mean, Sophie wasn't going to be here for long, surely she could have put up with the old furniture.'

'Sophie liked having nice things around her,' Jean said simply. Then she pointed in front of them and said: 'We are coming up to La Torre now.'

Kate looked up to see the top of the old, grey stone tower against the deep blue sky. When they drew level with the tower at ground floor level she saw there was a big glass window displaying a menu and people were already having lunch at the tables inside.

On an impulse she asked: 'Are you free to meet me here for dinner tonight? I would like to be introduced to Ernesto.'

Jean thought about it and then said: 'I'll be teaching till seven pm. But I could get back up here and leave my things at the apartment and meet you here for about eight.'

'That would be lovely,' Kate said. 'Will we need to book?'

'I wouldn't have thought so, not on a Monday night. I would think Ernesto will be glad to have some extra customers and I am sure that he will be interested to meet you.'

Later that afternoon, taking a rest back at her hotel, Kate lay with her head propped up on her pillows and her feet on the bed reading more of Edgar's book about Donizetti. She was interested in his account of Donizetti's early life in Bergamo. She had not realised the composer had come from such humble beginnings. He had been the fifth of six children born to a poor couple living in the dark basement of a house in Borgo Canale, just outside the city walls, towards the end of the 18th century. She was curious to find out more about what had changed his life and how he had gone on to become an internationally acclaimed composer of so many wonderful operas that were still regularly being performed.

Every now and then she thought sadly of Sophie and wondered what the book she had been working on would have been about.

Somehow, knowing Sophie as she did, she thought it unlikely that her book would have been just another straightforward biography. She must have found some new information, or a different angle to write about.

Having failed to find the manuscript or any notes for the book in the apartment her next line of enquiry would have to be with Aldo. Maybe the police had taken away the handwritten material for the book. She was guessing that they had removed Sophie's laptop and her mobile phone to look at what was on them.

She made up her mind to go round to the Commissariato there and then to ask about Sophie's possessions and got off the bed, grabbed her bag and left the room.

When she arrived in the entrance hall at the police station she was pleased to see only a few people on the seats in the waiting area. After giving her name and taking a seat there herself she took Edgar's book out of her bag and continued to read.

One of the best things about the book was the

quality of the photographs of Bergamo. She promised herself that while she was still in the city and had the opportunity she would visit all the places with Donizetti connections.

After a few minutes Aldo appeared in the waiting area with his shirt sleeves rolled up casually. He surprised her by saying: 'Kate, how lovely it is to see you again. Let's get out of here and go for a cup of coffee.'

They walked through a peaceful Piazza Mascheroni, Aldo pointing out to her the faded frescoes on the walls of some of the buildings, which were illuminated by the afternoon sun. Near the top of Via Colleoni he ushered her through a small dark wooden door into a bar.

Once they were seated at a table inside, she asked him: 'Would it be possible for me to have a look at Sophie's phone and laptop? I am assuming that you took them away to have them analysed, or something.'

Aldo stirred some sugar into his espresso and thought about it carefully with a faraway look in his brown eyes.

Eventually he replied: 'I don't see why not. Because of the nature of this particular case I don't think there would be any harm done if we returned them to you at this stage. If there was anything of significance on them, I am sure my officers would have found it by now and all your cousin's property will be coming back to you eventually, anyway. I will put a request in for them to be brought from the property store to my office when I get back and I will ring you to let you know when you can collect them.'

Kate said: 'Thank you. And the other thing I wanted to ask was whether any files of papers or notebooks were taken from the apartment by your officers at the same time.'

'I am not aware of any material like that being taken away by my officers but I will certainly make some enquiries.'

Kate said: 'Sophie was supposed to be writing a book and yet there is no trace of any manuscript or even rough notes for it in the apartment. I know Sophie often wrote in longhand in notebooks and that she was also going round the area interviewing people so I would have thought that she must have made some notes somewhere.

'I have had a look through the apartment again with the help of her neighbour, Jean Anderson, but we weren't able to find anything, so I wondered whether the police had taken it all away.'

Aldo said: 'What were you hoping to find out from her notebooks?'

'Just some indication of what her book was going to be about. I know my aunt would probably like to read it when she is feeling better so I would at least want to be able to take the working draft back with me.'

Aldo said: 'Leave it with me and I will ask my officers if they removed any books or notes and I will text you or ring you to let you know if I have something for you to collect.'

Kate thanked him again and then asked: 'When do you think you will be sent the results of the post mortem examination?'

He shrugged. 'Soon, I hope, but these things can take time, I'm afraid. I promise I will contact you as soon as I have received any news about it.'

Kate told him about meeting Sophie's American friends that morning and was surprised to find herself chatting and laughing with Aldo without any inhibitions. I feel as though I have known him for ages, she thought.

She walked back through the streets with him to the Commissariato and held out her hand to shake his hand when they reached the door, but he leaned forward and kissed her on both cheeks, saying: '*Coraggio*! Soon things will seem better for you, I am sure.'

8

Back at her hotel Kate dressed with care for her meal with Jean at La Torre. She was hoping to persuade Ernesto to talk frankly to her so she could find out as much as possible from him about his relationship with Sophie.

But when she studied herself in the mirror after all her efforts, as usual, she did not like what she saw. She sighed, resignedly. She was tall and well built, whereas Sophie had been small and very slim. She had long, straight dark hair, but Sophie's hair had been short and blonde and wavy. She had never been particularly interested in clothes or had much money to spend on them but Sophie had always been a stylish dresser.

When this is all over you are going to have to lose at least a stone and get yourself some new clothes, she told her reflection in the mirror sternly.

Ernesto will never believe that you are even related to Sophie, she thought and was then amused and slightly embarrassed to realise that she was even thinking about trying to compete with poor, dead Sophie. The important thing was to try to get as much information from Ernesto as possible while she had the chance.

She put the finishing touches to her make-up and took a final look in the mirror. Black skirt, black top. It was all just too black. She remembered grabbing some jewellery and putting it in her wash bag at the last minute before she had left for the airport. She found the bag and looked inside and spotted a necklace of coral beads she had bought on a previous visit to Italy. It would have to do. She put the necklace on, picked up her bag and left the hotel to walk through the narrow streets to La Torre.

In her eagerness she had allowed herself far too much time and she arrived at the restaurant about a quarter of an hour early. But it allowed her to scrutinise the menu on display in the window and she was pleased to find there were several local dishes that she hadn't yet tried that sounded tempting from their descriptions. After a while the door opened and a young waiter looked at her with a smile and said: 'Please, feel free to come inside, Signora.'

Kate said: 'I am waiting for a friend.' He indicated a table by the window and said: 'Well, you can sit here and they will see you as soon as they arrive.'

He asked if she would like something to drink and placed two copies of the menu on the table.

When Kate opened her menu she was interested to see that it contained a short history of La Torre, which provided information both about the tower itself and about the restaurant after it had opened there a couple of years before. There was a picture of Ernesto del Buono, who was described as the proprietor. He looked a few years younger than Sophie and had dark brown, wavy hair and a small amount of dark stubble round his jaw. He was dressed in a blue and white striped shirt and a navy blue jacket. He was rather attractive and looked nothing like a restaurant owner, Kate thought.

When the waiter brought her glass of wine she asked if Ernesto was in the restaurant that evening. 'He has gone upstairs to his apartment but I expect he will be coming back down again soon,' the waiter said.

Kate sipped her wine and continued to study the

menu while she waited for Jean. After a few minutes she glanced at her watch and saw that it was now nearly a quarter past eight.

Every time the door opened she looked up hopefully but it was other diners arriving and being greeted by waiters and shown to tables. Eventually Jean appeared in the doorway looking flushed and catching sight of Kate came over to the table and immediately started apologising.

'I really am very sorry but I just missed one bus outside the station and then had to wait ages for the next one,' she said.

Kate assured her that she was only a few minutes late and then summoned the waiter to order a drink for Jean. She passed her a menu. 'Ernesto is expected in the restaurant any time now according to the waiter,' she said.

She asked Jean for guidance about the dishes on the menu that had descriptions involving Bergamo dialect words and finally settled on *casonsei*, another local term for *casoncelli,* and *stinco al forno*, which was a pork shank braised in wine with vegetables.

'Sophie found all the meat dishes on menus around here a bit overwhelming,' Jean recalled. 'She was more of a cheese and salad sort of person.'

'Not the ideal person to be in a relationship with a restaurant owner, then,' Kate said with a smile.

'No, I suppose not.'

'What did she used to order when she came here?'

'Oh, she would often have the mushroom risotto and some grilled lemon sole with a salad afterwards,' Jean said at once.

'How did the relationship with Ernesto start?'

'Well, we used to come here a lot with Edgar and Marge because the food here is really good.

'Ernesto would always pay Sophie a lot of attention and bring us complimentary wine and desserts, that sort of thing.

'Then one night we were here and a young man came in selling red roses and Ernesto bought his entire stock and presented them all to Sophie. It was so romantic.

'She didn't confide in me about it at the time, but I found out later that she had started seeing him.

'She never brought him back to Palazzo Mattozzi to my knowledge but I think she sometimes stayed the night with him here. If she wasn't in by the ten o'clock bell she knew she would be locked out for the night in true Bergamo fashion,' Jean said with a smile.

Kate said: 'I'm sorry, but I'm not sure what you mean by that.'

'Well, at ten o'clock every evening the bell in the Campanone, the big bell tower in Piazza Vecchia, sounds 100 times. It is a tradition that dates back centuries to the time when they had a curfew. It was to let the residents of the Città Alta know they had to make their way back inside the city or they would be locked out for the night. It was all part of protecting the city from invaders. Nowadays they don't lock the gates to the city any more but they still ring the bell 100 times because it has become a Bergamo tradition. And, as a true *bergamasca*, Signora Mattozzi locks the gate to the courtyard after she has heard the ten o'clock bell. Anyone inside the Palazzo is in for the night and anyone outside has to stay outside.'

Jean suddenly stopped talking and Kate realised she was looking beyond her in the distance at something that had caught her eye. Kate turned to look and saw a small man with dark wavy hair and designer stubble wearing a plain white shirt and black trousers had come to the cash desk in the middle of the restaurant and was talking to one of the waitresses. He didn't look nearly as well and happy as he had done in his picture on the menu, but it was unmistakeably Ernesto.

He looks more like a musician or an artist than a restaurateur, thought Kate, but she could see why Sophie had been attracted to him.

Just then their first course was delivered to the table by the young waiter and Kate had to turn round again and start eating her pasta. But when their plates had been cleared and they had ordered a bottle of wine to accompany their main courses, Ernesto came over to their table.

'Jean, *come stai*,' he said bending down to kiss her on both cheeks.

'Ernesto, may I introduce you to Kate Butler,' said Jean. 'She is Sophie's cousin and is here in Bergamo to sort out her affairs.'

Ernesto looked shocked for a few seconds and then swallowed hard and said '*Piacere*. I am glad to meet you, Signora Butler,' holding out his hand to Kate who shook it.

Kate said: 'I am delighted to meet you because I understand you and Sophie had become very close.'

He laughed and said in an unnaturally high voice: 'For a while maybe, but she soon tired of me!'

Kate said: 'It must be very difficult for you to come to terms with her loss.'

'Very difficult, very difficult indeed. I always hoped she would change her mind and come back to me but all hope is lost now!'

At that moment a voice called out loudly: 'Ernesto, Ernesto!'

Kate turned in her seat and saw a tall, black man in

chef's whites wearing a red and white bandana around his head standing in the doorway of the kitchen. He was watching Ernesto talking to them with a worried expression on his face. He had a plate of pasta in one hand and a glass of red wine in the other.

Ernesto excused himself and went over to him and the two men had an aggressive exchange in low voices for a few seconds. Then Ernesto seized the pasta and the wine from the chef and took it to a table next to the kitchen doorway, where he sat down and started to eat.

'It must have been hard for him to lose Sophie to another man and then have to hear from someone else that she had died,' Jean said, still watching him.

'Yes, it must have been difficult to come to terms with,' Kate said as a steaming plate of stinco al forno was placed in front of her.

'Well, that's just it. I don't think he did come to terms with it,' Jean said, taking a forkful from the side dish of polenta she had just been given.

'He used to stand out on the street opposite Palazzo Mattozzi watching her window. He couldn't seem to accept that she didn't care about him any more.'

'Did you actually see him doing that?'

'Yes, quite a few times.'

'How recently did you see him?'

Jean thought about it for a while and said: 'It must have been the night before she was found dead. I needed to do some last minute shopping and I went down on the funicular to the Città Bassa because there is a really good supermarket practically opposite the station. When I came back with my shopping at about seven o'clock I saw him standing on the opposite pavement just staring up at her window. I remember thinking that he obviously hadn't seen me. He seemed oblivious of everything that was going on around him and was just staring up at Sophie's window.'

Ernesto went inside the kitchen after he had finished eating and Kate did not see him again until just before they were about to leave the restaurant. The meal had been excellent and she had enjoyed Jean's company. It was a relief to be able to talk about things to someone who seemed so straightforward and friendly. Jean had told Kate about her work as an English teacher in Bergamo and the different classes she had been engaged to teach. Kate had in turn talked about jobs in journalism she had done in the past and her attempts to make a living as a freelance writer since her redundancy.

Jean had told her more about what it was like living in the Città Alta in her apartment in Palazzo Mattozzi. 'I am sure that Signora Mattozzi is getting worse. She was not nearly as bad tempered and rude when I first moved into the palazzo as she is now. It is a shame because I really like the apartment, but she does make me feel uncomfortable about being there sometimes.'

Kate tried to steer the conversation on to Sophie and her recent falling out with Luisa but Jean could not really tell her much more about it. 'Luisa is normally quite sweet natured. I can't imagine what she could have done to upset Sophie. She is a single mother and spends all her time when she is not working looking after her little boy. I have seen them out together and she is marvellous with him. They live with her parents in the Città Bassa so she is able to leave him with them when she is working. I have no idea what she and Sophie could have fallen out about, but something must have changed between them recently, it was obvious to everyone who had anything to do with them,' she said.

When they had finished eating, their plates had been cleared away and they were waiting for the bill, Ernesto came back over to their table with two glasses of *limoncello* for them.

He said: 'I'm sorry about the interruption earlier but I'm afraid Anton is being a bit over protective towards me at the moment. He is behaving like my mother, trying to make sure that I eat something properly each evening.'

He looked directly at Kate: 'It is difficult for me to explain how I felt about Sophie to someone such as yourself, who is actually a member of her family. A few weeks ago I thought my world had ended when she told me she had met someone else. But this last week has made me realise what the end of the world really feels like. I loved her very much and was devastated when she ended our relationship, but I always hoped she would change her mind and come back to me in time. I just could not believe it when I heard she had died and that it really was the end of all my hopes.'

'When did you last see Sophie?' Kate asked.

'Oh, it was just a few days ago. I bumped into her in the street near the restaurant. She looked absolutely wonderful. You would never have thought there was anything wrong with her. I just can't believe what has happened. She was far too young to suddenly die like that.

'But I should perhaps not be talking like this to you. I don't want to cause you any more pain. I realise that it must have been terrible for you, too, to have lost her.'

He put the palm of his left hand across his

forehead as though his head was suddenly hurting. Sounding close to tears, he said: 'We are both suffering, I know, but it is difficult to talk about things now with a restaurant full of people.'

He paused, trying to compose himself, and then said in a calmer voice: 'I would like you to come back and see me some time so that we can talk freely in better surroundings. There are things I want to tell you about Sophie and things I would like to ask you about her. Here is my mobile number. Please give me a ring so that we can arrange a time for you to come and have a meal with me and then we will be able to talk properly.'

He placed a business card with his mobile number next to Kate's glass of limoncello and then turned to walk back in the direction of the kitchen. Kate saw that Anton was again standing in the doorway watching him anxiously.

Roberto was sitting on the leather settee in the reception area reading a magazine when Kate arrived back at the hotel. He stood up straight away when she came in and said: 'You look nice. Have you been somewhere special?'

'I have been out for dinner at La Torre with Jean Anderson, Sophie's neighbour. She introduced me to the owner, Ernesto del Buono.'

'Oh yes, of course, I believe Ernesto and Sophie were romantically involved for a while, weren't they,' Roberto said, with a little smile to himself.

Was there a hint of jealousy there, Kate wondered.

Then he said: 'Can I offer you a glass of wine, the bar is empty.' It crossed her mind then that he might have been waiting up for her, because he wanted to talk to her again.

They went through to the bar and he took a bottle

of Valcalepio Bianco from the fridge and placed it with two wine glasses on a small table with comfortable looking leather chairs arranged around it.

When they had sat down and he had poured the wine, Kate said: 'Jean was telling me that it was you who arranged for Sophie to rent her apartment in the Palazzo Mattozzi.'

He said: 'Yes, that's right. She said she would like a place of her own so that she had more space to work in. The apartment was standing empty so I offered it to her.'

'So you own the Palazzo Mattozzi, then?'

'I have a financial interest in it because my father was in business with Signora Mattozzi's late husband, Cesare, and when my father died I inherited all his businesses and his properties.'

Kate said: 'Jean was telling me that after Sophie moved in she said she didn't like the furniture in the apartment so you gave her permission to have it taken away and replace it with her own things.'

Roberto looked uncomfortable and said defensively: 'She had been living there for quite a while and she came to see me and said she really didn't like the big antique pieces. She offered to buy the new furniture at her own expense and she also said she was willing to pay to have the old furniture stored safely, so I couldn't see any reason not to agree to it.'

'But Signora Mattozzi wasn't happy about it, was she?'

'No, she wasn't,' Roberto said with a rueful smile. 'The furniture had been in her husband's family for generations and she did not want it taken out of the palazzo. I think she was offended by some of Sophie's comments about it. But why are you asking me about it now?'

'Well, it is just that it seems rather odd that on the morning she was found dead the men had come into the apartment to collect the old furniture to be put in store. Her body was not discovered until after they had taken away all the old furniture and left the apartment.'

'But that can't have had anything to do with her death, can it?'

'No, I don't suppose that there is any connection at all.' Kate said thoughtfully. 'But all the same, it just seems rather strange.'

9

Kate shivered as she looked down at the antique bed with its polished wooden headboard and footboard and golden yellow, silk cover. She could picture the gaunt face of the person who once lay in that bed, close to death. She could imagine the suffering that must once have taken place in it and now, more than 150 years later, she was looking at it in a museum.

She was standing next to the bed in which Donizetti had died on the eighth of April 1848. According to Edgar's book, Donizetti had returned to Bergamo a very sick man after being cared for in a sanatorium near Paris. Some of his devoted friends had looked after him in their home in the Città Alta until his death and the street where their house stood had since been renamed Via Donizetti. Kate thought the bed must have been donated to the Donizetti museum by a descendant of the family who had looked after him.

She wondered whether Sophie had found it inspiring to see the bed the composer had died in and the chair from the palazzo that he had sat in during the last few weeks of his life. Kate had spent a fascinating hour or more studying the documents, letters and original scores on display in glass cases in the museum and she could well believe that Sophie must have found them invaluable as sources of information for the book she had been intending to write.

Kate went back to have one last look at the large portrait of the composer and then at the piano that Donizetti was said to have played and she tried to imagine his hands touching the keys.

Leaving the museum, she made her way down the

staircase of the Palazzo della Misericordia Maggiore and out into the courtyard. Strains of piano music were coming from one of the practice rooms of the musical institute that was housed in the same building and the sound followed her down the tranquil Via Arena as she walked back in the direction of Piazza Vecchia.

She was so lost in thought with her head still full of music as she walked along the deserted narrow street that at first she did not hear her name being called out. Then she became aware of running footsteps behind her and turned to see that Edgar was trying to catch her up.

'Kate! I have been calling your name. What brings you to this quiet corner of the Città Alta?'

'I've just been to have a look round the Donizetti museum,' Kate explained.

'A fascinating experience, isn't it?'

'I thought I would visit all the places relevant to Donizetti's life while I am here in Bergamo, for Sophie's sake.'

'Absolutely, it would be a big shame for you not to see where the great man was born and lived during his early life,' Edgar said. 'I am on my way to the funicular bar to have some lunch before going back down to my house in the Città Bassa. Would you care to join me?'

Kate said: 'Thank you. I haven't got anything planned for the rest of the day.'

They walked down Via Arena and Via Donizetti to Piazza Mercato delle Scarpe and through the funicular station to the bar.

Edgar asked for a table on the terrace overlooking the Città Bassa and after they were seated the waiter brought a bottle of water and two menus out to them.

They both ordered a salad and Edgar asked for a bottle of white sparkling Franciacorta wine, explaining to Kate that it was a particularly good wine because it was made from grapes grown on an area of fertile land between Lago d'Iseo and Brescia.

'It is a part of Lombardia that is often compared to the Champagne region in France because some of the wines they produce there have achieved worldwide prestige,' he said.

He was very handsome, she thought, as she watched his animated expression as he enjoyed sharing his local knowledge with her. She took a sip of the wine he had carefully poured for her and wondered whether Sophie had ever been attracted to him and if there had been any hint of a romance between them before she had become involved with Ernesto.

She said: 'It is a great comfort for me to know that Sophie had made such good friends here in Bergamo.'

Edgar smiled at her: 'Well, we had some good times together, for sure. I am glad to be able to look back on those happy memories now. But at the time when we were just enjoying our lives out here, none of us could have possibly known what was going to happen to her.'

'What about Marge? Had she become good friends with Sophie?' she asked.

'Yes, they went shopping and out for lunch together plenty of times. But there would be the occasional fight between them because they were both such feisty ladies,' he said with a whimsical smile.

'Did Sophie talk to you at all about the book she was working on?' Kate asked.

'No, she kept that pretty much to herself, but then that was only to be expected. A lot of writers never want to talk about their work.'

'What first got you interested in writing about Donizetti?'

'Well, I just thought the music was so wonderful that I started reading up about him and the more I found out, the more fascinated I became with the man.'

'How did he become such a talented composer after being born into such a poor family?'

'A lot of it was due to the encouragement he received from the amazing Simon Mayr, who was *maestro di cappella* at Santa Maria Maggiore. He persuaded a local charitable institution to open a free music school, primarily to train choirboys, but also to provide a good musical education. Gaetano was in the first group of scholars to be enrolled. Mayr quickly spotted his exceptional talent and did his best to encourage it, eventually arranging for him to go on to study in Bologna to broaden his musical horizons. What a guy! But it is all in my book, you know,' Edgar said with a self-deprecatory gesture, as though he didn't want to bore her by talking about it too much.

Yes, it was in the book. Kate remembered reading about it. But he hadn't put it over nearly as well in his written account as he was doing now in conversation with her at this table, she thought.

'There wasn't much in your book about his death, was there? Donizetti must have suffered terribly towards the end.'

'Yes, it doesn't bear thinking about,' Edgar said with a shudder. 'But I wanted my book to be a celebration of his musical success.'

Just then Kate's mobile beeped inside her bag to

indicate she had a message. 'Excuse me, for a moment,' she said and got it out to look at it. 'It is from the Commissario, he is letting me know that I can pick up Sophie's laptop and mobile phone from the Commissariato this afternoon.'

Edgar looked concerned. 'I just hope you don't find it too upsetting reading whatever documents she has saved on the laptop and the messages she has sent and received on her phone. It will stir up all sorts of memories for you.'

Kate explained to him again that she felt she owed it to her aunt to find out as much as she could about Sophie's life in Bergamo and how her work had been progressing so that she could help her come to terms with her daughter's death. But then the finality of it dawned on her once again and she suddenly lost her appetite and put her knife and fork down, leaving a large part of her salad untouched.

'It is also hard for you to have to come to terms with losing her, isn't it?' Edgar said to her gently, and Kate once again felt near to tears.

Seeing her distress, he looked round and signalled for the bill to a waiter who had just come out on to the terrace.

'I am sorry, I didn't want you to have to rush your meal,' Kate said in embarrassment.

'Not at all, I need to get home and put some more work in on my new book this afternoon. I shouldn't really be spending my time drinking wine and lingering over lunch with attractive ladies.'

He gave one of his wry smiles again but Kate suddenly had the feeling that it wasn't actually meant for her. He wasn't really looking at her, but was looking past her at something in the distance. She turned to see what it was and realised he could see his reflection in the large, ornate mirror on the wall behind her.

Later that afternoon when Aldo had given her the laptop and mobile phone and Kate had signed a book to confirm that she had received them, he shared some new information with her.

'An Englishman came to see us after Sophie's death became public knowledge and gave us his contact details. He claimed he had recently been having some kind of a relationship with your cousin.'

'He must be the mystery man Marge and Edgar told me about,' Kate said thoughtfully.

When she saw Aldo looked puzzled she explained further. 'They told me that Sophie had been having a relationship of some kind with the owner of La Torre restaurant, Ernesto del Buono. But then recently she had met someone else and had ended it with Ernesto and afterwards he went round telling people how upset he was that she had left him. But no one seemed to know the identity of the new man in Sophie's life.'

'I can tell you that this man is called Simon Pargeter and he says he is a property developer, 'Aldo said. 'He is apparently renovating an old palazzo near Sarnico on Lago d'Iseo and is converting it into luxury holiday apartments.

'He came in to give us his name and other details because he had to go back to the United Kingdom for urgent business reasons, but he said he wanted us to be able to get in touch with him if we needed to.

'I'm telling you about him because I thought you might come across text messages from him on Sophie's phone when you look at it.

'He told us that he was in Sarnico the night before

Sophie was found dead because he was attending a business dinner at a local restaurant. He said several of his colleagues and associates would be able to vouch for his whereabouts until late that evening but he had then spent the night at his apartment alone.

'When he could not contact Sophie during Monday he left messages for her, which you will see on the phone. He had to come to Bergamo the next day for business reasons and after he had finished his meetings he called at Palazzo Mattozzi because he had still not heard from Sophie and was becoming anxious.

'Signora Mattozzi told him what had happened and so he immediately came round here to see us. He said he had urgent business in the UK that was going to take him away for a few days but he was very concerned that he made himself available to assist us with any enquiries we felt we needed to make.

'By then I felt that there was no reason to consider your cousin's death was suspicious and we said he could go back to the UK. He arrived back in Italy yesterday and rang me to say he was at his apartment in Sarnico and to ask if we had received the post mortem examination report yet.'

After a few seconds thought, Kate said: 'I shall contact him. He will be able to tell me a lot about Sophie's last few weeks here.'

Aldo smiled at her. 'Contact him by all means, but don't expect too much from him. He gave me the impression that he had not known your cousin for very long and that he did not consider their relationship as anything particularly serious.'

Walking back through the street to her hotel carrying the laptop as well as her shoulder bag, Kate almost collided with Marge coming out of a fashion shop in Via Colleoni holding several carrier bags.

'Kate, my dear! How lucky is this? I was going to ring you later. Come and have a drink with me in Piazza Vecchia.'

She led Kate to the bar on the opposite corner of Piazza Vecchia from the one they had been at the day before. They sat at a small table for two in a corner of the square that was still bathed in the afternoon sunshine.

'I wanted to fix up that dinner date with you. How about Thursday night? It will be my treat because I really want you to see the fantastic view of the Città Alta from the rooftop restaurant at my hotel.'

Kate was distracted, looking for somewhere safe to put Sophie's laptop, but had no choice but to lay it flat on the ground under the table.

'What's that you have there?' Marge asked.

'It's Sophie's laptop. I have just collected it from the Commissariato along with her mobile phone.'

'Wow! Are you expecting to find information about her life in Bergamo on there?'

'Not exactly. The main thing I am hoping to find is the draft of the book she was working on.'

'Oh, I see. I suppose you wouldn't expect to find anything about her personal life on it, would you?'

'Not really, although she might have kept a diary about her life out here, perhaps. I suppose that would be the best I could hope for.'

The waiter came to the table and Marge ordered a vodka martini while Kate asked for a glass of Valcalepio Bianco wine.

'Anyway, how does Thursday evening sound?' Marge asked when he had gone.

'Yes, that would be fine.'

'Great! Let's meet at seven-thirty in the bar next to

reception. We will have a drink in there and then I will take you up to the restaurant and show you that knockout view all lit up.'

Kate looked down anxiously at the laptop again and Marge sighed and said: 'I wouldn't expect you to find a completed book on that thing. I'm afraid Sophie always came over as a bit of a dabbler, to me. I mean, Edgar had already had a book about Donizetti published but she was only just starting out on hers.

'I guess it gave her something to do, and it was an excuse to live here in these lovely surroundings,' she said, gesturing at the piazza in the background.

Kate had often privately thought that it couldn't have been all that difficult for Sophie to produce just six books in about 20 years and she had often wondered how her cousin had spent the rest of her time. But she had no intention of sharing her opinions with Marge and just sipped her wine and remained silent.

Marge was clearly still thinking about what might be on Sophie's laptop, because she returned to the subject, repeating herself. 'I don't suppose you'll find anything about her personal life on it either,' she said. 'I mean she is hardly going to write anything about her friends or her love affairs is she?'

Kate said: 'The Commissario has just been telling me about a man who went in to see them and left his contact details with them. He claims to have been romantically involved with Sophie just before her death.'

'Did he give you his name?' Marge asked, leaning forward eagerly.

'Simon Pargeter, an English property developer living near Lago d'Iseo.'

Marge gave a little shriek and clapped her hands together.

'Well, the sly little madam! She never told me anything about him. I was at the cocktail party where they were first introduced to each other. It was in one of the bars up here to launch a new art exhibition at the Palazzo della Ragione. I remember him perfectly. He was absolutely gorgeous, tall, dark and handsome with piercing blue eyes. And we were told by someone that he's absolutely loaded. But I had no idea she had started seeing him. Wait till I tell Edgar. He will be completely blown away!'

Later, back at the hotel Kate struggled to hold on to both the shiny black laptop and her shoulder bag while taking the key from Roberto at reception.

Roberto helpfully preceded her up the stairs, unlocked the door of her room for her and held it open so that she could place the laptop on the writing desk.

She explained: 'I have just been to collect Sophie's laptop and phone from the Commissariato.'

She spent the rest of the afternoon going through the Inbox and Sent items on Sophie's mobile phone and soon realised her cousin had more in common with her than she had thought. Neither of them was a prolific texter. Sophie's Sent items were mainly phrases such as 'See u at 8' 'Thanks' 'OK' or 'Would love 2'. The last comment had been her regular answer to Simon's invitations which were the most recent messages to be found on her phone. Kate was surprised not to find romantic messages from Ernesto on the phone and came to the conclusion that Sophie must have deleted them all when she ended the relationship.

Kate rang Simon's number from her own mobile

but the call went straight through to his voicemail. She left a message explaining who she was and asking him to call her back.

Then she thought about plugging the laptop in and starting to go through Sophie's files but by now she was feeling hungry as she had not eaten much at lunch time.

She looked at her watch and saw that it was already six-thirty. She got ready quickly to go out for pizza or pasta, planning to return to the hotel early and settle in for the evening to study what was on the laptop.

She wandered along the streets of the Città Alta until she found a restaurant she hadn't tried before and went inside. Because it was so early there were hardly any other diners. She carried on reading Edgar's book until the wine and pasta she had ordered were delivered to her table.

Just as she was finishing her food, her mobile rang. She fished it out of her handbag and touched the glass screen to answer it. A gruff voice with a slight trace of a London accent asked: 'Is that Kate Butler?'

'Yes.'

'It's Simon Pargeter, you left me a message.'

'Yes, that's right. I'm Sophie Westmullen's cousin. I am here in Bergamo sorting out her affairs and I wondered whether we could meet up.'

'Yes, I suppose we could,' he said, sounding wary. 'But I'm going to be a bit tied up with business for the next few days. I'm not sure when I could get to Bergamo.'

'I could come to Sarnico to meet you if that is all right,' Kate suggested.

'Okay then, what about coming on Friday? I should have a couple of hours free around the

middle of the day and we could go for some lunch.'
'That would be great,' Kate said.
'Oh well, that's a date then. How will you get out here?'
'I will probably come by bus,' Kate said, having already considered the idea.
'Great stuff. Well, I will text you with directions from the bus stop to my office,' he said and then ended the call before she had the chance to say goodbye.

Back at the hotel there was no one behind the reception desk and Kate did not feel like waiting around until someone came. Because she was tall she thought she would be able to reach her key by leaning over the desk and stretching her right arm out to it.

She managed to help herself to it and then ran up the stairs to her room and quickly unlocked the door. She gasped with shock when she saw a figure sitting in the dark at the writing desk, illuminated only by the light from Sophie's laptop which was now switched on.

10

'What the hell do you think you are doing?' she shouted angrily, snapping on the light switch next to the door.

Suddenly the whole room was lit up. The figure at the laptop turned to face her and she saw it was Roberto. He looked momentarily scared but then quickly regained his poise.

'I am so sorry if I startled you, Kate. I can explain what I am doing here, I promise you.'

'I hope you can,' Kate snapped at him. 'You shouldn't be in here and you certainly shouldn't be touching the laptop. I have only just been given it by the Commissario and I haven't had chance to look at it myself yet. How do I know you haven't changed anything or deleted some files?'

'I can promise you that there is a reason for me being here,' Roberto reassured her. 'But I agree I shouldn't have come into your room while you were out. I am sorry if I frightened you, but please will you give me the chance to explain what I was trying to do.'

Kate was breathing hard, still shaken by her discovery. Roberto got up from the chair and moved towards the door and she stepped to one side instinctively to let him pass.

He turned in the doorway and said: 'I realise that I shouldn't have come into your room. We can't talk in here now, so I will go down to the bar. Please, I beg you, come down and sit with me in there for a few minutes and have a glass of wine. At least give me the chance to explain why it was so important for me to look at the laptop.'

At this point he left the room leaving Kate on her

own, shocked and unsure about what to do next.

She looked round the room. Everything seemed to be exactly as she had left it before she went out for dinner, apart from the laptop being plugged in and switched on.

She went over to see what Roberto had been reading on the screen. He seemed to have been looking at the list of the documents that were stored on it, but did not seem to have got any further than that.

She decided she wanted to hear what he had to say. She told herself he would pose no threat to her in a public area on the ground floor of the hotel. She would be safe in the bar, where anyone could walk in at any time. She had been trying to find out about Sophie's life in Bergamo and now was her chance to dig a bit deeper. Having been caught snooping in her room he would be on the back foot, she reasoned, and would be desperate to please her. She grabbed her bag and key, locked the room and made her way downstairs.

Down in the empty bar there were two wine glasses ready on the table they had sat at the previous time. Roberto came from behind the bar with a bottle of Valcalepio Bianco. She sat down and watched him pour a glass for her and then said: 'Well, I am ready to hear your explanation.'

He sighed deeply. 'It's hard to put it into words, but all I can say is that I had been having problems with Sophie. She had been making my life difficult for some time and when she died, sad though it was, I thought my life would become easier. But then you came in with the laptop and I started to worry that she might have written something about me on it.'

Kate stared at him in disbelief: 'But she was

supposed to be writing a book about Donizetti. Why would there be anything about you on it?'

He paused for a moment, looking embarrassed. 'Well, she had found something out about me, or at least she thought she had. She had some information about my family which I wouldn't have wanted her to make public.'

'I'm sorry, I still don't understand. Are you trying to tell me that Sophie was blackmailing you?'

'Nothing so crude, Sophie was too clever for that. But she believed she had a hold over me and that she was in a position to make certain demands.'

'This all sounds absolutely ridiculous.'

'You don't understand because you are not from Bergamo. The Città Alta is a very small place. To succeed in business you have to have a good reputation. If Sophie had carried out her threat and spread certain stories about my family around, however untrue the stories were, it would have damaged my reputation.'

'You'd better tell me the whole story and let me be the judge of whether she had a hold over you, or not.'

'But then what is to stop you spreading the stories around and damaging me?'

'Why would I want to? I will be going home to England in a few days time and will probably never come here again. There is no one here in Bergamo I could tell and in any case I have absolutely no reason to want to damage your reputation.'

She saw him hesitate and so she continued: 'But if you don't tell me now exactly what your problem with Sophie was, I will tell the Commissario that I found you in my room trying to look at the laptop without my permission.'

Roberto sighed and looked worried. Then he said:

'Well, I suppose that I have no choice but to trust you.'

'That's right, so start from the beginning and tell me everything.'

Roberto took a sip from his glass. 'When Sophie first arrived to stay at the hotel I really liked her. We became friends and often sat here in the bar talking until late at night. I have to admit I found her very attractive and I was beginning to hope that she felt the same about me.

'But while she was a guest in the hotel I felt that any kind of relationship with her would have been entirely inappropriate. When she said she would like to have her own apartment so that she could have more space to work in, I saw it as an ideal opportunity. There was an empty apartment in the Palazzo Mattozzi at the time. Tenants seemed to leave there rather regularly, I'm not exactly sure why, maybe because of Signora Mattozzi's attitude towards them. The top floor apartment had been standing empty for a while.

'I offered it to Sophie and she seemed to jump at the chance. Before she moved in I had it completely refurbished and redecorated and even installed a brand new kitchen and bathroom.

'She seemed to get on well with Signora Mattozzi when she first moved in. They are the same age and discovered that they were actually born on the same day. But of course there was a world of difference between them, not just the way they looked, but the lives they had led. However, I know that while they were on good terms Signora Mattozzi confided in her frequently about what a hard life she had had.

'Her husband, Cesare, was from an ancient and noble Bergamo family and had inherited the palazzo. He was a lot older than her and they had never had any children.

'He did some business with my father and they made a decent amount of money together to begin with but he had also made some foolish investments on his own. After a few years he got into severe financial difficulties and my father agreed to help him out. He paid off his debts in return for a majority share in Palazzo Mattozzi. You have to realise that if my father had not helped him out he would have lost Palazzo Mattozzi altogether.

'When Cesare Mattozzi died, my father paid to have the palazzo converted into apartments. He gave Signora Mattozzi the ground floor apartment with the terrace to live in for the rest of her lifetime in return for acting as a kind of concierge for the building.

'But since my own father died I have had to work with her and she hasn't made it easy for me. She made life so difficult for the tenants that many of them have moved on quickly. Signorina Anderson is the exception, she has stayed in Palazzo Mattozzi longer than most people have done.

'When Sophie moved in, it was strange, but Signora Mattozzi seemed to really like her to begin with. They became friends and she filled Sophie's head with all sorts of stories about how my father had cheated her husband out of Palazzo Mattozzi.

'Not long after Sophie had moved into the apartment I discovered that she had started having some kind of a relationship with Ernesto del Buono, the owner of La Torre restaurant, which I can tell you was a big disappointment at the time, but I suppose I realised I just had to accept it. I came to terms with the fact later that she had never really been interested in me in that way.

'But it was not long after she moved into the

apartment that she started to make certain demands of me.'

'What sort of demands?'

'Well, she asked for changes, silly little things really, to be made to the kitchen and the bathroom, even though they had only just been installed. When I wasn't prepared to make them she would soon hint about how sorry she was for Signora Mattozzi and her late husband and how badly they had been treated by my father. Eventually I gave in and had the work done that she had requested because she made me feel uneasy about what she might have been told about my family by Signora Mattozzi.

'She never asked for money or anything like that, she just made it clear she had the power to bring my family into disrepute. She once even mentioned writing to L'Eco di Bergamo, our local newspaper, about the way Signora Mattozzi had been treated, which is why I wanted to see if she had ever drafted any kind of letter about it on her laptop.

'More recently she came to me and said she wanted to get rid of most of the big pieces of furniture and replace them with her own things. By then she and Signora Mattozzi were no longer such good friends and the Signora was adamant that she did not want to see her husband's family heirlooms leave the palazzo, so I was stuck in the middle.

'Sophie left me no choice but to go into battle with Signora Mattozzi and it made me even more unpopular with that lady, I can tell you. Sophie always made me believe that she would not hesitate to tell people how badly my father had behaved towards Cesare Mattozzi. I couldn't stand by and let his good name be damaged, could I?

'I didn't want to be in the position where no one would do business with me because they thought I was part of the family that had ruined Cesare Mattozzi.

'I'm sorry to have to tell you this, Kate, but I really thought that Sophie was a lovely person when I first met her. However, I honestly believe that in the last few weeks she positively enjoyed tormenting me.'

'Unfortunately, the whole thing had a ring of truth about it and I could understand his point of view,' Kate said sadly to Steve over the phone from her room later that evening.

'I remember that even when she was a young child Sophie had a knack of getting people to do exactly what she wanted. Even if you didn't agree with her she would make you feel so uncomfortable and pile on the pressure with veiled threats that you ended up doing what she wanted you to do. She always threatened to tell my aunt or my parents about what I had been doing, but more often than not I hadn't done anything like what she was going to say I had. But I was always scared they would believe her over me so I usually ended up giving in and doing what she wanted me to. Sophie always managed to get the upper hand with me so I suppose I can sympathise with Roberto to a certain extent.'

'Well I think his story is ridiculous,' Steve said. 'There must be more to it than he is letting on. I mean, here we have a woman who is suddenly found dead in suspicious circumstances and then you catch him in your hotel room trying to look at her laptop without asking. And the best he can come up with is she nagged him to make changes to the bathroom and kitchen and wanted to replace the furniture in her apartment. His story is a bit thin, if you ask me. There must be more to it than that. He sounds as though he could be a very slippery customer.'

Kate smiled to herself fondly. 'You say that about everyone,' she said.

'And I'm proved right most of the time. Also, I'm not happy that he can let himself into your room at any time.'

'Oh, he's not going to harm me. I've given him my word that I am not going to tell anyone else here about Signora Mattozzi's claims about his father.'

Even so, after she had finished the call, she got out of bed and put a chair in front of the door, so that if anyone did try to come into the room during the night they would bump into it and almost certainly wake her up.

Kate could not find any material about Donizetti or Bergamo when she painstakingly went through every document saved on the laptop the next morning.

There were letters Sophie had written to individuals and businesses as well as material relating to her previous book but nothing that was at all relevant to her time in Italy. Without Sophie's password she could not get into her email account. She had tried a few obvious word and date combinations but without success.

Kate knew that computer experts could sometimes find and restore files that had been deleted and resolved to take the laptop back to England to see what could be done with it. But she found it hard to believe that Roberto had managed to delete all Sophie's Bergamo material in the time he had been looking at the laptop. And in any case, why would he have wanted to? Surely he would have just wanted to get rid of anything she had written about him or his father.

It made her even more curious about the whereabouts of Sophie's files and notebooks and she decided to go round to Palazzo Mattozzi to talk to Luisa about them.

She had slept late that morning after a restless night and had just managed to get downstairs before the end of breakfast and help herself to a coffee and a pastry from the buffet before it was cleared away.

There had been no sign of Roberto as she went through reception on the way to the breakfast room which had been a relief. Now she was ready to go out he was still nowhere to be seen and she left her key on the unattended desk, pleased to have avoided the hotel manager again.

She walked through an unusually empty and peaceful Piazza Vecchia and along the now familiar route through the streets to Palazzo Mattozzi.

Signora Mattozzi came out into the courtyard when she heard Kate's voice over the intercom. 'I would like to speak to Luisa if she is here,' Kate explained. Signora Mattozzi stared defiantly at her through the iron gates with a grim expression on her face for a few seconds.

Then she reluctantly opened one of the gates to let her in and preceded her up the stairs in the direction of Sophie's flat without saying a word.

She knocked on the door of Jean Anderson's apartment but there was no reply. She called out something in what Kate thought must be dialect words and after a few seconds there was a sound from inside the apartment and then Luisa opened the door looking red-faced and flustered, smelling of smoke.

She's been having a crafty cigarette, Kate thought to herself.

There were a few incomprehensible words

exchanged between the two women and then Signora Mattozzi went back downstairs leaving Kate on the small landing with Luisa.

'I wondered whether we could go upstairs to Sophie's apartment and if you could help me look for something?' Kate asked.

Luisa paused for a moment while she tried to understand what Kate had said to her in Italian and then she nodded and took a bunch of keys out of the pocket of her overall and led the way up the next flight of stairs.

She unlocked the door of Sophie's flat and stood back on the narrow landing to let Kate go in first.

When they were both in the sitting room Kate asked: 'Did you ever see Sophie writing in a notebook?'

'Yes, Signora.'

'Do you know what has happened to her notebooks?'

'No, Signora.'

'When you packed Sophie's things in the suitcases, before the big pieces of furniture were taken away, did you see any of her notebooks?'

'No, Signora.'

'So, where do you think the notebooks are now? Kate asked, raising her voice in exasperation.

'I don't know, Signora.'

'The day you found Sophie lying dead in bed, after the big pieces of furniture had been taken away from the apartment, do you remember seeing her notebooks?'

'No, Signora.'

'Well, they must be somewhere! Where was the laptop when you came in that day?'

'Over there on top of that desk,' Luisa said, pointing to the small antique bureau in the corner that Kate had searched when she had been in the apartment with Jean.

'Don't you remember seeing the notebooks that day?'

'No, Signora,' Luisa said, beginning to sound distressed.

'They have to be somewhere,' Kate repeated. 'Think hard, you must be able to remember something.'

'I remember that a drawer in the big desk was open as though someone had been looking for something, yet the Signorina would have known it was empty because it was one of the pieces that were going to be taken away later that day.'

'You don't think the notebooks could have been left in one of the drawers by mistake and taken away with the furniture?'

'No, Signora, because I checked every piece myself to make sure it was empty before I let the men take any of the furniture away.'

Kate couldn't think of anything else to ask for a moment and there was an uncomfortable silence in the apartment.

Then she asked the maid: 'Did you like Sophie?'

Luisa said nervously: 'She was very beautiful and could be kind and generous. When she first came here she seemed to like me. She asked about my little boy and gave me things, such as left over food, to take home with me.'

'But then you and Sophie had a disagreement, didn't you?'

The maid's face flushed and she looked defensive. 'It wasn't really a disagreement. It was just that suddenly she seemed to change towards me and I couldn't do anything right.

'It was stupid, I know, but one day I took some

cheese from the fridge because it had been lying there for a few days and I didn't think she wanted it, or would mind me having it.

'But she asked me what had happened to it and when I told her I had taken it she got very angry. She accused me of stealing and said she would report me. I don't know who she was going to tell. Signora Mattozzi, I suppose.

'I was very worried for a time, but after all that, I don't think she ever actually told anyone. But she asked me to do a lot more things for her after that and was never so kind and friendly towards me.'

Again it was all too familiar behaviour, thought Kate.

Aloud she said: 'When you came in that morning, the first thing you did was to go into the kitchen, reheat the coffee in the pot and pour yourself a cup, wasn't it?'

Luisa said: 'Yes, and that proves I have been telling the truth because I would never have done that if I had thought she was still in the apartment.

'But, in any case, I wasn't really helping myself to her things. There was some coffee left in the pot and I just reheated it. I often had the coffee left over from her breakfast, otherwise it would have just been thrown away when I washed out the coffee pot.'

'Are you sure that the furniture men did not go into the bedroom?'

'I am positive! All the furniture they took away was in this room and so they did not have to go into any of the other rooms.'

'And had they all gone before you went into the bedroom?'

'Yes, because the first thing I did was clean the floor in here, ready for the new furniture arriving.

And then when I went into the bedroom to start cleaning in there I saw her…' she stopped in mid sentence and put her hand to her mouth.

Kate asked softly: 'What did you see, exactly? Tell me what you saw.'

'She was lying in the bed in her grey, silk dressing gown. She looked far too still. I knew straight away that something was wrong and so I called for help.'

'Did she look at all distressed or as though she had been in pain?'

'No, not really. Her eyes were open and she just looked …. I don't know really.'

'Please, Luisa, tell me how she looked.'

'I suppose she just looked as though she was surprised about something.'

11

Kate wandered through the streets of the Città Alta afterwards, thinking. It had been an upsetting morning and she did not feel like any lunch. When she came to an empty table outside a bar in a quiet side street she sat down and ordered herself a glass of wine before ringing Steve.

'I have a really bad feeling about things,' she told him, after recounting the details of her conversation with Luisa. 'I have been trying to make myself believe that Sophie died in her sleep as a result of natural causes, but there are still too many odd things that don't make sense.

'She obviously wasn't very popular here and I'm beginning to realise that most of the people that she spent time with weren't real friends.

'Then there is the business with the laptop. I don't think Roberto deleted all her work but there is nothing on it at all relating to her time in Bergamo. Also, I have not been able to find any of her files and notebooks.

'Jean Anderson was obviously jealous of her, the maid was frightened of her and Signora Mattozzi seemed to hate her. As a consequence she now seems to have moved on to hating me.'

'I'm coming out to Bergamo to help you,' Steve said immediately.

'But what about Aunt Edna? I want you to keep an eye on her because she is so vulnerable at the moment. She needs you to visit her regularly.'

'Don't worry about Edna, I've had an idea about that. Trust me, I will sort things out at this end. But I can't help worrying about you and how you are feeling at the moment. I think you could do with some support right now.'

Kate was sorry then that she had made him anxious and was eager to put his mind at rest. 'Please don't worry about me. I will be fine, I promise you. And you can rest assured that tonight, at least, I will be having dinner with the one person in Bergamo who could see no wrong in Sophie.'

That night when Kate arrived at La Torre she was shown up two flights of stairs to Ernesto's private dining room. The walls of bare stone were broken up by niches with white candles burning in them and the grey flagstone floor was softened by red patterned antique rugs.

It was like a room in an English castle and nothing like the décor of the smart restaurant that occupied the two floors below.

The waiter gestured to her to sit at the table set for two in the middle of the room. From her seat she could see through the window how high up they were as she had a bird's eye view of the tops of the towers and cupolas of the Città Alta.

Ernesto came in to join her, saying: 'Thank you for ringing me. I am really glad to have the opportunity to talk to you about Sophie. It will be wonderful to be able to hear about her from someone else who cared about her.'

He was wearing a smart, pale blue shirt that suited his olive complexion and Kate thought he looked happier and less tense than when she had seen him on her previous visit to the restaurant.

Ernesto handed her the menu and said: 'Please choose what you would like to eat and I will make sure that when they have brought in the food we are not constantly disturbed.'

Kate asked him why he had chosen to open a

restaurant in one of Bergamo's 12th century towers.
Ernesto leaned back in his seat and seemed happy to tell her about the restaurant's history.
He said: 'I used to work as a waiter in a restaurant near here but I always wanted my own place one day. I passed this tower on my way to and from work every day but it had been empty for years and needed a lot of restoration work.
'When my grandmother died she left me some money and so I approached the local authorities here in Bergamo and asked if I could renovate the tower and open a restaurant in it. Luckily they agreed. It needed a lot more work and cost more than I had originally expected but eventually we were able to open. We didn't do as well as I had hoped to begin with, in fact we weren't even breaking even, but fortunately then I discovered Anton.
'I read about him in an article about the restaurant scene in Milan that I came across in a magazine. He had become well-known for his unusual interpretations of classic Lombardian dishes.
'I went to the restaurant where he was working to sample his cooking and was immediately won over. Fortunately I managed to tempt him to come here and bring his talent to La Torre in return for a share of the profits. His contribution made all the difference and we started to do much better. The restaurant was full most nights and sometimes we even had to turn people away. But then I met Sophie…'
The waiter came in to take their order at that point and Kate asked for La Torre's version of *casoncelli alla bergamasca* again and Ernesto said he would have the same. She chose a veal dish, *vitello alla bergamasca*, for her main course and was surprised when Ernesto again said he would have the same.

Ernesto reeled off the long Italian name of a wine he wanted them to have with the meal and then the waiter left them alone.

When she was sure the waiter was out of earshot, Kate said: 'Tell me, how you first met Sophie.'

Ernesto smiled at the memory. 'It was here in the restaurant,' he said. 'She came in with a group of friends one night and I was intrigued by her immediately. She seemed so delicate and fragile, but I came to realise that she was actually very strong and highly intelligent. I was fascinated by her.

'Each time she came in I talked to her more and I became sure that she felt something for me. So eventually I asked her to come to the restaurant on her own without her friends one night as my guest and we had a meal together up here. That was the start of something very special between us.'

'Did you ever go to her apartment in Palazzo Mattozzi?'

'No, I never went inside. I would walk with her to the gates at the end of the evening sometimes, that's all.'

'Did she ever stay here?'

'Oh yes. I have a private apartment above here, right at the top of the tower. She said she preferred to stay the night with me here in my apartment and that she would not feel comfortable if I stayed with her because of the unpleasantness of the concierge.'

'How long were you together?'

'I suppose it was just for a few weeks. But I knew very quickly that I had fallen in love with her. I had never really been in love before, even though I had had plenty of girlfriends in the past. I always knew this was completely different. I was sometimes worried that I did not really know her very well. There was always something mysterious about her.

What do you think made her like that? Was it her family?'

Kate said: 'Sophie was an only child with parents who were older than average. She wanted for nothing in life, but her father died when she was just a teenage girl. I am sure that it affected her badly at the time. However, she has always had a devoted mother who is now, of course, devastated by her death.'

When the waiter had delivered two dishes of *casoncelli* and a bottle of wine to the table, Ernesto asked: 'And how close were you to Sophie?'

'My mother was the younger sister of Henry Westmullen, Sophie's father, although I am actually a few years older than Sophie. Her parents had been married for quite a while before she was born.'

Ernesto smiled and said: 'But no one would realise, looking at you tonight, Signora.'

Kate smiled at the compliment but made sure it did not distract her from what she felt she had to tell him. She said: 'To be honest, we have never been particularly close. There was always the age difference, which caused problems when we were told to play together when we were children and for various reasons we have not had a lot to do with each other since we became adults.

'But I am very fond of Sophie's mother, who is my aunt. She is far too unwell to come to Bergamo herself and so I am determined to do my best to find out what I can for her about what happened to Sophie while I am here.'

Ernesto shook his head in disbelief and said: 'Sophie looked outwardly so well and strong. Her mother must have been stunned by her death just as I was.'

When the waiter came in to take their plates away

a few minutes later Kate noticed that Ernesto had barely touched his *casoncelli.*

Once the waiter had served their second courses and refilled their wine glasses, Kate plucked up the courage to ask: 'How did Sophie end her relationship with you?'

Ernesto sighed and immediately put down his knife and fork again.

He took a sip of wine and said: 'She had seemed a bit distant and elusive for a couple of weeks. Then one day she told me she thought it would be best if she stopped seeing me because she had met someone else. She said nothing had happened with him yet but she hoped the relationship would develop and she wanted to be completely honest with me about it.'

He gave a rueful smile and said: 'It was just a few days later that I saw them together in one of the bars in Via Colleoni. I saw them through the window sitting at a table together laughing and talking. I guessed straight away that this must be the new man she had talked about meeting. As I stood there outside the bar looking through the window at them I felt as though I had been stabbed through the heart.

'I always hoped that she would come back to me if the relationship didn't work out and that's why I gave her some space. I waited and I desperately hoped that I would get her back. But then I heard that she was dead and now I have no hope left.'

Kate pushed the food around her plate while she considered her next question carefully.

'But when you say you gave her some space, didn't you try to get her back at any time?'

'No. I respected her wishes and left her alone.'

'It's just that I heard you sometimes went to Palazzo Mattozzi and stood outside in the street watching the window of her apartment.'

'That's ridiculous.'

'I'm sorry, Ernesto. I know it's painful, but you can be honest with me. Did you ever stand on the opposite pavement looking up at her window? I have been told that you were actually there the night before she was found dead, staring at the balcony outside her living room.'

'I may have gone past the palazzo occasionally on my way to and from the funicular railway station and I suppose I may have glanced up at her window out of curiosity, but you make it sound a lot worse than it actually was.'

'I'm sorry,' Kate said, anxious that she might have offended him and that he would stop talking to her.

He put down his knife and fork again and Kate realised he had eaten hardly any of his main course.

'It's okay. I know that you loved her too. She was your cousin and you are trying to make sense of it all and come to terms with her loss, just like me. I admit I did make a point of going past Palazzo Mattozzi from time to time in the hope of bumping into her because I hadn't given up all hope of her coming back to me.

'That's why it is impossible to explain to you how terrible the last few days have been for me. I know now that she is gone for good and that I no longer have any hope.'

He topped up Kate's glass with the last of the wine and said: 'There is only one thing we can do now.'

'What's that?' Kate asked.

'I must send for some Prosecco. At least we can drink a toast to the memory of the beautiful Sophie Westmullen.'

Aldo was sitting on the red leather settee in the

reception area when Kate arrived back at the hotel later.

'Have you been waiting to see me?' she asked in surprise. 'I have been having dinner with Ernesto del Buono at La Torre.'

'Can we go somewhere and talk privately?' Aldo asked.

'We could try the hotel bar, it is usually empty at this time of night,' Kate said.

There was no sign of Roberto, or any of the other guests. When they were both seated at one of the tables, Aldo said: 'I am sorry to call on you at this late hour but I have some news for you. I wanted to tell you in person rather than over the phone. We have had the results of the post mortem examination.'

He paused for a moment and then said: 'It is not good news, I am afraid. Traces of a sedative were found in Sophie's blood stream.' He paused to let the impact of this sink in with Kate and then added: 'There were also other indications that Sophie did not die from natural causes.'

Kate's heart pounded and she said: 'All day I have had this terrible feeling that things just weren't right. Poor Sophie, who do you think could have done this to her?' Her voice trailed away and she could not stop herself from breaking down in tears.

She was aware that Aldo had got up from the table and was standing behind her. She felt his hand stroke her shoulder in an attempt to console her.

Kate said: 'It's all right, I'll pull myself together in a minute. Please tell me everything you know.'

Aldo sat down opposite her again and said: 'I am afraid that you will find this upsetting, but in addition to the sedative in her blood stream they found signs that indicate she was smothered, probably with one of her own pillows. There were some tiny bruises around her mouth and her eyes were slightly bloodshot. These signs were noticed by one of the officers called out to the apartment just after Sophie's body had been discovered. He put these details in his initial report and unfortunately the information was conveyed to your legal representatives that the death was being treated by us as suspicious.

'But after I had been to the apartment myself I came to the conclusion that no one from outside could have got in during the night or have got out again before Luisa arrived the next morning. After speaking to Signora Mattozzi, Luisa and the neighbour, Jean Anderson, I formed the opinion that none of them would have wanted to harm your cousin.

'I was inclined to think that my officer's initial findings were misleading and that the post mortem examination would show your cousin died of something that had occurred naturally such as a heart attack or a stroke. It was entirely possible the bloodshot eyes and the small bruises did not have a sinister cause.

'But now I realise that he was right in the first place. I am so sorry Kate, I feel that I have let both you and your cousin down.'

Kate said: 'There were just too many little things that didn't quite add up. Sophie was young and healthy and had everything to live for. She spoke to my aunt the night before her death and said the research for her book was going well and yet there is nothing about it on her laptop and there are no papers or notebooks in the apartment relating to it.'

'I promise you that I have checked and ascertained that my officers did not bring any such material away from the scene,' Aldo said.

'She was supposed to have a new man in her life, but none of her so-called friends knew any details about him. Also I have been told that her previous boyfriend has been seen watching her apartment, which I find worrying. When I was with him tonight I could see he is still in a highly emotional state, even though he was perfectly pleasant to me.'

Trying to stifle her sobs she continued: 'It has become clear that both Sophie's landlady, Signora Mattozzi, and the maid, Luisa, had grown to dislike her. It also now seems as though her neighbour, Jean Anderson, who I had thought was so nice to begin with, was jealous of my cousin for some reason. My poor Aunt is going to be horrified when she finds out about all this!'

She could not stop the tears from coming and she felt Aldo put his arms round her to try to comfort her. 'I am worried that the shock will kill her!' Kate sobbed into his shoulder.

12

The grey, overcast sky matched Kate's mood as she sat at a table outside the bar next to Palazzo della Ragione the next morning, drinking a cappuccino.

There were only a few people in Piazza Vecchia and she felt that the young music student standing under the archways of the palace had chosen the haunting melody he was playing on his flute especially for her.

She had slept badly after Aldo's visit to the hotel and felt tired and washed out. She was still shocked by what he had told her the night before. She was also thinking about Steve, who had volunteered to drive down to Warwickshire and break the news to Aunt Edna about the post mortem examination results when she had telephoned him first thing.

Aldo had asked her not to give anyone from Sophie's circle of friends in Bergamo details about the exact circumstances of her death because of the risk of jeopardising the police investigation which was now getting under way.

But despite the horrifying thought that someone from Sophie's circle of friends could have been responsible for her violent death, she was determined to keep going for Aunt Edna's sake and carry on with her plans to meet Marge for dinner at her hotel that night and travel to Lago d'Iseo to meet Simon Pargeter for lunch the next day.

As she gazed across the square she became aware of a very young boy on a small tricycle circling the white marble Contarini fountain in the middle. A young man in jeans and a white baseball cap was running in front of him in mock terror, pretending to be chased. A slim, dark-haired young woman in jeans and a T-shirt stood to one side smiling as she watched them.

Eventually the man and the woman sat down together at the edge of the fountain. He put his arm round her and started to talk to her intently, looking into her eyes, while the little boy on the tricycle turned his attention to chasing the pigeons that had landed to peck at crumbs on the ground.

It suddenly dawned on Kate that the dark-haired girl was, in fact, Luisa the maid. She looked completely different out of her uniform and with her long, dark hair worn loose.

Jean had mentioned that Luisa was a single mother who lived with her parents and small son in the Città Bassa, the night they had gone out for dinner together at La Torre. She had said nothing about the whereabouts of the little boy's father, but maybe this young man had only come into Luisa's life recently, Kate thought.

She could not take her eyes off the couple as they sat chatting and laughing and watching the little boy play. Eventually he came to a halt in front of them on his tricycle and started talking to the young man. Occasionally she would hear him laugh delightedly at what the young man was saying to him.

Despite her low spirits, she thought it was such a charming little scene that she could not resist taking a picture of them to show to Aunt Edna. But the square was so quiet and empty that the young man was alerted by the flash from her camera and looked straight across at her. He said something to Luisa who also looked in Kate's direction before she said a few words to him in reply. Whatever she said caused the young man to look at Kate again.

Kate felt guilty and wished she had not taken the photograph as they clearly regarded it as intrusive and she was sure Luisa had recognised her.

As she sat finishing her cappuccino she had the uncomfortable feeling they were still talking about her although she tried to avoid looking in their direction again.

After a few minutes she was aware of them getting up and walking slowly across the square in the direction of Via Colleoni with the little boy pedalling his tricycle in front of them. The young man turned and looked over his shoulder at Kate one more time before they left the square and turned down the street.

Kate felt relieved when they were out of sight and put some money down on the table to pay for her coffee. She left the square in the opposite direction going under the archways beneath Palazzo della Ragione to reach Piazza Duomo. She stopped and put a coin in the basket in front of the flautist before taking sanctuary in the calm interior of the Basilica di Santa Maria Maggiore where she spent the rest of the morning listening to the organist practising while walking slowly round the cool, musty-smelling church looking for Donizetti's tomb.

Steve sat staring at the two pints of beer that the landlord had just placed on the polished wooden table in front of him. After a while he lifted one up to study it in the light from the window behind him and then took a sip, savouring the taste. He placed the glass back on the table and relaxed against the padded back of his seat. 'You've definitely earned that,' he said to himself.

He had been up early to answer the phone to Kate and then driven down to Warwickshire, where he had spent a difficult morning with Edna at Hampton House. He had to admit that she had taken the news about the results from the post mortem examination remarkably well. There had been moments when she had shed a few tears, but her main reaction seemed to have been relief that she finally knew the truth about what had happened to Sophie. At least now she knew that something was going to be done about it. She had said that she would not be able to rest until she knew that the wicked person who had killed Sophie had been caught and punished. But she had also said she did not trust the Italian authorities to commit enough time and resources to be successful in catching Sophie's killer and had begged Steve to fly out to Bergamo to help Kate with her enquiries.

After leaving Edna's room he had gone to speak to Adam Leighton to put him in the picture but there had been no sign of the nursing home manager in the reception area.

Steve had opened a few doors to see if there was anyone about and eventually came across Adam sitting with three other men at a table in a corner of the residents' dining room.

They were speaking in raised voices and Steve formed the brief impression that the other men were behaving aggressively towards Adam. However, as soon as Adam saw him in the doorway, he rushed across the room and almost pushed Steve back into the entrance hall, quickly closing the door behind him.

Steve told him about the results of the post mortem examination and asked him to take particular care of Edna over the next few days. Although Adam still looked flustered and preoccupied, he had assured Steve he would keep an eye on Edna to make sure her health did not deteriorate.

As Steve took another sip of his beer he wondered

what Adam had been discussing with the other men so heatedly. He had noticed a couple of flashy cars in the car park, along with a van from a building supplies company, as he drove away from Hampton House.

He had promised Edna he would get a flight to Italy as soon as possible but he had not told her that before he left Warwickshire he had some business to deal with in the Rose and Crown in the next village.

He was just reaching for his glass again when a shadow fell across the table and he looked up to see a huge figure looming over him.

'So this is the sort of thing you get up to now you've retired,' the man observed. Steve pushed the second glass across the table towards him. 'Good morning, Detective Chief Inspector Batts,' he said. 'Sit down and sample this very fine ale while I tell you about the little job I have lined up for you.'

With plenty of time on her hands, Kate started getting ready early to go for dinner with Marge at the Majestic Hotel that evening. When she was dressed she was glad to be able to leave her room and try to distract herself from the horrible thoughts she had been having all afternoon about the way Sophie had died. She went for a walk around the Città Alta in the evening sunshine, looking in shop windows and reading the menus outside the restaurants to pass the time.

But some unconscious pull took her in the direction of Palazzo Mattozzi and she eventually found herself standing on the pavement on the opposite side of the street looking up at the double windows of Sophie's living room with the small balcony in front of them.

This must be where Ernesto had stood the night

before Sophie was found dead. Jean had said she saw him when she came back from the shops although Ernesto appeared not to have noticed her. But what happened after she went inside to put her groceries away?

Suppose Ernesto had managed to persuade Sophie to let him into the apartment? If he had begged her to take him back, to give him another chance, what would Sophie have said? If she had turned him down again, what would Ernesto have done?

The only person who might possibly be able to shed any light on these matters was Jean. Kate realised she had not yet asked her for more details about the events of that night after she returned from the shops, but she now had specific questions she wanted answers for.

On a sudden impulse she crossed the road and pressed the brass call button next to the name Anderson. She was pleased to hear Jean's voice answer immediately and said to her: 'I was wondering whether you would like to go out for a glass of wine. I have some time to kill before I go down to the Città Bassa to meet Marge and wondered whether you would come for a drink at the funicular bar with me.'

'Actually, I would be glad of an excuse to leave all my marking for bit. Give me a couple of minutes and I will come down to you,' Jean answered.

Kate loitered outside for a few minutes, hoping not to be spotted by Signora Mattozzi, until Jean came out through the iron gates to join her.

They walked down the street to the funicular bar and took seats at a table on the terrace overlooking the Città Bassa.

While Kate was ordering the drinks she noticed Jean take her phone out of her bag and look at it anxiously before putting it back again.

She started telling her about her dinner with Ernesto the night before but then Jean's phone made a buzzing sound and she whipped it out of her bag again eagerly.

'Have you got a message?' Kate asked.

'Yes, but not from the person I'm waiting to hear from,' Jean said, pulling a face.

The drinks arrived then and when the waiter had gone Jean said: 'Sorry Kate, what were you saying just now?'

'I was just wondering whether you heard any sounds coming from Sophie's apartment after you had gone inside the building to put your shopping away the night before her body was discovered.'

Jean shook her head and said: 'One of the good things about Palazzo Mattozzi is that the rooms are all soundproof. The walls are very thick and the floors must be extremely solidly made. I never, ever heard anything from Sophie's apartment while she was living there'.

'So you wouldn't know if she received a visitor after you got back from doing your shopping in the Città Bassa?'

'No, I'm sorry, I don't. You could try asking Signora Mattozzi but her apartment is even further away so I don't think she will be able to help you either.'

'It's okay, it was just a thought. My aunt is pretty certain that Sophie was on her own in the apartment when she rang her later that evening.'

Jean looked puzzled and said: 'Why do you want to know, anyway?'

Kate could not tell her about the results of the post mortem examination and so she just said: 'I wondered whether Sophie had seen Ernesto in the street and invited him in. It's just curiosity really.'

Jean said: 'I suppose you could ask Ernesto, but he might think it is a bit strange that you want to know about it now.'

Kate decided to change the subject because she was clearly getting nowhere. She told Jean she was going to Sarnico in the morning to meet Simon Pargeter and asked her what she knew about Lago d'Iseo. Jean was able to give her some interesting information about the different resorts around the lake and the minutes passed quickly.

She realised suddenly that it was time to get the train down to the Città Bassa. She gave Jean the money to pay the bill and left her at the table to finish her wine.

As Kate left the bar she turned in the doorway to wave goodbye to Jean but saw that she had once again taken her phone out of her bag and was hunched over it, studying it anxiously.

13

The acres of thick carpet, the gold-coloured velvet settees and the heavily embossed wall coverings came as a shock to Kate when she stepped into the foyer of the Hotel Majestic later. It could not have been more of a contrast with the elegant simplicity of the décor of the Albergo Milano in the Città Alta.

She also felt decidedly under-dressed in the skirt and top she had chosen to wear when she walked into the bar and saw Marge sitting on a stool in an expensive- looking little black cocktail dress and smart, high heeled black patent leather shoes.

The hotel restaurant also turned out to be ornately decorated and rather grand but the food was better than Kate had expected it to be. She enjoyed every morsel of her ravioli with taleggio cheese and truffles and her main course of Veal Marsala and savoured every sip of the excellent wine the waiter had recommended.

She also had to agree with Marge that the night-time views through the windows of the rooftop restaurant of the illuminated skyline of the Città Alta were spectacular.

Kate carefully avoided mentioning either the Commissario or the post mortem examination results and fortunately it never occurred to Marge to ask if Aldo had been in touch with any news about them.

Marge spent most of the meal telling her anecdotes about her friends back home in America. They meant little to Kate because she did not know any of the people involved and they were not even particularly amusing.

It was not until they were relaxing over coffee in

the bar after the meal that Kate was able to bring the conversation round to Sophie's life in Bergamo by telling Marge that she was going to Lago d'Iseo the next day to have lunch with Simon Pargeter.

'Oh, lucky you! He's absolutely drop dead gorgeous and I have been told he is a very successful businessman. You have to hand it to Sophie – one thing she did have was very good taste in men. I mean, Ernesto is quite good looking in a Latin lover type of way, don't you think?'

Kate murmured some words of agreement and then asked casually: 'Was there ever any hint of a romance between Sophie and Edgar?'

Marge gave a peal of laughter: 'Good heavens, no! I mean, he was perhaps a bit smitten with her when they first met, but then I think we were all taken in by her 'little miss innocent' act.

'No, Edgar soon realised what she was like. I know she was your cousin, but take it from me, she could be a right little madam. She always wanted her own way and she was constantly arguing with him. Even though he's an acknowledged expert on Donizetti, she always used to think she knew better. Sometimes she was like a dog with a bone and wouldn't let things drop. It was quite irritating for me and Jean, having to listen to it all.

'I remember on one occasion when she kept going on and on about one of Donizetti's letters where he mentions a woman with a long, unpronounceable Italian surname, she was called Marianna something or other. She kept saying this woman's name over and over again. She was obviously just enjoying showing off her Italian accent but I can tell you, I got sick of hearing it.'

'Do you remember what the letter was about?' Kate asked curiously.

'It was nothing very exciting, they weren't involved romantically or anything like that. I seem to think it was about this woman paying to have him excused from military service, that's all.

'But Sophie just kept repeating this woman's long name over and over again until I thought I was going to scream. I think her charms had started to wear a bit thin with Edgar as well by then, to be honest.'

'What about Jean? Do you think she got on well with Sophie on the whole?'

'No, not really. Poor Jean always seemed to be in her shadow and I think she resented it. In my opinion Jean has always had a bit of a thing about Edgar, but she allowed Sophie to muscle in on him after she introduced them to each other. I bet she regretted bringing Sophie along to the opera group with her in the first place.

'To be honest though, I don't think Jean was ever going to have bagged Edgar even if Sophie hadn't got in the way. She isn't his type really.'

Marge took a sip of the martini the waiter had just brought her and chuckled in a self-satisfied way.

'I think it annoyed Jean to see Sophie getting all the male attention. Mind you it was a bit obvious, the tactics she used. Sophie always encouraged men to think they had a chance with her even if she wasn't really interested in them. Of course, I could see right through her act but it was obviously a little game that she enjoyed playing.'

'Sorry, I'm not sure exactly what you mean by that,' Kate said.

'Well, she would have a way of looking at every man when he was talking to her as if he was the only person that mattered to her. I remember an occasion once when we had been to Milano for the day. We had just got off the train here in Bergamo and were coming up the stairs at the station. We had got to about half way when a very tall, good looking black man put his hand on Sophie's arm to get her attention and spoke to her. I have no idea who he was or how she came to know him.

'She stopped dead in her tracks in the middle of the steps and started talking to him really intensely. People hurrying down the steps for trains had to somehow manoeuvre round them to get past. She just stood there talking to him, looking into his eyes and nodding very seriously at everything he had to say.

'All the while she was completely oblivious of everything that was going on around her. She had obviously forgotten that I was there, standing around like a fool holding all my carrier bags waiting for her.'

'What was he asking her about?'

'I've no idea. I couldn't hear a word they were saying. But the way she looked at him, it was as if he was the only man in the world. That's how she behaved with most men. And they used to fall for it to begin with until they got to know her a bit better and found out what she was really like.'

Kate felt she needed to clear her head and chose not to ask the staff on the reception desk to order her a taxi when she decided to call it a night, telling Marge she would go back up to the Città Alta on foot.

Although she knew there was a grain of truth in what Marge had said about Sophie it was hard to have to listen to such a sustained attack on the character of her cousin.

Fuelled by several vodka martinis, Marge had

ended the evening by making several even more vitriolic comments about Sophie and, as she walked up the road towards the Città Alta, Kate even wondered whether Marge had hated her cousin enough to have crept into her bedroom, put a pillow over her face and killed her.

She banished the thought as ridiculous. Marge Ransom was a respectable, well-off woman who lived a very comfortable and enjoyable life travelling about in Europe. She might be a bit of a bitch and had found Sophie's behaviour irritating but it did not make her a murderer.

Kate went under Porta Sant'Agostino through the pedestrian entrance and turned left into the narrow winding road that led up to Piazza Mercato delle Scarpe still thinking about what Marge had said about Sophie's way of getting attention from men. It had been quite an accurate assessment, Kate had to admit to herself.

However, although Sophie may have been self-centred and frequently infuriated people by the way she carried on about things, she hadn't deserved to die. It was hard to believe that someone she had met in this beautiful city had come to hate her so much that they had actually killed her. Although she now knew all the medical facts, Kate realised that she still could not really come to terms with that.

She couldn't imagine Signora Mattozzi, Jean or Luisa killing Sophie in such a brutal way and the Commissario had proved to her that no one could possibly have got into the palazzo from outside. But there had to be some kind of logical explanation for the suspicious signs discovered during the post mortem examination. Someone had inflicted those injuries on Sophie, someone had murdered her. There was just no other explanation.

As she continued to climb the hill towards the centre of the Città Alta, still thinking about Marge's comments about Sophie, she did not hear the car until it was right behind her. She turned round to look when she heard the noise of the engine and had a brief impression of a dark face wearing sunglasses behind the steering wheel.

Then, to her horror, the car accelerated and drove straight at her. She flattened herself against the wall of a house and the car roared past her, the wing mirror missing her stomach by little more than a couple of centimetres.

The car sped up the road and turned left at the top with a screech of brakes, leaving Kate gasping and holding on to the wall for support.

She made herself start walking up the road again in the direction of the Città Alta and tried to keep calm. Yes, the car had been driven recklessly but maybe the driver hadn't seen her. However unnerving it had been, she tried to tell herself, it surely couldn't have been deliberate.

But as she neared the top of the road and could see Piazza Mercato delle Scarpe ahead of her she heard the sound of the car engine again. Some instinct made her start to run as fast as she could. She hoped and prayed that when she got to the top of the road there would still be people in the square, sitting at the tables outside the bars or going towards the funicular railway station to catch the train to the Città Bassa.

She hadn't quite reached the top of the street before the car caught up with her again. She threw herself at the door of a house and hoisted herself up off the road by holding on to the ornate stonework above the lintel. She was just high enough off the ground for the car to miss her legs as she hung there, her arms hurting with the strain of holding on to the stonework. With a supreme effort of will she continued to hang on to the stonework until the car had reached the top of the street and turned left again and then she dropped down and ran for all she was worth up the street and across the by now deserted square into Via Gombito.

She thought her heart was about to burst but she kept running until she reached Piazza Vecchia. She forced herself to run across the side of the big, empty square in the direction of Via Colleoni, stumbling along as fast as she could even though she was finding it difficult to breathe. But as she passed the colonnades in front of the white, marble Civic Library, a dark figure stepped out from behind a pillar and grabbed her arm. Kate screamed in terror and heard her voice echoing for what seemed a long time afterwards around the empty square.

14

'Kate, I am sorry, I did not mean to frighten you,' she heard someone say in English and then she felt herself gently pulled towards him. When she recognised Aldo's voice she fell into his arms and sobbed with relief.

'Kate, try to be calm, do not be afraid of me, I am so sorry that I scared you,' he said, holding her close to him.

She stopped crying and tried to compose herself so that she could speak to him. 'I think someone has just tried to run me over with a car.'

'Do you think it was by accident,' Aldo asked, stepping back from her and looking into her eyes in concern.

'No, it can't have been an accident because they came back and tried to do it again,' Kate said and let out another sob.

'Kate, don't cry. You are safe now, I promise. Please, come with me.' With one arm still supporting her he led her into Via Colleoni. She leant against him, glad of his strength, strangely surprised that she did not seem to be towering over him on this occasion.

'I'm sorry, I can't seem to get my legs to move properly,' she said as she stumbled along.

They turned into a bar a few metres down the street and he signalled to the woman behind the counter who showed them into a wood panelled alcove with padded red velvet seats around three sides of a dark wood table.

'I will order you a brandy.'

'No, not brandy. Could I have white wine please,' she said quickly.

Aldo called out a few words in *bergamasco* dialect and two glasses of wine were placed on the table in front of them within a matter of seconds.

'Now tell me about it right from the beginning,' he said.

Kate took a sip of the wine and then put down her glass and tried to compose herself.

'I had been having dinner with Marge Ransom in the restaurant of the Majestic Hotel opposite the *funicolare.* I decided to walk back afterwards because it was such a warm night and I felt I could do with some fresh air.

'After I had been through Porta Sant'Agostino I turned up the street that leads to Piazza Mercato delle Scarpe. There wasn't much of a pavement to walk on at the side of the road but there were no cars about and so I thought it would be fine. I was about halfway up when I heard a car behind me. I turned to look and I thought the driver must surely have seen me. But then the car suddenly accelerated and seemed to drive straight at me. Even though I flattened myself against the wall of a house the car passed very close to me and it was a miracle that I wasn't injured.

'It was very frightening, but even then I thought that it might have just been a mistake and that the driver perhaps hadn't seen me until the last minute. But before I got to the top of the street I heard a car engine coming up behind me again.'

She drank some more wine and then described how she had hoisted herself off the ground and held on to the stonework above the door of one of the houses to avoid being struck by the car.

'*Oh mio Dio*!' exclaimed Aldo, looking shocked.

'Afterwards I ran as fast as I could in the direction of the hotel. When you appeared from behind the pillar on the library steps I thought for an awful moment that it was the driver, that he'd parked his car and was lying in wait for me.'

'I'm sorry I screamed so loudly,' she added, with an attempt at a smile.

'Could you give me a description of the car?' Aldo asked, sounding serious.

'Not really, it all happened so fast. I think it was some shade of dark grey but I couldn't tell you what make it was.'

'Did you get a look at the driver?'

'Yes, I think he may have been dark-skinned, or perhaps very tanned and I seem to remember he was wearing sun glasses.'

'Do you remember anything else about him?'

'No, not really. I couldn't see his hair. I think he may have been wearing something on his head, like a baseball cap, covering it up. We're assuming it was a man, of course and not a woman.'

'Who knew you would be walking back from the Città Bassa at this time?'

'No one, that is apart from Marge, of course. Jean knew I would be coming back from the Majestic Hotel after the meal but she had no reason to think I would walk back. Unless someone followed me down to the Majestic earlier and waited for me to come out again,' Kate said with a shiver.

Aldo sipped his wine thoughtfully and then asked: 'What are your plans for tomorrow?'

'I'm going by bus to Sarnico to meet Simon Pargeter.'

'Do you think that is wise, after all this?'

'Well, to be honest, after what has happened tonight I think I will be quite glad to get away from Bergamo for the day. In any case I was looking forward to seeing Lago d'Iseo.'

'I suppose you will be safe enough on a coach with lots of other people. I will come to your hotel first thing in the morning to see how you are. If you are sure you feel well enough to travel to Sarnico I will walk with you to Colle Aperto and make sure you get safely on to the bus to the Città Bassa.'

Aldo finished his wine and put down his glass. 'Do you feel up to walking back to your hotel now?'

'I think so, if my legs have got back to normal.'

Aldo put his arm round her and supported her again as they walked through the deserted streets to the hotel. There was no one on reception and so Aldo reached over to take her key and then followed her up the stairs to her room. He unlocked the door and put the light on.

'Does everything seem to be in order here?' he asked.

Kate had a quick look round. Everything seemed to be in the right place and the laptop was still closed and had not been moved from where she had left it.

'What time shall I come round tomorrow?' Aldo asked.

'I was planning to leave at about half past nine to walk to the bus stop at Colle Aperto.'

'Well, I will make sure that I am here in good time then. *Buona notte*, Kate. Please be careful from now on and lock the door safely behind me.'

He set off towards the stairs again and Kate quickly shut the door and turned the key in the lock.

Back inside her room she felt safer. It was very late to be calling Steve now and in any case she was too exhausted to go through it all again on the phone. She undressed quickly and got into bed. After a few minutes she got out again and put the chair up against the door as she had done previously. Then she got back into the bed again but lay awake for some time thinking about things, still shivering occasionally.

The sun shone on the grapes ripening on the vines for the next season's Valcalepio Bianco wine as Kate gazed through the bus window at the fields they were passing and at the mountains in the distance.

She sat on her own spread out over a double seat, trying to make herself as comfortable as she could although her arms ached from hanging on to the stonework and her legs were still stiff from running. But she had slept for a few hours, showered and had breakfast and as the bus sped further and further away from Bergamo she started to feel brighter.

Aldo had been leaning on the reception desk chatting and laughing with Roberto when she came out of the breakfast room. She had collected her things from her room and then they had walked up Via Colleoni and through Piazza Mascheroni and Piazza Cittadella to the bus stop in Largo Colle Aperto.

'On a beautiful morning like this the events of last night just seem like a bad dream,' Kate said to Aldo as they waited for the bus to arrive.

He sighed. 'I am afraid that without a vehicle number or details of the manufacturer it is difficult to see how we will ever be able to trace the driver. So I would suggest that you stick to well lit streets where there are plenty of people about from now on.'

He stood patiently waiting with Kate until the bus arrived and she was safely on it. As the bus set off along Viale delle Mura, Kate caught a glimpse of his curly hair as he went through the archway into Piazza Cittadella on his way back to the

Commissariato and she suddenly became aware that she was smiling.

She got off at the stop before the railway station and made her way to the bus station where she bought a return ticket to Sarnico. With so many people about she felt reasonably safe and she bought a copy of L'Eco di Bergamo to read while she passed the time with a pastry and cappuccino in the bar until the bus was due to leave.

It left the city along Via Borgo Palazzo and once it had gone through Grumello del Monte, which had a pretty square with a fountain, and Castelli Calepio, she began to get the occasional glimpse of Lago d'Iseo in the distance, with its blue water sparkling in the sunshine. After going through Villongo, the bus turned off the main road and went downhill towards the lake.

Kate got off outside the municipal building as Simon Pargeter had suggested in his text. Her journalist's habit of being early for everything meant she had plenty of time to spare before she had to go to his office.

She followed her instincts and walked in the direction of the lake, finding her way to Via Garibaldi where she was able to walk along at the side of the water to the landing stage from where the boats departed.

The sun was shining and she joined the people strolling along at the side of the lake admiring the views. She stopped and looked down at the still blue water where white gulls were floating peacefully on the surface. She began to feel more relaxed knowing she was out of Bergamo for the day and unlikely to run into anyone from Sophie's circle of friends.

Simon Pargeter had only recently met her cousin and had surely not had time to develop any resentment towards her. He had also been a considerable distance from Bergamo the night before Sophie's death. What she was hoping to find out from him was whether he thought Sophie had been happy just before her death.

She might also have confided in him about whether she had been having problems with any of her friends in Bergamo. She hoped deep down that he would tell her that Sophie had been happy so that she could go home and reassure her aunt. It might give her some comfort.

She reached a point on the path at the side of the lake from which she could go no further. The water went round the corner and because of the shape of the land she could not see the rest of the lake. She was disappointed that there was no view of Monte Isola, 'the cute little island', that Marge had mentioned visiting.

She looked at her watch and thought that it was probably time to start making her way back into the centre of Sarnico where Simon Pargeter had an office.

His directions took her through a series of pretty squares and up a steep winding street lined with shops where she found the *agenzia immobiliare*, a type of estate agency that he had told her was on the ground floor of the building where he had an office.

Inside, the young woman sitting behind the reception desk picked up the telephone to let Simon Pargeter know that she had arrived.

While she waited, Kate looked at the pictures on display of properties available for rent with lake views and wondered what it would be like to live in the area.

A tall man, smartly dressed in a suit with short, sleek, dark hair and the unusual, pale blue eyes

Marge had mentioned, advanced towards her, smiling. As they shook hands, he said in his slightly hoarse, southern accent: 'Thanks for coming, Kate. There's a good restaurant only a short walk from here. I suggest we go and get a table so we can talk privately.'

They walked back down towards the lake and he led Kate in the opposite direction from where she had just been walking, towards the point where the lake joined the River Oglio. They left the path and went up a flight of steps to the terrace of a restaurant where there were just a few diners enjoying the excellent view of the lake while they ate.

After they had both ordered risotto and main courses that featured fish caught from the lake, Kate asked him about the property he was currently developing in the area.

'It's an early 20th century palazzo set back on high ground above the town with stunning lake views from many of its windows. It has lots of interesting period features that they call *stile liberty* in Italy, or art nouveau as we know it.

'I'm turning it into 12 luxury apartments but I am trying to retain as much of the original character of the building as possible.'

'Will you sell them, or rent them out?' Kate asked.

He smiled and she noticed that attractive grooves appeared in his suntanned cheeks. 'Ideally I will sell them to get my money out as quickly as possible. But renting them to get some short term return on the investment is another possibility if I don't get enough buyers immediately.'

'How did you first meet Sophie?'

'It was at the launch of an art exhibition in Bergamo. Art isn't really my thing but you have to work with other businesses and suppliers in my game and keeping in with the right contacts is crucial. Some business associates of mine had put money into the restoration of the paintings that were going on display so they sent me a couple of tickets for the launch and I felt I should attend to show them some support.

'Sophie was talking to someone who worked for the local authority in Bergamo that I had met before and so I went up to them and asked him to introduce me to her.'

'I think it was instant attraction on both sides. It all happened only a few weeks ago, but it seems a lot further back in time than that,' he said with a wistful smile.

'What was it that attracted you to Sophie?'

'Oh, lots of things. She was obviously very pretty but she also had a sharp mind. For a scholar and an academic she knew a lot about business.

'She was very interested in the apartments I was developing so I arranged for her to have a look round even though they are not finished. I took her out for dinner afterwards and we found that we got on really well together.

'I arranged to see her the next time I was in Bergamo and then she came out to Sarnico the following weekend to stay with me at the apartment I am renting here. It was a nice weekend and I enjoyed her company. It was only early days but I think we were beginning to get close.'

'Did you ever stay at Palazzo Mattozzi in Bergamo?'

'No, I never even went inside the building. I think Sophie thought it was more private and peaceful here. And she had been having issues with some of the people living there.'

'What did she say about them?'

'Oh, just that Signora Mattozzi could be in a bit of a grim mood sometimes. Apparently she had had a difficult life and looked years older that she actually was. But she wasn't an easy person to deal with about tenancy issues, as I understand it.

'And Sophie was very concerned about Luisa, the maid. She said she was basically a decent girl and had worked very hard to bring up a child on her own but that she had apparently just met an unsuitable man.

'I think she was pleased for Luisa to begin with that she had met this man, Massimo, because he was very good with the child and took them out to places in his car. But then she found out he was running some kind of house clearance and antiques business that seemed a bit dodgy and she suspected him of exploiting his workers. I don't know all the details, but she and Luisa had argued about it only recently, I think.'

'What did she think of her neighbour, Jean?'

'Oh, I think she liked Jean and thought she was basically a decent person, but they didn't have a lot in common. I think she went about with her socially when she first arrived in Bergamo. But I suppose it was inevitable that she ended up having less to do with her recently because she had met a lot of other people.'

'Did she mention two Americans staying in Bergamo, Edgar and Marge?'

'Oh yes, she often mentioned them. In fact I met them at the same party where I met Sophie. I think Sophie found Marge a bit overbearing at times but she liked Edgar. He seemed a nice enough bloke, for an American,' Simon said, looking at Kate with a hint of a mischievous smile.

'Did she ever mention Roberto Mariotto. He is a

businessman who owns the majority share in Palazzo Mattozzi?'

'She never really talked about him, she only mentioned to me once how she had found her apartment. She said that he had offered her the apartment when she was staying as a guest at his hotel. That's about all really.'

'Do you think her life in Bergamo was happy?'

'I think so. In fact, I'm sure of it. But like I said, it was early days for the two of us. The sad thing is that I didn't have the chance to get to know her any better. Her death was a terrible shock to me and I wish we could have been together for longer.'

He sighed and said: 'If only things hadn't come to an end so abruptly. Who knows what might have happened between us?'

On the bus back to Bergamo, Kate closed her eyes and pictured Simon's handsome face as he'd said those words. He had seemed genuinely sad about Sophie's death but nowhere near as distraught as Ernesto had been. As Aldo had said, he had not known Sophie for long and there was no way of knowing whether the relationship would have lasted any length of time or become more serious.

As the bus neared the centre of Bergamo she received a text message from Steve. It said: 'Booked flight to Bergamo. Arriving tomorrow at three. Will get bus to Città Alta. Please book me a room at your hotel. x.'

Kate's heart pounded. She was both excited and unnerved by the text. She would be glad to see Steve. She had been missing him and it would be great to be able to talk to him in person about all the things she had been finding out in Bergamo rather than over the phone. She had not been looking forward to telling him about the car that had tried to run her over the night before because she knew that it would worry him. But it would be a lot easier to tell him about it face to face.

She wondered why he had asked her to book him a room of his own. He had used the words 'please book me a room'. He obviously did not want to move into her room at the hotel and yet when they had taken holidays together before they had always shared a room.

They had been growing apart over the last few months. Was this an indication that he also recognised this and wanted to maintain the distance between them?

15

Later that afternoon, when Kate had arrived back in the Città Alta, as she walked from Colle Aperto to the hotel, she saw the tall, slim figure of Roberto in the street a few metres ahead of her and forced her aching legs to break into an ungainly run so that she could catch him up.

'Ciao, Roberto,' she greeted him when she found herself walking alongside him. She thought he looked anxious when he turned and saw her.

'Sorry to be chasing after you but I was wondering whether there were any rooms available in the hotel at the moment. A friend of mine is coming out to visit me here in Bergamo for a few days and he has asked me to try to get him a room at the Albergo Milano.'

'That shouldn't be a problem,' Roberto said, looking relieved. 'I think there will be a room available, but I'll just have to check in the hotel register to see what bookings we have coming up in the next few days.'

When they were back in the reception area of the hotel he went behind the desk and picked up a leather-bound book from the shelf in front of the key rack.

Another charming example of the hotel's old fashioned style, Kate noted, unlike other hotels where everything has been computerised.

'How long would your friend wish to stay?' Roberto asked, frowning as he studied the neat, handwritten entries in the book.

Using her journalist's knack of being able to read writing upside down, Kate spotted among the entries her own name, with her room number and the date recorded for each of the nights that she had stayed so far.

'I'm not completely sure, but could you reserve the room for a week provisionally, running from Saturday to Saturday?'

Roberto turned the page and continued to concentrate on the book. Then he said: 'Yes, I can give him a room on the floor above yours.'

'That will be fine,' Kate said quickly. She was disappointed they were going to be a floor apart but she had done what Steve had asked and booked him a room at the hotel. At some stage she would try to find out why he had requested a separate room. She would let him settle in first and see how things were between them over the next few days.

As she went upstairs to her room she was looking forward to showering and changing but as soon as she unlocked her door and went inside the room she was aware of a strange scent in the atmosphere. It was a heavy, musky type of fragrance. Was it a man's aftershave, or could it be a rather overpowering woman's perfume?

It was certainly not one of the fragrances she had brought with her. Then she saw that the laptop lid was up and remembered that it had definitely been folded down when she had returned with Aldo last night and she had not touched it again before she left the room that morning.

She grabbed her key and bag and ran out of the room, locking the door behind her before she rushed downstairs again.

'Roberto, have you been looking at the laptop in my room again?' she called out to him from halfway down the stairs.

He looked up from what he had been reading as he stood behind the desk and seemed genuinely surprised. 'No, I haven't been in your room again. Since our talk the other night I have not been near your room, or the laptop, I swear.'

He looked so worried that Kate said: 'It's okay, I believe you. But then someone else must have touched it. The lid was definitely closed when I went out this morning and it is open now. Also there is a strong smell of aftershave or perfume in my room that I don't recognise. Who do you think it could have been?'

Roberto thought about it and said: 'Well, I suppose someone could have taken your key while the desk has been unattended. I have been out of the hotel for quite a while today and when the staff were all busy in the restaurant over the lunch period there might have been a few occasions when the desk was left.

'Guests who can't be bothered to wait sometimes help themselves to their keys, so I suppose it is possible that someone from outside who knew the layout of the hotel could have done the same thing.

'At times when the restaurant is busy the staff would not think it was odd if they came through reception and found a non-resident in here.'

'Okay, thanks, Roberto,' Kate said absently. She believed him and her mind was now ranging over all the other possibilities.

Signora Mattozzi would know the layout of the Albergo Milano and have a good idea of when the restaurant was likely to be busy and the desk unmanned. She could easily have helped herself to the key and gone into Kate's room to look at the laptop. But then judging by the type of clothes she wore, she couldn't imagine Signora Mattozzi wearing perfume like that.

However, what about Ernesto del Buono? The hotel was only a short walk from La Torre and she could imagine him wearing a man's cologne that smelt like that. He was obsessed with Sophie and may have had a reason for wanting to look at her laptop.

Or there was Jean? She knew Kate had asked Aldo for the laptop to be returned to her and she knew where Kate was staying. If she had really been jealous and resentful of Sophie, as Marge had suggested, she might have been curious enough to come to the hotel to try to see what information had been stored on the laptop.

It was probably not very likely, but Kate decided to walk round to Palazzo Mattozzi to see Jean anyway. She had made no firm plans for dinner that evening and would ask whether Jean wanted to go for a meal with her. Following her talk with Simon Pargeter at lunchtime, she had a few more things to ask her about.

Within minutes she was outside the gates of Palazzo Mattozzi pressing the brass button next to Jean's name. When Jean heard Kate's voice over the intercom she said: 'I'm just on my way out actually. I'll come down straight away.'

Jean looked terrible when she appeared at the iron gates. Her normally sleek blonde hair looked limp and wispy as though she had not had time to style it and she had bags under her eyes indicating she hadn't slept well.

'Jean, are you all right?' Kate asked in concern.

'Yes, I'm okay, it's just that I've got something urgent to sort out. I'm going down to the Città Bassa.'

'Have you got time for a drink in the funicular bar before you go? There are a couple of things I wanted to ask you.'

'No, I'm sorry, Kate. I've got to go straight away.'

'Okay, well I'll walk down with you then. I just wanted to ask you about Luisa's boyfriend Massimo. What do you think of him?'

Jean looked puzzled. 'Oh, I don't know really. I've hardly ever spoken to him. He seems nice enough. He has been very good to Luisa's little son, apparently. He takes them on days out into the countryside in his car.'

'I've heard from someone that Sophie wasn't convinced about the legitimacy of all his business dealings.'

'Oh, what would Sophie know about any of it?' Jean burst out angrily. 'It would be just typical of her to try to put doubt in Luisa's mind in order to split them up.'

'Well, apparently Sophie not only thought his business was dodgy but that he exploited his workers.'

'Sophie, Sophie, Sophie! I am sick to death of hearing about what Sophie thought and what Sophie said about things. It's unbelievable. Even though Sophie is dead, she is still dominating everything!' Jean exclaimed. She then started to run in the direction of the funicular railway station, leaving a stunned Kate standing alone in the street.

The next morning Kate sat in the shadow of Palazzo della Ragione drinking a cappuccino and reading that day's edition of L'Eco di Bergamo.

She was tense, but in a pleasant, excited way, as she looked ahead and imagined meeting Steve off the bus that afternoon. It would be good to see him again and tell him about what had been happening in Bergamo. She did not like keeping things from him but had felt reluctant to tell him over the phone about being chased by the car when she was walking back up to the Città Alta. She would also welcome his opinion on the people she had met so far while in Bergamo, who she was now beginning to think of as 'Sophie's circle.'

She did not like to think of them as suspects, but the fact was that someone must have given Sophie some kind of sedative if she hadn't taken it herself. And someone, probably the same person, had put a pillow over her face and smothered her. That person was almost certainly connected with the driver of the car that had tried to run her down.

She had experienced Signora Mattozzi's overt antagonism towards her every time they had met and she had also been told that Sophie had felt she could no longer trust Luisa and had criticised the business methods of her boyfriend, Massimo.

Also, Marge had shown her true colours after all those martinis the other night and had revealed how much she resented Sophie. And it had been just after having dinner with Marge that she had been chased by the car. Could Marge have disguised herself somehow and been behind the wheel?

If you are planning to commit murder you don't worry too much about being over the alcohol limit for driving in Italy, Kate thought to herself.

Her phone beeped in her bag at that moment. It was a text from Aldo asking if he could see her. She texted him back straight away to let him know she was having coffee in Piazza Vecchia.

A few minutes later he appeared at the end of Via Colleoni and crossed the square towards her. He sat down at the table with her but waved away her offer of coffee.

He said: 'I am sorry Kate, but I am afraid that I have to bring you some upsetting news. I have just been informed that the body of Jean Anderson was discovered early this morning in a small area of parkland in the Città Alta.'

Kate gasped in horror. 'But I saw her only last night. What could possibly have happened to her?'

She thought Aldo looked tired and worried. He said: 'It is too early to know for certain but the patch of ground where she was lying was in front of one of the old lookout towers in the walls. According to the officers who attended the scene, the injuries she appeared to have sustained were consistent with having fallen from a considerable height. Obviously we will have to wait for the results of the post mortem examination to be sure, but it is a possibility that she may have fallen from the top of the tower.'

'But how would she have got up there in the first place?' Kate asked.

'Oh, there are old steps inside all the towers leading to the top. People like to climb up them and take photographs of the views from high up. When you saw her last night, did she mention going to visit one of the old lookout towers for any reason?'

'No, she was on her way to the funicular to go down to the Città Bassa. She said she was in a hurry because she had something urgent that she needed to sort out, but she didn't say what it was.'

'And how did she seem?'

'Well, to be honest, she didn't look well. She seemed a bit on edge and looked tired and as if she was upset about something. She was not nearly as pleasant and friendly towards me as usual. She said she didn't have time to have a drink with me and when I started asking her questions about Luisa and her boyfriend she got very angry. She said she was fed up of hearing about what Sophie thought about things all the while and that even though she was dead she was still dominating everything. They may not have been her exact words, but that was the gist of it.'

'How curious,' Aldo said thoughtfully. 'Well, now we are going to have to try to ascertain whether she fell accidentally or whether she jumped from the top of the tower deliberately.'

'Maybe someone was there with her and seized the chance when there was no one else in sight to push her off,' Kate suggested.

'We certainly can't exclude that possibility so I would urge you again to take great care of yourself. Try to avoid walking about on your own, particularly at night, and stay away from deserted areas.'

'Well, thankfully, from this afternoon I will have someone to look after me. I have a friend coming out to join me in Bergamo for a few days. He is a retired police officer and so I will feel safe going out in the evenings with him for company.'

Aldo looked surprised, even annoyed briefly, Kate thought. But after a few seconds he seemed to recover and said quickly: 'Good, I am glad you will have some protection. Perhaps you will be kind enough to introduce me to him at some stage. I would like to make the acquaintance of an English police officer.'

16

That afternoon as Kate waited in the sunshine in Colle Aperto for Steve's bus to arrive from the airport she thought sadly about her last meeting with Jean. She could still picture her tired, worried face and the wispy blonde hair that for once had not been straightened into its usual smooth bob.

If only Jean had been willing to go for a drink with her and had stopped for a chat last night she might have revealed where she was going in the Città Bassa or who she was planning to meet. There had obviously been something worrying the English teacher. She had seemed to be in a hurry and had been less friendly than usual. She had become impatient when Kate had asked about Luisa's boyfriend, Massimo. But she had not seemed suicidal, Kate thought to herself. So how had her body ended up lying in parkland in front of one of the city's ancient lookout towers?

Her thoughts were interrupted when she became aware of a small shape in the distance coming up the steep hill towards her and her heart leapt as it got nearer and she realised it was the Number 1 bus from the airport.

When she saw the familiar figure carrying his suitcase off the bus she felt overwhelmed with different emotions and ran forward to meet him. Steve put down his case on the pavement and swept her up in a hug.

Then he said: 'I know it is the middle of the afternoon, but I am absolutely starving. Do you know of anywhere that will still be serving hot food?'

Kate smiled at him and said: 'Let's take your case

to the hotel and get you checked in and then I will take you to a place where they do wonderful pizza.'

She stood back and took a good look at him. Steve was taller than most of the Italian men she had met during the last few days but he looked as though he belonged in these surroundings. He would never be taken for an English tourist because he was of southern Italian descent. His short dark hair was beginning to get a bit thin on the top but he had a naturally olive skin and very dark eyes.

'You're looking well, considering the circumstances,' he said studying her in turn. Then he pulled out the handle of his suitcase ready to wheel it along and said: 'Well, come on then, lead the way to this hotel.'

As they walked through Piazza Cittadella, Steve looked round at the fortifications and said: 'Bergamo is absolutely amazing, isn't it? It is not at all what I was expecting. I've never been this far north in Italy before. I was expecting a pretty little alpine place, I suppose. But I couldn't believe the size of the walls when we came through them on the bus.'

Kate said: 'Yes, even the Città Alta, the medieval part, is on a much bigger scale than I thought it would be. I can't wait to show you round everywhere.'

After Steve had signed in and left his passport with Roberto, he carried his case up to his second floor room. When he came back down the stairs into reception, Kate led the way through the narrow streets to the restaurant she had in mind.

Although there were only a few other people at the tables, Kate made her way to a quiet corner away from everyone else. After they had ordered a jug of wine and both chosen a pizza from the long list on offer, Steve's face took on a serious expression and he said: 'Right, tell me everything I need to know right from the beginning.'

'Well, first I must tell you about the terrible news I received this morning,' Kate said. 'Jean Anderson, Sophie's neighbour has been found dead. Her body was found early this morning in front of one of the old lookout towers in the walls and it seems as though she had fallen from the top of it. Apparently, it could have been an accident, or it could have been suicide. It is even possible that it could have been murder. But whatever happened to her, it is shocking, isn't it?'

Steve said, with a severe look on his face: 'It certainly is shocking, considering the fact that Sophie was found dead only a few days ago. Surely, it is too much of a coincidence for two English women living in the same building to die within a matter of days of each other. There has to be a connection between their deaths.'

'And that's not all,' Kate said quickly. 'The other night when I was walking back from the Città Bassa after having dinner with Marge Ransom, a car tried to run me over.'

'Do you think it was deliberate?'

'Yes, I'm afraid so. It missed me the first time and although I was very shaken up I tried to tell myself that it could have been an accident. But the car went round the block and then came back up the street and tried to do it again.'

'But that's terrible! I hope you reported it to the police,' Steve said, looking concerned.

'I didn't have to. Aldo was waiting for me in Piazza Vecchia. He could see I was upset and took me for a drink to calm me down and then saw me safely back to the hotel.'

'Why on earth didn't you ring me to tell me about it?'

'Well, it happened late at night and by the time I got back to my hotel room I just felt worn out and all I wanted to do was get into bed. I couldn't face going through it all over again with you on the phone.'

'Tell me exactly what happened now,' Steve said looking grim.

The waitress put a pizza in front of each of them at that moment. As Steve started to eat his, Kate calmly described what had happened on Thursday night and he listened to her carefully.

Afterwards he said: 'Haven't you been worried that whoever was behind the wheel of the car might try to have another go?'

'I suppose so, but the next day I went to Sarnico to meet Simon Pargeter and so I was some considerable distance away from Bergamo. Since I returned I haven't left the Città Alta. I feel reasonably safe up here. It isn't an easy place for drivers. They would struggle to run me over in broad daylight on these narrow cobbled streets full of tourists. But I must admit that I am glad you are here now. I will feel safer, particularly at night.'

'But in the light of what's happened to Sophie's neighbour…' Steve's voice trailed off in a worried way and he took a sip of his wine.

'Can I just ask you about Aunt Edna? You said you had something planned.'

'Yes, that's right. Do you remember Terry Batts? You met him at my 50th birthday do. We became good friends during that detection course I went on and have managed to keep in touch since. He's now a Detective Chief Inspector with West Midlands Police and so I've asked him to pop in and see Edna from time to time and do a bit of digging into Adam Leighton and his business affairs. There's something about that smarmy character that makes me suspicious, I'm not sure exactly what it is. But it won't do any harm to have Terry look into it for me and he's a strong enough personality to keep Adam in his place while we are away.

'Anyway, he rang me last night to say he had already been in and had a cup of tea with Edna and that it had gone really well. I don't know why, but he seems to have a way with the ladies, despite being so massive. I'm sure Edna will love him. And he has promised to keep texting me with progress reports from time to time so hopefully it will enable you to relax a bit more, knowing someone is looking out for her. I promise you, he will make sure she has everything she needs and if she is at all unwell at any time he will deal with it. You don't have to just rely on Adam and his staff any more.'

'Thanks, that is a relief. I feel guilty that I haven't texted Aunt Edna myself for the last day or so but I didn't want to tell her anything about this car business,' Kate said, cutting herself a piece of her pizza.

'Don't worry, Terry is on the case now. Look, finish your pizza and let's order some more wine and then I want you to take me through everything that has happened here right from the beginning.'

As Kate finished eating her pizza she began to feel less tense. Now Steve had joined her she wasn't alone any more. To her relief he seemed just the same as always.

Eventually she put down her knife and fork and sat back in her seat. Steve refilled their glasses from a fresh jug of wine he had ordered and said: 'Tell me about everything you have managed to find out in chronological order if you can.'

Kate said: 'Right, I will try my best.'

She took her notebook out of her shoulder bag and opened it, had a sip of wine as she studied it and then took a deep breath: 'Okay. The night before Sophie died she went down to Signora Mattozzi's apartment for a chat. The Signora has said that she seemed perfectly well and gave her the impression that she would be staying in for the rest of the evening.

'She later phoned Hampton House and had a chat with Aunt Edna on their land line so we know that it was about half past eight UK time and therefore about half past nine Italian time. That means we have absolutely reliable evidence that she was safe and well at that point, seemed in good spirits and gave every indication that she was on her own and planning to stay in for the rest of the evening and get on with her book.

'Jean Anderson has told me that she went down to the Città Bassa on the funicular and went round the supermarket opposite the funicular station returning to Palazzo Mattozzi with her shopping at about seven o'clock. So, knowing that both women were in for the night, Signora Mattozzi locked the iron gates to the street after the ten o'clock bell as usual.'

Steve said: 'Sorry, but what exactly is the ten o'clock bell?'

'It's a Bergamo tradition. The big bell, which is known as the *Campanone*, in Piazza Vecchia rings 100 times at ten pm every night. It dates back to when the Città Alta had a curfew and the gates in the walls were locked at ten pm. It gave anyone outside the walls the chance to get back inside the Città Alta and anyone who didn't return while the bell was ringing knew that they would be locked out for the night.'

'But how would Signora Mattozzi have known that both women were at home?'

''I wouldn't put it past her to have listened at their doors,' Kate said darkly. But then she added: 'Although, to be fair, Jean did say that they both knew that this was Signora Mattozzi's routine and they would either ensure they were home in good time or make some sort of arrangement with her in advance.

'Signora Mattozzi said that she unlocked the gate again early the next morning as usual so that Luisa could get in to do the cleaning.

'Luisa's story is that after she arrived at Palazzo Mattozzi she went straight upstairs to start in Sophie's apartment because she was expecting some men to arrive to collect some of the old furniture.

'Apparently Sophie didn't like some of the heavy antique furniture and had ordered new pieces to replace them.'

Steve frowned: 'That seems a bit over the top considering she wasn't going to be staying in Bergamo for long.'

'That was Sophie all over. She always liked to have nice things around her and arrange them exactly the way she wanted them. Anyway, the men arrived and Luisa supervised them to make sure they took the right things away with them and then cleaned the marble floor tiles to remove the marks where the furniture had stood. She went into the bedroom to start cleaning in there and says that is when she found Sophie lying dead in the bed. She went to the door of the flat and screamed for help and so Signora Mattozzi came rushing upstairs. Jean also heard the noise and came out of her apartment and followed Signora Mattozzi up the stairs.

'Signora Mattozzi and Jean went into the apartment. They said they saw Luisa in the bedroom looking shocked and upset and that Sophie was lying in the bed and seemed to be dead. Signora Mattozzi called for an ambulance but it was too late to save her, apparently. The ambulance people must have told the police about it because they came to look at Sophie's body in the bed and spoke to Signora Mattozzi and Luisa and, presumably, Jean.

'Then the police arranged for her body to be taken away and did a post mortem examination.' Kate said taking a deep breath. She sat back in her chair and drank some of her wine.

'And I have already told you about the results of the post mortem examination,' she added.

Steve nodded and said: 'Isn't it possible that when Luisa arrived she made Sophie a cup of tea or coffee, put the sedative in it and took it to her in the bedroom? Then when the furniture men arrived and the sedative had had time to work, one of them could have gone into the bedroom and put the pillow over her face and smothered her.'

'But why would they do it? Aldo said he was inclined to believe Luisa's version of events.'

'Do we know how many men came to collect the furniture and who they were working for?'

'No. Signora Mattozzi didn't seem to want to talk about it and told me that Luisa had arranged it all for Sophie.'

'Have the police interviewed the men?'

'I don't know.'

Steve took a small notebook and a pen out of his jacket pocket and wrote something down.

He said: 'I would like to talk to Luisa and the Commissario.'

'Well, Aldo has already said he would like to meet

you. I could text him and perhaps arrange a time when we could go and see him at the Commissariato.'

'You sound as though you are on good terms with Aldo.'

'He has been very kind to me, particularly since the car incident.'

Steve frowned and then said: 'In addition to Luisa, of course Signora Mattozzi had access to Sophie's apartment and could have gone and let herself in at any time of the day or night. But what about Jean?'

Kate said: 'I've been thinking about that. Jean may not have had a key, but then there would have been nothing to stop her going up the stairs at any time and just knocking on the door. Sophie would have let her in, I suppose, because she would have no reason not to trust her.'

'So, all three of them had the opportunity to kill Sophie. But what about their motives?'

'Apparently Luisa and Sophie had fallen out recently. Luisa told me it was about some cheese that she had helped herself to from the fridge, but Simon Pargeter, Sophie's latest man, told me they had argued about Luisa's new boyfriend, who Sophie had thought was unsuitable, Apparently she had told Luisa this, but of course Luisa had other ideas.'

'Why did she think he was unsuitable?'

'Well, you know Sophie. She was a wealthy woman who enjoyed having left wing sympathies. She seemed to have got the idea that he exploited his workers. I don't know whether there was any truth in it, but Luisa wouldn't like to hear her criticise him, presumably.'

'And what about the Signora?'

'According to Roberto Mariotto she and Sophie

got on well to begin with but their friendship didn't last. She had told Sophie quite a lot about her life and how badly she had been treated. Maybe she regretted confiding in her. Maybe she was jealous of Sophie. They were the same age, even born on the same day, but their lives were so different. Sophie had lots of money, a good social life and always had plenty of men interested in her. The Signora looked years older than Sophie, lived in a small flat in her husband's former family home and did the work of a concierge. You could understand it if she resented Sophie.

'Then there was the issue of the furniture. That could have brought things to a head.'

'Yes, tell me more about that,' Steve said, intrigued.

'They were apparently big, old pieces that had been in the Mattozzi family for generations and when Sophie said she didn't like them and wanted to replace them, Signora Mattozzi was offended. She was absolutely against the idea of them going into storage. But it's not exactly a motive for murder, is it?'

'People have been killed for a lot less, believe me.'

They considered this for a moment and then he said: 'Tell me about Jean. Can you think of a motive for her? It would be a nice, neat solution for the Italian police to have one English visitor kill another English visitor and then kill herself out of remorse.'

'I really can't see it being Jean. She seemed to be a really decent person!'

'Honestly, Kate, that makes no logical sense!'

'Well, she is the only person in Bergamo who reacted the way you would have expected her to react after Sophie's death. Even though she and Sophie weren't particularly close friends she seemed genuinely sorry that she had died.'

'Could there have been some bloke that they were both after?'

'I think she was keen on Edgar and didn't like Sophie muscling in on him. I have been told that she resented Sophie getting so much interest from the men she met around here. Both Signora Mattozzi and Marge said they had noticed that.

'But the day we went up to Sophie's apartment together, she couldn't even get the door open with the pass key, I had to do it. I can't imagine her going up there, murdering her, getting out again and then going up with Signora Mattozzi after Luisa had discovered the body as though nothing had happened. She just seemed too nice and normal to be able to behave like that.'

'Well, what about Marge, then?' he asked, sipping his wine thoughtfully.

'She and Sophie were supposed to have become good friends, but the other night after she had had a few drinks, she let the act slip and showed that she really couldn't stand her.'

'Why was that, do you think?'

'It was probably partly because Sophie took Edgar's attention away from her and partly because she knew Sophie looked down on her. Sophie had made spiteful remarks about her lack of purpose in life, her lack of intellectual substance.

'She had made it clear to everyone that she saw through Marge. She had worked out that she was just on a long holiday really and was only interested in the shopping side of Italy. She was just paying lip service to being interested in music and art, or in the history and wonderful architecture here.'

'What about Edgar?'

'So far as I can tell he seems to have been a nice

guy who was happy to go around Bergamo with three women. He perhaps enjoyed the fact that they were all competing for his attention. I think he just liked being the celebrity author they all admired and doesn't seem to have had any particular romantic interest in any of them.

'Marge says he was a bit smitten with Sophie when he first met her but then began to see through her, although I only have her word for that. He never admitted to having had any romantic feelings towards her when I tried to draw him out.

'I had lunch with him the other day and he seemed genuinely sorry Sophie was dead. But I had wondered whether there might have been any romance between them at some time because he is rather good looking.'

'Oh, is he?' Steve said raising his eyebrows, pretending to have taken offence.

'I think Jean fancied Edgar but was perhaps too timid to do anything about it. I don't think there was ever anything going on between Edgar and Marge, I think they were just old friends from the same kind of background back home.

'To outsiders they would seem like a happy foursome as they went around Bergamo together, but there were obviously undercurrents going on.'

'And then there were all Sophie's Latin lovers,' Steve said.

'Only one that we know of,' Kate corrected him. 'Roberto obviously fancied her when he first met her but went off her when she became so demanding about the apartment.'

'Yes, I want to speak to him,' Steve said making another note in his notebook. 'Has it occurred to you that he could have had keys to all the apartments as well as the main gate and could have let himself into Palazzo Mattozzi whenever he felt like it?'

'No, I hadn't thought of that.'

'He might have decided to shut Sophie up once and for all to protect his father's reputation.'

Kate thought about this and then said: 'But the man she did end up having an affair with is Ernesto, the owner of La Torre restaurant. He was seen outside in the street watching her apartment the night before she died and we know he was devastated that she had ended their relationship.'

'How do we know that he didn't ask her to let him into her apartment? Then he could have drugged her and killed her and let himself out again before Signora Mattozzi locked up for the night,' Steve said.

'But she sounded perfectly well and happy when she spoke to Aunt Edna at about nine thirty Italian time. I don't think he would have had time to get in and sedate her and kill her before the ten o'clock bell.

'Also, he might have people that can vouch for him being in the restaurant between nine thirty and ten pm. We could ask him.' Steve wrote something in his notebook again and then asked: 'What about this new guy that she dumped Ernesto for?'

'He was in a restaurant in Sarnico surrounded by his business associates until late in the evening. Also, it was just the start of the romance between them and he seemed genuinely upset that she had died.'

'I'm always suspicious of people with good alibis,' Steve said with a smile.

'But he hadn't really got to know her properly. He hadn't had time to grow to dislike her enough to want to kill her.'

'Well, the problem we have is that someone did dislike her enough to want to kill her. And the same person then made an attempt to run you down. And if Jean is not that person, then she was almost certainly another victim. So for the sake of Edna and Sophie and, perhaps also for Jean, we are not going to stop until we have found out exactly what happened.'

17

Kate filled Steve in on everything she had been doing in Bergamo over the last few days while they finished their wine. Then they left the restaurant and she took Steve through the streets to Piazza Vecchia.

'It's absolutely stunning,' Steve said gazing round at the buildings. 'I have read that this is the square most admired by architects in the whole of Italy.'

'Where did you read that?' she asked in surprise.

'Oh, it was in a book about northern Italy that I bought at the airport to read on the plane.'

'Well, this white marble building is the Civic Library where Sophie used to come and do her research. It was on the steps here that Aldo was waiting for me on Thursday night after the car tried to run me down. He gave me the fright of my life suddenly stepping out from behind one of those pillars.'

'It seems odd that he was waiting for you here rather than at the hotel. Did he know you would be coming up from the Città Bassa and walking through the square?'

'I hadn't really thought about it, I suppose he must have decided that it was a possibility,' Kate said.

'That white marble fountain in the middle was a gift to Bergamo in the 18th century from one of the Venetian rulers of Bergamo, Alvise Contarini, to mark the end of his time in charge of the city. Apparently the Venetians liked to have beautiful fountains built here to impress people who visited the city with their wealth and power,' she continued.

'Across the other side of the square that dark building is the 12th century Palazzo della Ragione.'

'Shall we go and sit at the bar next to it and have a coffee,' Steve suggested.

As they sat at a table in the sunshine Steve glanced at the statue a few feet away and said: 'Oh look, there's good old Torquato Tasso! He got around a bit during his short life, didn't he? He was actually born in Sorrento and there is a statue of him in the main square, Piazza Tasso, which is named after him.

'I remember being taken to see it for the first time when I was a child and staying with my grandparents during the summer holidays, so I've always had a soft spot for him even though I've never read any of his poetry. I didn't know he had a connection with Bergamo as well.'

Kate pointed to the open archways of the ground floor of the Palazzo behind Tasso's statue and said: 'Apparently they used to hear court cases through there out in the open air and put the prisoners on show so that the good people of Bergamo could come and look at them and hurl insults at them.'

'Oh, I approve of that. It is an early example of community punishment. I might ring the Chief when I get back and suggest the force gives it a try.'

After they had finished their coffee they walked through the archways into Piazza Duomo.

'This is considered to be one of the finest Renaissance buildings in Italy,' Kate said pointing out the Colleoni chapel.

'It's very pink and white and pretty, but what was its purpose?'

'Would you believe it was built on the orders of a famous Bergamo military leader to house his own tomb?'

They went inside the chapel and looked at the ornate sarcophagus that still housed Bartolomeo

Colleoni's remains.

'He commissioned an architect to design it for him,' Kate said. 'Can you imagine looking ahead to your own death and seeing the designs for the tomb where your body is going to lie?'

'But isn't that better than dying suddenly without any warning and having no say in your own funeral arrangements?'

'I don't know.'

After they left the chapel they walked along until they found a bench to sit on and then Steve said: 'One thing I haven't asked you yet is how you actually feel about it.'

'About what?'

'About Sophie's death, of course. We have discussed all the events leading up to it and what you've found out about her friends and associates here. But you have been so busy worrying about Edna and how she feels that you've never told me about what it means to you.'

'Well, I have shed some tears since I have been here and seen where she was living, more than I would have thought I was capable of. But you know how I felt about Sophie when she was alive. She was difficult to like, let alone to love. She never let me get close to her.'

'I always used to think she looked down on me,' Steve said reflectively.

'She looked down on a lot of people,' Kate said smiling. 'Sometimes I have even found myself feeling sorry for the people she became friends with out here, because of the way she treated them.'

'But we come back to the undisputable fact that no one had the right to kill her.'

'That's right.'

'Who was it who said: 'Murder offends me.' It was

someone famous, I'm sure.'

'I think it was Hercule Poirot, actually,' Kate said and they both laughed.

That evening Kate took Steve down to the Città Bassa on the funicular railway and they walked along the main street until they reached Via Sentierone, where she showed him the grand buildings that lined both sides of the wide thoroughfare. In the little park next to Teatro Donizetti they came across the white marble monument to Donizetti that Kate had read about. The composer was sitting on a bench gazing thoughtfully at the figure of a female playing the lyre.

'You could almost imagine he was looking straight past her because he was far more interested in the theatre over there,' Kate said.

'So, this is the man Sophie had come here to find out all about. What was the attraction, do you think?' Steve asked thoughtfully.

'It was his wonderful music, of course,' Kate said at once. 'I now realise it was one of the few interests we had in common.'

They continued to stroll along Viale Papa Giovanni XXIII towards the railway station until they found a restaurant advertising typical Bergamo cuisine.

Steve sampled *casoncelli alla bergamasca* topped with bacon, sage and melted butter. He even dipped a tentative spoon into Kate's dish of *polenta taragna* that she had ordered to go with her main course.

'All this hearty, northern Italian food is a bit of a culture shock for a southern Italian boy, but I'm not denying that it is very tasty,' he said.

'This is a Bergamo speciality, *polenta taragna*, made with the local *taleggio* cheese. It's much nicer than ordinary polenta, isn't it?' By taking a second spoonful Steve showed that he agreed with her.

After they left the restaurant they were waiting to cross the road to walk back to the funicular when Kate noticed a grey saloon car parked on the opposite side of the road with the engine running.

She felt a moment of anxiety until she saw the curly hair of the driver illuminated by the street lamp and realised that it was Aldo sitting in the car with another man next to him in the passenger seat.

'Look, it's the Commissario sitting in that parked car. Let's go across and say hello to him.'

But Steve pulled her back by her arm and said: 'They look as though they are carrying out a surveillance operation. You could ruin everything by going up to the car and talking to them.'

They watched the car from across the road with interest.

After a few minutes they saw two men come out of a building further down the street and start to walk off in the opposite direction from them. The grey car set off and began to follow them slowly. The smaller of the men wore a white baseball cap and the taller man was black and had a shaven head.

'The police are obviously watching that pair for some reason,' Steve said.

As Kate watched the two men walk away down the street, a good distance ahead of the car, she had the odd feeling that there was something familiar about the smaller man wearing the baseball cap. Then she realised with a jolt that it was Massimo, the boyfriend of Luisa, the maid. It was definitely the same man she had seen out with Luisa and her little boy in Piazza Vecchia and who had seemed annoyed when she had taken a photograph of them two days before.

18

Kate woke feeling refreshed and having enjoyed a much better night's sleep. She was reassured to have seen Aldo working on the investigation into Sophie's death. His interest in Massimo and his companion in the Città Bassa the night before suggested he must think Massimo and Luisa were involved somehow.

She had texted Aldo to ask about a convenient time for her to take Steve to meet him at the Commissariato on Monday and was looking forward to being able to find out more about how the investigation was going.

She had also texted Marge and said she would like to introduce Steve to her and Edgar if they were going to be anywhere near Piazza Vecchia that day. But in the meantime she was looking forward to spending Sunday with Steve in Bergamo and having arranged to meet him for breakfast at nine o'clock, she went to more trouble than usual styling her hair and choosing something to wear after showering.

They lingered over fresh bread rolls with ham and cheese and had several cups of coffee while they talked in the hotel's small breakfast room. Kate could see through the window that it was another lovely, sunny day and suggested that they went for a walk around the walls of the Città Alta.

As they were leaving the hotel later, Roberto called out from behind the reception desk: 'Signor Bartorelli, I have your passport here to return to you.'

Steve turned back and went over to the desk to collect his passport and Kate seized the opportunity to take a photograph of the front entrance of the hotel, with Roberto in the background behind the desk talking to Steve.

Steve said: 'Thanks for finding me a room at such short notice and letting me have an open ended stay because I don't know how long it will take Kate to sort her cousin's affairs out.'

'That's no problem,' Roberto replied smoothly. 'What do you think of Bergamo's Città Alta now you have seen it?'

'I think the architecture is superb and I'm also fascinated by the Bergamo traditions, such as the ancient curfew. Can you hear the ten o'clock bell this far away from Piazza Vecchia?'

'Yes, if you stand out in the street you will hear it.'

'Do the bars and restaurants close after the bell rings? I wondered whether Bergamo was an early closing city like Venice?'

'No, not at all. The bars and restaurants in Piazza Vecchia and also in Via Colleoni and Via Gombito all stay open till late.'

'I just thought it was a bit odd when Kate told me that Signora Mattozzi locks up at ten pm after she has heard the bell each night.'

Roberto smiled and said: 'Yes, she is very old fashioned. She has always been an early riser and therefore she goes to bed early at night.'

'What if there was a fire in Signora Mattozzi's apartment. How would the other tenants get out of the building and through the gate?'

Roberto looked displeased but answered him politely: 'When we had the building converted into apartments we took expert advice about the fire safety regulations. The tenants can get into the courtyard and out on to the terrace without going through Signora Mattozzi's apartment. And I have a key to the main gate as well, just for emergencies.'

'What about the three apartments?'
'Yes, I have keys for them as well in case of a problem or if Signora Mattozzi should be taken ill. I also gave both of the residents my mobile number so they could call me in an emergency.'
With a relaxed smile, Steve turned to Kate, who had been standing a few feet away looking at the pictures she had taken on her camera, and said: 'Right, are you ready to go for this walk?'
Kate led the way to Colle Aperto from where they turned down Viale delle Mura to walk down to Porta San Giacomo.
After they had strolled along for a while in the sunshine Steve said: 'Let's sit on this bench and take in the view.'
The Città Bassa was laid out before them and it was such a clear day that they could look down on the buildings and at the long, straight Viale Papa Giovanni XXIII stretching towards the railway station.
Steve said: 'I've been thinking about Sophie's book. How do we even know that there was one? I mean, she wasn't under any pressure to write it, was she? She didn't need the money. She may not have actually got started on it. She seemed to have been having a bit of a jolly out here, what with art exhibitions, operas and concerts, not to mention all the love affairs. She might not have had time to get going on the book.'
'But she told Aunt Edna that the book was going really well.'
'Well she might have just said that to give her a reason for staying out here longer.'
'Luisa and Jean both said they had seen her writing in a notebook, but I haven't been able to find one in the apartment.'

'Roberto could have stolen it on one of his visits to the apartment to see if she had made any notes about his father's business dealings.'

Kate said: 'Apparently she threatened him with writing to L'Eco di Bergamo about it. But it's ridiculous. Why would a newspaper be interested in Signora Mattozzi's grievances?'

'I suppose the Italian press might be different from ours, Maybe they would have been interested. And it could have led to a reporter doing some investigating and digging into Roberto's business dealings. That might have been what he was afraid of, if he had things he wanted to keep quiet about.

'Also, you told me that the apartment wasn't left untouched after Sophie's body was taken away as the Commissario had requested. Signora Mattozzi says she didn't go in there, but we know Luisa went in there to tidy up and strip the bed. You were told she had taken all the bed linen and covers away to wash them. She could have taken other things away from the apartment as well. Who would have known about it afterwards?'

Kate thought about it for a while and then said: 'You know, there were quite a few days available for Roberto to get in using his pass key before the Commissario took me round to see the apartment.'

Steve said: 'Yes, the police seized the laptop right at the beginning so he had to go into your room to check it out when you got it back. But he could have helped himself to any notebooks she had left in the apartment at any time after her death.'

Kate's mobile beeped in her bag at that moment. After she had looked at it she said: 'Good! Marge is suggesting we meet them for a drink at the bar next to Palazzo della Ragione at noon.'

They got up from the bench to continue their walk

and then Steve said: 'I don't trust Roberto. He has very watchful eyes.'

'What do you mean by that?'

'He's constantly on his guard. That probably means he's concealing something from you.'

'You always think you can spot a wrong'un, don't you?' Kate said fondly.

'Yes, just in the way that if you decide you like someone you can't imagine them lying to you or trying to deceive you.'

'That's interesting. You see the worst in people and I see the good in them.'

'Well, in theory we should make a good detective team.'

They continued walking until they reached Porta San Giacomo, which they passed through to walk back into the centre of the Città Alta.

Edgar and Marge were already sitting at a table outside the bar when they arrived in Piazza Vecchia.

Edgar stood up and greeted Kate warmly, kissing her on both cheeks. When she introduced Steve they both looked at him with interest.

'An English detective, wow! Well, maybe you can find out exactly what happened to poor Jean,' Marge said at once. She turned to Kate and asked her: 'I take it you have heard about it? Some English people were talking about it in the hotel this morning. Apparently there was a piece in the newspaper about an Englishwoman's body being found in a park in Bergamo. I couldn't believe it when I found out that they were talking about Jean.'

After they had all ordered their drinks from the waitress, Marge turned to Kate again and asked: 'Do you know any more details about it? I was wondering whether you had spoken to the police at all.'

Kate said guardedly: 'I have spoken to the Commissario about it and he said that they think she may have fallen from one of the old lookout towers in the walls on to the patch of grass where her body was found, but I don't know any more than that.'

'She must have had a pretty good reason for killing herself, if she decided to throw herself from the top of a tower,' Marge said.

'To be fair, we don't know that's what happened. It could have been some kind of accident,' Edgar protested.

Marge said: 'Well, suppose it turns out that Sophie didn't die as a result of natural causes after all. I think it will be pretty clear that it was Jean who was to blame for her death. I can just imagine her creeping upstairs and killing Sophie while she slept.'

'How would she have got through the locked door?' Steve asked.

'She could have knocked on the door and asked Sophie to open it on some pretext, like saying she wanted to borrow something.'

'Well, then, she couldn't have killed her while she slept,' Kate pointed out.

'Did you ever visit Jean and Sophie in Palazzo Mattozzi?' Steve asked, looking at them both.

'Hell, no. I've never set foot in the place,' Edgar said at once.

'Me neither,' Marge said. 'We used to meet them up here. This was always our stomping ground. We had some great times in the bars and restaurants around Piazza Vecchia.'

There was silence for a moment and then Steve gave a chuckle. 'I must say it sounds like something out of a Victorian novel, two single women being locked in the palazzo after ten pm each night and not allowed to have a man in their rooms.'

'Yes, but it didn't stop Sophie enjoying herself, did it? She was able to stay the night at La Torre whenever she wanted to,' Marge said quickly, reaching for the glass the waitress had just placed in front of her.

'And then when she found someone better, she dropped poor old Ernesto like a hot potato, didn't she?'

'Steady on, Marge,' Edgar said mildly, but Kate thought he looked embarrassed.

'When did you last see Jean?' she asked.

Edgar said: 'Well now, let me think, it must have been here at this bar with you last Monday.'

Marge said: 'Yes, that's right, she was going teaching in the afternoon, wasn't she? She seemed perfectly all right, just her usual self.'

Kate said: 'I went to La Torre for dinner with her that same night and she introduced me to Ernesto. She seemed fine at that point. Then I met her for a drink at the funicular bar on Thursday evening before I had dinner with you. But on Friday evening I called on her at Palazzo Mattozzi when I got back from Sarnico to see if she was free for dinner or to go for a drink and she seemed different.'

'Really!' Marge said, agog with curiosity. 'How did she seem?'

'Well, I suppose the best way to describe it is that she was not very happy. She was in a hurry and didn't want to hang around talking. She said she had to go down to the Città Bassa to sort something out, but I don't know what, she didn't say. She got angry with me when I tried to ask her about something else and then she ran off in the direction of the funicular station in Piazza Mercato delle Scarpe.'

'That's very interesting,' Marge said, looking at

her closely. 'Do you realise, Kate, that you were probably the last person to speak to her before she died?'

19

Kate wanted to introduce Ernesto to Steve so she suggested having dinner at La Torre that evening. When they arrived at the restaurant the waiter showed them to a quiet table in an alcove but Ernesto soon noticed them and brought them a jug of wine.

'Please accept some Valcalepio Bianco with my compliments,' he said placing the jug and two glasses on the table. He then kissed Kate on both cheeks.

After she had performed the introductions, Steve said: 'Would you care to sit down and have a drink with us for a few minutes.'

Ernesto hesitated for a few seconds and then pulled a chair away from a nearby table and sat down with them. He leaned behind him and took a wine glass from the next table and then poured them all half a glass from the jug. 'Salute!' he said as they raised their glasses.

'Can I take a picture of you with Steve to show to Sophie's mother when I get back to England?' Kate asked.

Ernesto said: 'Of course!' and smiled for the camera as Kate stepped back a few feet from the table and took the picture. Steve in turn photographed her with Ernesto, before sitting down to begin the conversation.

'It is a very sad reason for me to have come to Bergamo, to help Kate sort out Sophie's affairs.'

'Yes, it must be. The loss of such a beautiful young woman is terrible,' Ernesto agreed.

Steve said: 'I still find it hard to believe that someone as healthy as Sophie could suddenly die like that. It doesn't seem possible. How did she seem to you the last time that you saw her?'

Ernesto said: 'As far as I could tell she was absolutely fine. I saw her walking along in the street quite near the restaurant and I thought that she looked as wonderful as always. I never remember her complaining of feeling tired or ill the whole time I knew her.'

Kate said: 'You didn't by any chance catch a glimpse of her the night before she was found dead? Jean said she noticed you on the opposite side of the street from Palazzo Mattozzi?'

Ernesto sighed and looked down at the wine glass he was holding between his slim fingers.

'No, I promise you, she never came out of the building and I didn't even have a momentary view of her through the window, but then I wasn't there for very long really.'

'Do you think Sophie knew you were outside her apartment that night?'

Ernesto looked surprised and said: 'No, I don't think so. How would she have known?'

Steve said: 'But, weren't you tempted to ring her and ask her to let you in?'

Ernesto looked embarrassed. 'To be honest I was waiting to see if this new man in her life was going to make an appearance, but no one came out of the building or went into it while I was watching, apart from Jean who looked as though she had been out shopping.

'After a while I realised I was being stupid just standing there waiting around in the street and so I walked back.'

'What time was that?' Steve asked.

'I honestly can't remember and in any case I didn't come straight back here. I walked around the streets of the Città Alta for a while thinking about things and then I came back to the restaurant.'

'Did anyone see you arrive back? They might be able to tell you what time it was.'

'No, I don't think anyone saw me. I came into the restaurant and got a bottle of wine from the fridge and then went straight up to my apartment. The restaurant was very quiet because it was a Sunday night and so I just went upstairs and had some wine and then went to bed. I knew Anton would be able to cope with the few diners we had in that night and that I could leave him to lock up. We weren't doing very well at the time, mainly because I had become so distracted by Sophie leaving me, which I know was extremely frustrating for Anton, but it meant that he could manage without me.'

'So you have no idea what the time was when you stopped watching Palazzo Mattozzi and left the street?'

'No, I'm sorry, I don't. Why do you want to know? Do you think it is important?'

Kate said: 'We're not sure at the moment. But we are trying to piece together the last few hours of Sophie's life, for my aunt's sake at least. I think it would comfort her to know who she saw and what she did the night before she died.'

Ernesto's voice suddenly became high-pitched and he sounded close to hysteria. 'Well, I am sorry that I can't be of more help! I thought Sophie would probably be in her apartment because it was a Sunday evening. But I never saw her and I never saw anyone arrive to visit her. As far as I am aware she was inside her apartment on her own all that evening and therefore I am sorry to have to tell you that she must have died all alone!'

Later that evening after they had enjoyed an excellent meal and were ready to leave La Torre they looked round to say goodbye to Ernesto but there was no sign of him in the restaurant.

Steve left enough euros on the table to cover the bill and they walked back through the streets to the hotel.

'I thought Ernesto seemed a bit young to have been having an affair with Sophie,' he said thoughtfully, after a few minutes.

Kate said: 'There would have been quite an age difference, but then Sophie looked good for her age and people often thought she was a lot younger than she actually was. Roberto is probably several years younger than her as well and yet he has admitted that he was attracted to her at the start.'

'Also, Ernesto has no alibi for the crucial time between her finishing her phone call to Edna and the ten o'clock bell,' Steve said.

Kate smiled and said: 'You don't like people who have good alibis but you are also suspicious of people who haven't got one. There's no pleasing you.'

'Well, actually I'm suspicious of everyone.'

Kate laughed and then after they had walked along in silence for a couple of minutes she said: 'Feel how warm it is, even at this time of the evening. And yet Sophie was lying in the bed wearing her grey silk dressing gown, according to Luisa. You don't sleep in your dressing gown at this time of the year. It makes me think she must have got up and put her dressing gown on, possibly to answer the door.

'Luisa also said that she helped herself to the left over coffee when she arrived. But it wouldn't have been from the day before, would it? So Sophie must have made herself some fresh coffee after getting up. She perhaps got up really early to work on her book and just sat in her dressing gown, drinking coffee and writing.'

'And then someone could have dropped a sedative into her coffee,' Steve said.

'But only Signora Mattozzi, Jean or Luisa could have got into the apartment in order to do that.'

'Or, one of these mysterious furniture removal men that we don't know anything about yet,' Steve said thoughtfully.

Aldo looked tired and harassed when he came to meet them in the reception area at the front of the police station the following morning. He had kept them waiting a few minutes, despite having previously texted Kate to suggest a time when he expected to be free to see them.

Once inside his office he shook hands formally with Steve and after a nod in Kate's direction pulled two chairs up in front of his desk for them to sit on.

After asking Steve questions about the police force he had been working for until recently, he suddenly exclaimed: 'Bartorelli! But that sounds like an Italian name.'

Steve said: 'My grandparents are from a village in Campania near Sorrento but my father came to work in England and eventually married a Yorkshire girl.

'He encouraged me to learn Italian when I was young and I was brought over to Italy regularly to visit my grandparents.

'But I have never been as far north as this in Italy before. Bergamo has been a complete surprise to me.'

'I hope it has been a pleasant surprise.'

'Oh, absolutely, I think it is a beautiful city.'

When the conversation halted for a moment Kate asked: 'Would you ask Signora Mattozzi if I can take Steve to see Sophie's apartment?'

Aldo said: 'Of course, I will telephone her this morning and will let you know later when it would be convenient for her to show you round again.'

After another awkward pause, Steve asked: 'How's the investigation going?'

Aldo said: 'Unfortunately we won't have anything definite to go on until we have received the post mortem examination results.'

Steve said: 'Sorry, but I meant the investigation into Sophie's death.'

Aldo seemed irritated by this and said: 'Well, it is not inconceivable that the two deaths are linked. If Jean was responsible for Sophie's death she may have been full of remorse later and decided to kill herself. But we will know more about how she died when we get the post mortem examination results.'

Steve nodded thoughtfully and then said: 'In that case do you think it is likely that Jean was behind the attack on Kate?'

Aldo looked even more annoyed. 'We don't even know if Jean Anderson could drive.'

'So, what steps have you taken to trace the car and the driver?'

Aldo shrugged: 'It is difficult, if not to say impossible to trace them, without knowing either the registration number or the make of the vehicle.'

Steve then turned to Kate and said: 'I never thought to ask you this, but the next day, after you were pursued by the car, did you ring Marge and tell her about what had happened to you on the way home after seeing her.'

Kate said: 'No, I decided to keep all the details to myself. I had already agreed with Aldo that I wouldn't tell anyone here about the results of the post mortem examination on Sophie. By then I had begun to think that someone from Sophie's circle of friends could have been involved so I wanted to keep the information about the car to myself as well.'

'That was the right thing to do, Signora,' Aldo said, nodding approvingly.

Steve then said: 'I wanted to ask about the men who came to take the furniture away from the apartment. How many of them were there that morning?'

'Two, as far as I recall.'

'And have you interviewed them yet?'

'Two of my officers went out to the furniture warehouse to speak to them. They seemed satisfied that what they were told confirmed Luisa's version of events.'

Steve said: 'It seems rather curious to think that they were in the main room of the apartment taking furniture away while Sophie was lying dead in the bedroom. Have you considered the possibility that Luisa could have administered a sedative to Sophie in a cup of tea or coffee and then one of the men could have gone into the bedroom later and smothered her while she was unconscious?'

'Yes, of course I have considered the possibility, but we have absolutely no evidence to support that theory,' Aldo said, with an edge to his voice.

Kate said: 'Last night, we saw you with one of your colleagues down in the Città Bassa. It looked as though you were watching Massimo, Luisa's boyfriend. It made me think that you now suspected Luisa of being somehow involved in Sophie's death.'

Aldo looked puzzled and asked: 'I'm sorry, but

who exactly is Massimo?'

Kate said: 'One of the men you were following last night near the railway station was definitely Luisa's boyfriend and I have been told by someone that his first name is Massimo.'

Aldo shook his head and said: 'The two men we were watching last night are being investigated in connection with another matter entirely. I had no idea that one of them was the boyfriend of Luisa.'

While Kate was still trying to take in this new information, Steve said: 'Could we have the address of the warehouse where the furniture is being stored so that we can go and talk to the people who run it, informally, of course.'

Aldo looked uneasy and said: 'I shouldn't really give the address out to you.'

Steve said: 'We would be very tactful and just ask about the furniture. We could say that Kate is looking for an item that belonged to her cousin and wondered if it had been left in a drawer in one of the pieces of furniture by mistake.'

Aldo pressed a few keys on his computer keyboard and looked at the information that came up on the screen. His expression quickly changed to a look of astonishment. He said: 'I am sorry, but I can't allow you to visit the warehouse. I hadn't realised before, but it seems there is a connection between the firm that operates from that furniture warehouse and some of the people we are investigating in connection with the other matter I was just telling you about.'

Steve said: 'So, it would seem that Luisa is the common denominator in all this. She arranges for the furniture to be taken away by the firm that operates from this warehouse. You are watching her boyfriend Massimo and his mate because of something else that you are currently investigating. And now you have found that they have a connection with the firm that operates from this warehouse, where the furniture is currently being stored. The furniture was taken away from the apartment only a short time before Sophie's dead body was found. Surely this is all rather significant.'

Aldo looked exasperated and said: 'I am sorry, but at this stage I am not sure what the connection is or what it could mean in relation to Signorina Westmullen's death. I can't give you any more details about the other matter we are investigating. It is at a delicate stage and therefore has to remain completely confidential. But as a police officer yourself, I am sure that you will understand.'

20

'It's so frustrating!' Steve exclaimed later as they sat at a table outside a bar having a glass of wine in the sunshine. 'I hate not having access to all the information.'

'But you can understand why Aldo couldn't tell us more. He doesn't want to risk jeopardising another case,' Kate pointed out.

'Yes, so we are just going to have to do it on our own, aren't we? We have to find out what really happened to Sophie, and to Jean as well. I feel sure that the furniture has something to do with it. We now know that there is something suspicious about the firm that came to take it all away. So we are going to have to look into it further. Anyway, there is nothing to stop us from talking to Luisa and asking her for more details about it.'

'But remember that Simon Pargeter told me that Sophie was worried about Luisa getting too involved with Massimo. We must tread very carefully because Massimo could be mixed up in it all. If he is exploiting his staff and doing shady business deals he could be dangerous. It was not all in Sophie's head, as Jean seemed to think it was. We know now that Aldo is investigating the firm based at the warehouse and that he was actually following Massimo and his companion down in the Città Bassa to see what they were getting up to.'

Steve said: 'To be honest I think we will do a lot better on our own. I can't believe how slack the Italian police have been so far. Fancy not realising that the place where Signora Mattozzi's furniture was being stored was connected with the firm mixed up in the other operation.'

He took a sip of wine and then said: 'And another thing - yet again the Commissario seems content to sit back and wait for the results of the post mortem examination before he is prepared to do anything else to investigate a suspicious death in the city. And why hasn't he at least tried to ask around to find out if anyone among Sophie's friends owned, or had access to, a car?

'I think the most likely explanation for that car trying to run you down is that someone wanted to scare you off because you had been asking too many awkward questions. I know they are probably strapped for resources here, just like we are at home, but a few enquiries among Sophie's mates to see who might have had access to a grey car wouldn't have been all that taxing, surely?

'I'm sorry Kate, your Commissario seems a nice chap, but I'm not terribly impressed with the way he's been running this investigation He probably wouldn't have bothered helping you with anything at all if you hadn't been an attractive woman.'

'That's very unfair,' Kate said immediately, but she was pleased he had revealed that he still thought she was attractive.

Then she said thoughtfully: 'But, I'm not sure that you can call him 'my Commissario' any more. He wasn't nearly as pleasant and helpful to me today as he has been in the past.'

As she spoke her phone beeped in her bag and after she had taken it out and looked at the message she said: 'Anyway, he has fixed it with Signora Mattozzi for us to go and look at Sophie's apartment this afternoon.'

'Well, we're making some progress then, aren't we?' Steve said. 'Come on, drink up and then we will go and look for somewhere to have lunch. I rather fancy a pizza!'

When Signora Mattozzi came to let them in through the iron gates of the palazzo that afternoon Kate thought she looked even older and more haggard than before.

She handed them the key and gestured to them to go up to the apartment and then went back through her own front door again looking disinterested.

'She seemed less aggressive than usual,' Kate said to Steve as they climbed the stairs. She pointed out Jean's door as they passed it and Steve said: 'You know Jean could have been in the habit of regularly nipping upstairs to have a chat with Sophie.'

'I don't think they were all that close, actually. She told me she found Sophie difficult to become good friends with and I knew what she meant. Sophie was good at keeping people at arms length.'

'Apart from the men she met out here, it would seem.'

'Yes, but even though she had at least two lovers she seems to have had the upper hand with both of them and conducted the relationships entirely on her terms.'

'Maybe one of them, Ernesto perhaps, lost patience with her. Despite everything he said to us last night, he could have snapped suddenly and murdered her because she didn't want him any more.'

Kate did not reply because she was struggling to turn the key in the lock of Sophie's apartment but eventually she managed to get the old wooden door open and they went inside.

Steve stood in the middle of the main room and looked round, carefully taking in his surroundings. Then he went over to the small antique desk and looked inside each drawer in turn as Kate had done before him.

He examined the stack of suitcases and carefully went through the contents of each one.

'These are very well packed,' he observed. 'Who do you think was responsible, Sophie or Luisa?'

He held up a dainty, white cotton sun dress that he had removed from sheets of folded tissue paper. 'Look how tiny this is!' he said in amazement. Kate, who was uncomfortably aware of the difference between her and Sophie's dress sizes, said nothing.

Steve walked over to the window and opened the double doors out on to the balcony. He stepped outside and looked down at the street. Kate stood just behind him and said: 'See how high up we are. From here it is a sheer drop to the street below. There would be nothing to hold on to if you tried to climb down. The killer can't possibly have got out this way.'

After a moment Steve said: 'I'm just trying to imagine Ernesto standing over there on the opposite pavement watching this window to try to catch a glimpse of Sophie or her new boyfriend. The poor devil!

'You can't help but feel sorry for him, although, of course, we only have his word for it that he didn't demand to be let in so that he could have another attempt at changing her mind about finishing with him.'

'But if he got so exasperated that he ended up killing her, it would have been a spur of the moment thing. He wouldn't have drugged her first and then waited until she was sedated to smother her, surely,' Kate pointed out.

They went back inside and as Steve closed the balcony doors he exclaimed: 'Look down there. Those scuff marks on the paintwork look quite recent.'

Kate looked down at the marks at the bottom of the wooden door frame that he was pointing to. 'I wonder what caused that?' she said.

'It's hard to say but they are fairly recent marks I'm sure. The doors look newly-painted.'

'Roberto told me that he had the apartment completely redecorated before Sophie moved in.'

Kate opened the door of the bedroom and again experienced the uncomfortable churning feeling in her stomach as she imagined Sophie's body lying still and cold in the bed.

Steve went over to the small side window and opened the shutters to look down at the street below. He said: 'Again it is hard to imagine how anyone could have possibly got in or out this way.'

Back in the main living room he said: 'Of course it is difficult to visualise what the room would have looked like with all the furniture in it. We don't know what has been taken away.'

Kate said: 'Well, we could ask Luisa for more information about it if you think it is important.'

They left the apartment, pulling the door shut behind them and went back downstairs.

When they knocked on Signora Mattozzi's door she answered it within seconds to take the key back from them.

Steve said: 'Thank you for allowing us to look round the apartment. I hope it hasn't stopped you from going out this afternoon.'

'No, it is no problem, Signore,' she said in a subdued manner.

Steve said gently: 'These last couple of weeks must have been very hard for you. It is bound to have been upsetting to have experienced the shock of first one of your tenants and then the other dying so suddenly.'

Signora Mattozzi just nodded in agreement.

Steve said: 'The flat looks empty without all the furniture, doesn't it? You will presumably be having it all brought back again soon.'

Signora Mattozzi said, with a brief look of irritation: 'But I have been told to do nothing to the apartment until the Commissario has finished making his enquiries.'

Steve said: 'It must have annoyed you that Sophie moved in and then wanted to make changes to the apartment.'

Signora Mattozzi said: 'She wanted to get rid of genuine antique pieces that had been in my husband's family for generations and replace them with flimsy, modern furniture. It was ridiculous.'

Steve said: 'When Sophie came down to see you the night before she died, what did she talk to you about?'

Signora Mattozzi said: 'She said she wanted to tell me about the arrangements she had made for storing the furniture but I wasn't really interested in hearing about it. I am sure she just wanted to gloat because she had persuaded Mariotto to take her side against me.'

Then she looked at Kate and said: 'I can't pretend to be upset now that she is dead and I am sorry if that offends you, but I think I have made my feelings clear about what I felt about your cousin.'

A strange expression came over her face then and she said: 'Jean Anderson's death is different. She was basically a good woman. I am sorry she had to die as well."

With a flash of anger, she said: 'I wouldn't really blame her, whatever she may have done. Sophie's behaviour was enough to drive people to do almost anything!'

She then abruptly closed her door and Kate found herself staring at a piece of solid oak while she tried to take in what Signora Mattozzi had just revealed to them in her sudden outburst.

That evening, Kate and Steve walked out of the Città Alta through the huge stone gateway of Porta Sant'Alessandro and up the hill to Via Borgo Canale, the street where Donizetti was born and had lived as a young child. They found the composer's birthplace marked by a simple plaque in the middle of a row of similar looking tall, narrow houses.

The house was open to the public only at weekends and so after taking some photographs they made their way back down to Porta Sant'Alessandro. On the way down the hill they noticed the funicular railway station for the train that linked the Città Alta with the village of San Vigilio, a tiny hamlet perched high above Bergamo. On an impulse they bought tickets and boarded the waiting train.

Once at the top they paused for a while to enjoy the view of the domes and towers of the Città Alta spread out far below them. They both took photographs from the terrace next to the funicular station before walking round to see San Vigilio's solidly built Castello, which had been standing there for hundreds of years as a defensive post protecting Bergamo from invaders.

Near the castle Kate noticed a restaurant and stopped to look at the menu on display outside. Steve, reading the menu over her shoulder, said there were dishes he would like to try so they went inside and he asked for a table on the terrace.

After they had ordered their meal they sat back to admire the views of the rolling hills and the lush,

green countryside between Bergamo and the Alps.
As they gazed at the scenery while sipping their wine, Kate said: 'If only life could be simpler and we could just come to places like this to see the countryside and enjoy the local food and wine. But all the while I have Sophie at the back of my mind and the horrible thought that someone killed her. It is hard to imagine ever feeling relaxed and happy again.'

Steve said: 'I promise you we will find out what happened and then you and Edna will have to try to come to terms with it.'

There was a pause and then he said: 'I know that you are not going to want to hear this but I am afraid that I still think Jean is the person most likely to have killed Sophie. She could have gone upstairs early in the morning, slipped a sedative in Sophie's coffee while her back was turned, waited till it started to work, carried her into the bedroom, put a pillow over her face and smothered her with it.

'Then out of guilt, or because she was scared of what would happen to her if she was found out, she decided to kill herself.'

'I suppose it is possible, but how do you explain the fact that her mood and behaviour seemed to change in a matter of a few days. She was really pleasant to me and seemed happy when I met her the first few times but she almost ran away from me on the Friday night before she killed herself.'

'I don't know yet, but there must have been a reason for the change in her behaviour. Also, we need to find out whether she owned, or ever hired, a car and could have been the person that tried to run you down.'

Kate shook her head. 'I'm fairly sure the driver of the car was dark skinned and Jean was very fair and pale,' she pointed out.

'Also, I can't get Signora Mattozzi's strange behaviour out of my head. She has now openly admitted that she disliked Sophie. She might have been so angry about Sophie coming down to her apartment to gloat about the furniture that she went upstairs early in the morning, let herself into the apartment, somehow managed to drug her and then dragged her into the bedroom and smothered her. She might have said those things about Jean earlier to divert our suspicions away from herself and make us think that it was Jean who killed Sophie.'

Steve said: 'On the other hand, it is entirely possible that the murder could have been committed by Luisa, either working on her own or with the help of the furniture removal men because it now seems that she had some kind of connection with them.'

Kate said despairingly: 'Or, it could have been Roberto Mariotto, because you have found out that he had keys both to the main gate and to Sophie's apartment and could let himself in whenever he wanted to, so we are no further forward, are we?'

Steve said: 'No, so we need to lean on Luisa a bit and get the address of the furniture warehouse from her and then go and take a look at the furniture. We can make a show of going through the drawers and say we are trying to find something that you think is missing from the apartment. But it will also give us the chance to find out a bit more about what is going on at that warehouse.'

Their first course arrived then and while they ate Kate brought up their visit to Donizetti's home in Via Borgo Canale. She said: 'I have read that he lived with his parents and all his brothers and sisters in the basement. If it wasn't for a charitable institution he would never have received a musical education and gone on to compose all that wonderful music.'

They continued to talk about places in Bergamo associated with Donizetti for the rest of the meal, avoiding all mention of Sophie as if by some unspoken agreement.

But as they were getting up from their table to leave the restaurant, Kate noticed a group of men wearing smart suits being shown to a table at the opposite end of the terrace. As she glanced in their direction she said: 'Oh look, there's Simon Pargeter sitting at the end of that table with the big group over there.'

Steve looked across with interest and then made a point of taking a rather roundabout route as he led the way out of the restaurant so that they could go past the table. Simon noticed Kate as she went by and smiled and lifted his hand to acknowledge her.

'He's a handsome chap, isn't he? Sophie certainly had good taste when it came to choosing men,' Kate said to Steve as they rode back down to the Città Alta on the funicular railway.

But Steve did not reply and when she turned to look at him she saw that he was frowning to himself in deep concentration.

After they got off the train and were walking back down the hill to Porta Sant'Alessandro he suddenly came to a halt in the street and turned to her. He said excitedly: 'I felt sure I had seen Simon Pargeter before somewhere. His face seemed really familiar when I looked at him in the restaurant but I couldn't quite place him. But now I have remembered where I encountered him. I wasn't actually introduced to him at the time so I didn't know his name, but I've told you before, I never forget a face.'

He looked at Kate and said: 'I know that this is going to sound utterly bizarre, but I am sure that I saw him only last week standing behind the reception desk talking to Adam Leighton when I went to visit Edna at Hampton House.'

21

An hour later as they sat at a table inside a bar in Via Colleoni, Kate was still trying to make sense of it all.

'Aunt Edna has never mentioned Simon Pargeter to me, I am positive about that. It may be that Sophie had not even got round to telling her about him because it was still early days in the relationship. I am sure if Aunt Edna had met Simon she would have told me before I came out here that he lived near Bergamo and suggested I meet up with him. So, what was he doing at Hampton House just a short time after Sophie's death?'

Steve said: 'He was standing behind the reception desk looking very chummy with Adam Leighton so he wasn't just visiting his old Granny, was he? I wouldn't mind betting there is some kind of business connection between them.'

'But surely Sophie would have known about it if there was one? Yet, Simon told me that he met her for the first time at a party to launch an art exhibition in the Città Alta. He never mentioned any connection with Hampton House.'

They were both silent for a moment and then Kate said hopefully: 'You could be wrong, you know. He may just look like the man you saw behind the reception desk at Hampton House.'

'I'm not wrong. It was definitely Simon Pargeter that I saw with Adam,' Steve insisted.

Kate took a sip of her wine and when she had put her glass down again Steve leant across the table and placed his hand over hers.

He said gently: 'If the story he told you is true and he met Sophie for the first time at that party in the

Città Alta, you have to ask yourself whether it was by accident or by design.'

Kate said in a horrified voice: 'Do you mean that he may have somehow contrived to get himself introduced to Sophie?'

'Well, it would explain why Adam Leighton has shown interest in what you have been doing in Bergamo. He may have been anxious about you finding out that he had some kind of a connection with Sophie's new boyfriend.'

'But how can we find out what Simon Pargeter's true motives were for getting to know Sophie and what he was doing at Hampton House last week?'

'The simplest way is to confront him with it and see what he has to say about it.'

Kate said: 'I could text him and ask him if he can spare the time to meet me in Sarnico tomorrow. I won't mention you at all and then you can appear suddenly and surprise him. I will introduce you to him and then you can tell him that you saw him with Adam last week. It will be interesting to see what his reaction is. Then hopefully we will be able to find out everything we need to know from him.'

Although the blue waters of the lake had looked enticing in the morning sunshine, Kate and Steve made their way straight to the restaurant after getting off the bus outside the municipal building in Sarnico.

Simon had suggested in his text message to Kate that they should meet at the same restaurant where he had taken her for lunch the Friday before. They made sure that they arrived well in advance of the time he had proposed and Kate was sitting alone at a table on the terrace reading the menu when the tall, smartly-dressed property developer bounded up the steps to join her.

'This is an unexpected pleasure,' he said smiling at her and then kissed her on the cheek. She was again struck by his unusually pale blue eyes.

'There were a few more things about Sophie I wanted to ask you about,' she began as he sat down next to her. Then she noticed Steve appear on the terrace from inside the restaurant and said: 'And I also wanted the chance to introduce a friend of mine to you.'

When Steve reached the table Kate performed the introductions and the two men shook hands.

Simon smiled charmingly and asked: 'Did you have a good journey on the bus from Bergamo?'

He doesn't remember seeing Steve before, Kate thought to herself.

Steve said: 'Yes, the journey was very pleasant and we went through some interesting places. I must say the glimpses we had of Lago d'Iseo were extremely tantalising. Hopefully we will have the time to walk down to the lakeside before we have to head back to Bergamo.'

Simon said: 'Well, let's order our food and then Kate can ask me whatever it is she wants to know.'

After the waitress had taken their order, Steve took a picture, using Kate's camera, of Simon sitting at the table with her in front of a view of the lake below them.

'The photo is to show Aunt Edna when I get home. I know she will be interested to see pictures of all Sophie's friends,' Kate explained.

Simon seemed completely at ease and did not mind having his picture taken. He was just raising his wine glass to drink from it when Steve asked: 'What's your connection with the Hampton House care home?'

Simon put his glass back down on the table. When he spoke his voice sounded even more hoarse than usual. 'Who says I have a connection with Hampton House?'

Steve said: 'I saw you the Sunday before last standing behind the reception desk talking to the manager Adam Leighton when I was over there visiting Kate's aunt.'

Kate could see that Simon looked less sure of himself as he picked up his glass again to take a sip of wine. He seemed to consider his next words carefully and then said: 'Well actually, Adam Leighton happens to be my cousin.'

Steve said: 'Fair enough. And are you particularly close?'

'Yes, I suppose you could say that we are. We have always looked out for each other and we visit each other from time to time.'

'I see. And on any of these visits did he mention Edna Westmullen and her daughter Sophie?'

Simon looked down at the glass he was still holding and seemed to think about the question before he said: 'He talked about many of the residents at the home.'

Steve said: 'The story you told Kate about meeting Sophie for the first time at a party in the Città Alta, was that true?'

'Yes. That really was the very first time I met Sophie.'

'And when you were introduced to her did you mention that your cousin was the manager of the care home where her mother was a resident?'

For the first time Simon looked ill at ease. He said: 'Look, what is all this? Why are you asking me about my family business? I thought you were here to collect anecdotes about Sophie's life in Bergamo to relay to her mother. The poor woman is dead and it is very sad. I have already told you that we were starting to get close. Even though I had not known her for very long I had started to care about her. But what more is there to say about it now?'

The waitress brought their first courses to the table at that point and the three of them started to eat in silence.

After a couple of minutes Kate decided to try to calm the situation. She said: 'I know that you cared about Sophie and you are bound to be sad that you have lost her. So I am sure you can understand how I feel. My cousin has died suddenly in odd circumstances and the police still aren't certain what happened.

'My aunt is old and not very well and she is going out of her mind with worry. When Steve said that he recognised you last night after he had seen you in the restaurant, I was bound to be curious. You gave me the impression that your meeting with Sophie was entirely coincidental. So I was bound to be intrigued when I heard that you have actually been to Hampton House. Did you know that it was the house where Sophie was brought up when she was a young girl?

'My aunt sold it to Adam Leighton and bought a smaller house in the village when she became too old to look after such a big property. But since she suffered a stroke she has found it difficult to take care of herself and so she took the decision to move back into Hampton House as a resident to get the benefit of all the facilities they have for the elderly.'

Simon put down his fork and smiled at Kate. Her soothing tone had clearly helped him recover his poise.

He said: 'Of course you are bound to be curious

and I will try to reassure you.' He took a forkful of his fish risotto, held it in mid air while he tried to choose the right words and then put it down again.

He said: 'When Adam first heard that Sophie had moved out to Bergamo he told me that if I ever encountered her socially I should make a point of getting to know her because it could turn out to be useful.'

'Why could it turn out to be useful?' Steve asked.

'Because her mother is one of his residents and it is helpful in his business to have a good relationship with members of the family.

'Anyway, our paths didn't cross naturally but then he heard a few weeks ago from Mrs Westmullen that Sophie had been invited to a party to launch a new art exhibition in Palazzo della Ragione in the Città Alta. He suggested that I somehow managed to secure myself an invitation and contrive to be introduced to her. So I made a few calls and one of my contacts got my name added to the guest list.'

'How did you know who Sophie was?' Kate asked curiously.

Simon gave a wry smile and said: 'Adam had described her to me because he had seen her on many occasions when she had been visiting her mother. But he needn't have bothered really because my eyes were drawn to her as soon as I entered the room. She was the most stunning woman I had ever seen and I found myself immediately attracted to her.

'From then on, everything I have already told you is true. The relationship developed quickly from her coming to look round the apartment to us spending the weekend together here in Sarnico. I was starting to care a lot about her and I think she felt the same about me. But then this terrible thing happened...'

He looked down at the table and Kate saw the corners of his mouth twitch. Then he put his hand over his eyes. He looked as though he was trying to hold back tears.

Steve said: 'So when Adam found out that Kate was coming out to Bergamo to do a bit of digging and talk to Sophie's friends out here, he was understandably nervous.'

Simon said: 'Well I wouldn't go that far. And in any case I have nothing to hide from anyone. Everything I have told you is true. I wasn't anywhere near Bergamo when she died and I was as shocked to hear the news as you were. And the police still haven't told me whether she died from natural causes or not.'

Kate already knew the post mortem results and felt uncomfortable. Simon had sounded completely genuine but she made herself keep silent, helped by the presence of the waitress who had come to clear away the plates at that moment.

Steve waited until they could talk openly again and then said: 'Why didn't you tell Kate all this when she came out to Sarnico to see you the first time?'

'I didn't think it was necessary,' Simon said stiffly. 'Kate told me she wanted to hear about Sophie's life here and about what she thought of her friends in Bergamo. I didn't think it was necessary to go too deeply into how I came to meet Sophie. The fact is after I met her I developed feelings for her. It was completely unexpected and as far as I am concerned nothing that happened before then is important.'

That afternoon after they had finished their meal and Simon had gone back to his office Kate and Steve strolled along at the side of Lago d'Iseo in the afternoon sunshine.

'There has to be more to it than he is letting on,' Steve said, finally breaking the comfortable silence. 'It was a lot of trouble to go to if all Adam wanted him to do was develop a useful connection with the relative of one of his residents.'

'What do you mean?' Kate asked. She led the way to sit on a bench at the side of the water and leant back and stretched out her long legs. She was still feeling full from lunch and felt like having a rest in the afternoon sunshine.

'Well, he rang round his business contacts until he found someone who could get his name added to the guest list for the party to launch the art exhibition. He's supposed to be a shrewd businessman for whom time is money, but he put in a lot of effort doing all that for what seems to be a rather vague reason. It just seems like a lot of trouble to go to, just to get to know a relative so that you can get her on side if you needed her backing at some stage in the future.'

'Yes, and I can tell you now that Sophie was nobody's fool. She wouldn't have agreed to anything that might disadvantage Aunt Edna just because she had started to date Adam Leighton's cousin.'

'No, that's what worries me,' Steve said thoughtfully.

They sat looking out at the view of the lake for a couple of minutes and then Kate asked: 'What was his real motive then?'

'I don't know yet, but we are going to have to dig a bit deeper.'

'We can't ask Aunt Edna about Simon because it would only upset and worry her if she thought Sophie had somehow been conned or used by him.'

'No, but we might be able to get a bit more

information out of Adam Leighton.'

'Do you think you could get him to tell you the real reason he wanted Simon to meet Sophie?'

'No, probably not while I am still out here. But on the other hand I think I know a man who can,' Steve said thoughtfully.

Kate suddenly found herself shivering, despite the warmth of the afternoon sunshine.

'Do you think any of this could be connected with Sophie's death?'

Steve turned to face her and looked her straight in the eye. He said: 'If Sophie had found out that Simon had a connection with the care home she may also have stumbled on the real reason he had started to go out with her.

'And if it was because of something criminal or immoral that Simon didn't want anyone to know about, he may have been desperate enough to want to silence her for good.'

Later that evening Kate and Steve were standing together in Piazza Vecchia in Bergamo's Città Alta listening to the bell in the Campanone mark the traditional ten o'clock curfew.

After a good meal and some wine, surrounded by a happy, laughing crowd of holidaymakers, they felt relaxed and when Steve put his arm round her shoulders it was the most natural thing in the world, as though there had never been any distance between them.

But Kate knew there was something still bothering her at the back of her mind. It was something that she was trying to remember but she couldn't think what it was. Eventually the chimes came to an end and she could hear only the buzz of conversation from the crowd surrounding her as she tried to identify what was worrying her.

Steve said: 'Well, I'm pretty useless. I'm afraid to say that I lost count. It could have been 100 chimes or it could have been even more, I'm not really sure.'

Then Kate remembered what Jean had said to her about the ten o'clock bell while they had been having dinner together at La Torre restaurant, something about anyone who wasn't back by ten o'clock having to stay out for the night and everyone who was inside Palazzo Mattozzi having to stay in. Why had that suddenly come into her mind?

As they walked back to Albergo Milano Kate asked: 'Why did you ask me to book you a room of your own at the hotel? Before, whenever we went on holiday together we used to share a room.'

Steve was silent for so long that Kate felt uncomfortable. Then he said: 'Well, to be honest I felt awkward about asking if I could move into your room. I knew Edna was picking up the tab for it and I didn't want it to seem as though I was freeloading. Also I didn't know how much space you had and whether it would even be practical. And I suppose I was worried about what the hotel would think if I didn't have my own room, ridiculous as though it might sound.'

Kate hadn't thought of any of those things and did not know what to say in reply.

Back at the hotel they collected their keys from the man on duty on the desk and climbed the stairs to the first floor. Steve came with her to the door of her room and they stood outside looking at each other. Then he gently pulled her towards him and kissed her.

Kate said: 'Do you want to come in?' He stood

looking into her eyes for a few seconds and then said: 'Of course I do.'

22

When they were still some distance away from Palazzo Mattozzi the next morning, Kate noticed through the iron gates that Luisa and Signora Mattozzi were in the courtyard in full view, folding a large quilt together.

She quickly got her camera out of her bag and took a picture of the maid and the concierge together in front of the palazzo without either of them realising.

Then they continued to walk slowly up to the gates and it was only when they were standing by the row of bell buttons on the wall at the side that Signora Mattozzi looked round and noticed them. She came across to them reluctantly with a weary expression on her face.

'Good morning, Signora,' Steve said cheerfully. 'We would like to speak to Luisa if that is convenient.'

'What do you want to speak to her about?' Signora Mattozzi demanded.

'We wanted to ask her about the place where the furniture from Sophie's apartment is being stored.'

Signora Mattozzi sighed in exasperation and then turned and called across in dialect to Luisa, who was still folding the laundry, before grudgingly opening the gate and allowing them to come into the courtyard.

Luisa looked scared as they approached her and dropped the sheet she was in the middle of folding on top of the pile in the laundry basket.

'Good morning, Luisa,' Steve said in Italian, with a pleasant smile. 'We wondered whether you could tell us a bit more about the items of furniture that were taken away from Sophie's apartment.'

Luisa gave a quick glance over her shoulder but Signora Mattozzi had already disappeared inside the building in the direction of her own apartment.

'What do you want to know about them?' she asked uncertainly.

'Well, could you tell us precisely which pieces were removed and give us some idea as to why Sophie didn't want them any more?'

Luisa chose to answer the second part of the question first.

'She said she did not like the heavy pieces of furniture because they were too dark and they made the apartment feel overcrowded.'

'I see. So can you tell us which pieces of furniture she asked to have removed?'

'There was a big old desk, but she said she didn't want it because she never used it.

'There was also a big chest of drawers but she said the drawers smelt of mothballs and she didn't want to put any of her clothes in them.

'The Signorina had some very expensive clothes and she always liked to take good care of them,' Luisa added.

'Were there any other pieces she didn't like?' Kate asked.

'Yes, there was a wardrobe and a big circular dining table that took up a lot of space in the *salone*. It used to stand right in the middle of the room and sometimes she would sit at it when she was looking at her laptop. But she insisted that she didn't like it and said that it had to be taken away with the rest of the furniture.'

Kate said: 'Am I right in thinking that she planned to replace it with a more modern table?'

Luisa nodded. 'Yes, there was a shop in the Città Bassa that she liked and she had chosen some new things from their catalogue. She had ordered a small, square white table, a tall, narrow white cupboard with a hanging rail and two lovely, white chests of drawers. My boyfriend Massimo knows the people who own the shop and so he was able to get her a good discount and he also agreed to look after all the old furniture at his warehouse. But, of course, I had to cancel the delivery of the new furniture after what happened to the Signorina, it was so sad.'

Steve said: 'So the situation at the moment is that the original furniture from the apartment is still in store.'

'Yes, Signore, it is being kept in Massimo's warehouse just outside San Pellegrino Terme. But I would imagine that Signora Mattozzi will have it brought back again to the apartment quite soon.'

Kate said: 'I have been worried that I have not been able to find some of Sophie's possessions here in the apartment. I have looked in all the places where they should have been and so I have been wondering whether any of them could have been accidentally left in the drawers of the desk, or even whether there is a possibility they might have been in the chest of drawers.'

Luisa flushed and said quickly: 'I checked all the drawers the day before the furniture was taken away. Every item they removed from the apartment was empty, I can promise you.'

Steve tried a different approach. 'Sophie's mother is elderly and not very well and she is living in an old people's home. We want to be able to reassure her that all Sophie's possessions have been brought back to England by us when we return. You can understand how upset she has been during the last two weeks and I feel that if we can tell her that we have checked every drawer in the furniture ourselves it will make her feel better.

'Could you be very kind and give us the address of the warehouse where the furniture is being stored so that we can go and have a quick look at each item. As long as we can tell her that we have checked every drawer, I think she will stop worrying about Sophie's belongings.'

Luisa relaxed a little and said: 'I understand Signore. The warehouse is just outside San Pellegrino Terme after you have been through the small village of Gonzago. It is on one of the roads that lead off the main square going in the direction of San Pellegrino Terme. The road is called Via della Chiesa and the warehouse is at number 14.'

'Thank you, Luisa, you have been very helpful,' Steve said, smiling at her.

'I will ring Massimo and tell him that you will be coming,' Luisa said, sounding relieved that she had managed to answer all their questions.

'Thank you. That will be a great help to us. Tell him to expect us to arrive there some time this afternoon.'

Later in the day as they travelled by bus towards San Pellegrino Terme, Kate said: 'Do you think it was a good idea for Massimo to be warned in advance that we were coming? He could look through the drawers of the furniture before we get there.'

'But why would he want to look through them now? Luisa was probably telling the truth and all the furniture was empty when it left the apartment. But if she had left anything inside one of the items, he would have been able to help himself to it by now. At any time since he fetched the furniture from

Bergamo he could have gone through the drawers to see if there was anything he fancied in them.

'To be honest, I am not really expecting to find anything, I just want to be able to have a look at the furniture and try to imagine it set out in that room.'

'Why?' Kate asked in surprise.

'I don't know exactly, I just have a feeling about it. I think in a way it is a good thing that Luisa has prepared Massimo for our arrival because if we had just turned up out of the blue he might have refused to let us into the warehouse at all and we wouldn't have been able to get anywhere near the furniture.'

They got off the bus at the small village Luisa had mentioned, just before San Pellegrino, and found the road that led off the main square she had told them about, using a map that Steve had bought earlier at the bus station news stand. When they reached the warehouse they were able to walk straight in through a door that had been left propped open into a large open space filled with items of furniture.

Kate recognised Massimo, who was once again wearing his baseball cap. He was standing at the other end of the room talking to the tall black man he had been with the night they had seen Aldo following him in the Città Bassa.

Massimo looked across at them but his face remained expressionless when Steve walked towards him. Steve said politely: 'Good afternoon, I believe Luisa will have rung you to say that we would be coming here to look at the furniture that you are storing for Palazzo Mattozzi.'

Massimo shrugged and said dismissively: 'Raz will show you where it is being stored.' Kate thought that he then made a point of turning and walking away as if he had better things to do with his time.

The tall black man, Raz, led them through the large main room past row after row of pieces of furniture, both new and old, which had been lined up neatly.

'Are you storing these items for other people?' Steve asked interestedly.

Raz said: 'No, this furniture is all from houses and apartments that we have cleared after people have died. We send it out to be sold at furniture auctions. We are only storing the furniture from Palazzo Mattozzi here as a favour for someone that Massimo knows.'

When they reached the end of the room, Raz pointed to a gloomy corner where there were several large pieces of antique furniture made from what looked to Kate like solid oak.

There was a circular dining table, a chest of drawers, a wardrobe and an impressive desk decorated with ornate carving.

Steve studied each piece of furniture carefully and then went across to the desk and opened the drawers one by one.

'They are all empty,' Kate said in disappointment.

Watched closely by Raz, he repeated the process with the chest of drawers and then he looked inside the wardrobe. 'Again, nothing,' he said, turning to Kate.

Then he went over to the circular dining table and ran his hand over the highly polished top. 'It is made from beautiful old wood,' he remarked.

'Is it valuable?' Raz asked with interest.

'I'm not really sure,' Steve said thoughtfully, continuing to study the table.

'I just wondered whether that was why the other people were so interested in it.'

'What other people?' Kate asked sharply.

Raz said: 'Twice I've come into this area and

found people looking at the furniture. They had no right to be in here because the warehouse isn't open to the public. They hadn't asked anyone's permission, they had just managed to get in here somehow.'

'When was that?' Kate asked.

'Oh, it was just a few days ago.'

'Could you describe these people?' Steve asked.

Raz looked evasive. 'I'm not sure,' he mumbled, as though he wished he had not mentioned anything about it.

'Well, how many different people have you seen in here?' Steve asked patiently.

'There was one person in here looking at the furniture not very long after we got back from Bergamo with it.

'I was out of the room for a while after we had put the furniture in this corner and when I came back I found a man in here looking at it. He asked me if any of it was for sale but I told him that it wasn't so he just went away again.

'Then a couple of days later I came in and there was a woman looking at these pieces. But when I tried to speak to her she just walked out without saying anything to me, so I don't really know what she wanted.'

Kate had a sudden flash of inspiration and whipped out her digital camera and switched it on. She started to show Raz the images stored on the camera of the various pictures she had taken of Sophie's friends and acquaintances since she had arrived in Bergamo.

'That's him,' Raz said eventually, pointing at one of the images. 'He's the one I found in here on the day we collected the furniture.'

Kate felt a shiver of excitement but held herself in

check and continued to show Raz the images.

'Yes, that's the woman I found in here,' Raz said pointing at another image after a few seconds.

'She managed to get in here somehow and I found her looking at the furniture about two days after the man had been in. I don't know why either of them would have been interested in it, unless we find out that it is really valuable or something,' he said, turning to look again with interest at the huge items in dark wood that had been grouped together out of the way in the furthest corner.

Later that evening Kate and Steve sat in silence in a secluded alcove in a restaurant in the Città Bassa. They had stopped off near the bus station to have a pizza after arriving back from San Pellegrino Terme.

They had already talked about it endlessly, but after a while Kate found herself saying yet again: 'I just do not understand why either of them would have been so interested in the furniture that they would have gone to all the trouble of travelling out to San Pellegrino Terme to see where it was being stored.'

Steve put down his knife and fork, having finished his meal, and answered again: 'No, neither do I. It seems really strange.'

After another silence he said: 'Another thing I don't understand is how they got that furniture out of the palazzo in the first place. You saw those pieces this afternoon, they were all huge. I would have thought the staircase between Jean and Sophie's apartments was far too narrow for the men to have carried that furniture down it.'

Kate thought about it and then asked: 'Do you think they showed us the right furniture?'

Steve said: 'Well, it was all exactly as Luisa had described it to us. And, in any case, why would they try to keep the real furniture away from us?'

Kate sighed and said: 'That's what I don't know. Jean might have been able to tell us if she was still alive, but she isn't here to ask. And I know that Signora Mattozzi will not want to help us. So what can we do now?'

Steve took a sip of his wine and then answered her. 'There's only one thing we can do, we have to keep going. We have to keep asking the questions until we get all the answers we need.

'At the moment I just have the awful feeling that we are missing something obvious. There must be a piece of information that we don't have that would make everything else fall into place.'

'So what do we do now?' Kate asked again, helplessly.

'I am afraid to say that however unwelcome we might be made to feel by the good Signora, tomorrow morning we will have to go back to Palazzo Mattozzi again.'

23

When Signora Mattozzi came to the iron gates of the palazzo after they had rung her bell the next morning she looked angry rather than just exasperated.

'What do you want with us now? Why can't you just leave us alone?' she demanded.
'Go back to where you came from and leave us in peace!'

Steve said: 'I am really sorry to have to bother you, but it is very important that we have a word with Luisa again.'

'Wait there!' Signora Mattozzi said, leaving them on the other side of the iron gates. She turned abruptly and disappeared inside the palazzo again.

'She's not exactly friendly today,' Steve said in a low voice to Kate.

'Well, she hated Sophie and so she feels under no obligation to be polite to us. I think we have tried her patience once too often and she really can't be bothered with us any more,' Kate replied.

After a few moments Luisa appeared in the doorway of the palazzo in her pale green uniform looking wary and when she saw them she came reluctantly towards the gate.

Steve said: 'I'm sorry to trouble you again, Luisa, but a question has occurred to us after seeing the furniture yesterday afternoon at San Pellegrino Terme.'

'Did you find anything in the drawers?' Luisa asked anxiously.

'No, you were quite right, they were all empty. You had obviously checked them thoroughly,' Steve answered.

Kate thought that Luisa seemed to relax a little then.

Steve said: 'I was just a bit puzzled when I saw the furniture. They really are very big pieces for what was not a particularly big room. I could see why Sophie might have thought the apartment looked overcrowded. But I just wondered how the men got it down to the ground floor and out of the building because, if I am remembering correctly, the flight of stairs up to the top floor apartment is very narrow.'

Luisa nodded in agreement and then explained. 'Massimo brought special equipment with him to move the furniture because I had told him it was very big and heavy. He has a special ladder with a platform on top of it that he was able to put up to the window from his truck. Raz and he manoeuvred each piece of furniture out on to the balcony and then on to the platform. Then Massimo went down to the street again and lowered the ladder to get each piece on to the truck.

'I had told him that it was all old and very valuable and he knew that he would be in trouble with Signora Mattozzi if any of it was damaged. Lowering the pieces from the balcony was much safer than trying to carry them downstairs and risk them catching on the walls.'

'Oh, I see! It all makes sense to me now,' Steve said, smiling at the maid. 'Thank you Luisa, you have answered my question.'

'So where does that leave us, then?' Kate asked a few minutes later as they sat at a table outside their usual bar in Piazza Vecchia.

'Well, we've seen the furniture and checked that all the drawers were empty and we now know how Massimo and Raz got it out of Sophie's apartment, hence the scratch marks I noticed on the balcony door frame. Thank goodness Luisa was willing to tell us all the details about it. It's a good thing that it never occurred to her to wonder why I was asking so many questions.'

'She was probably too dazzled by your charming smile to think straight,' Kate said waspishly.

'You're a fine one to talk, considering you have the Commissario of Bergamo eating out of your hand.'

'Oh, don't be ridiculous,' Kate said, suddenly feeling rather embarrassed. 'Anyway, we know now that two people from Sophie's circle of friends were also interested in the furniture and went to the trouble of travelling out to San Pellegrino Terme to look at it in the warehouse. So what does that tell us?'

'I'm afraid that things are still not clear at the moment, but I am sure that if we're patient we will get all the answers we need in the end. I think we need to start tying up all the loose ends and see where they take us.'

Steve looked at his watch and then said: 'I would imagine now would be a convenient time to try to get hold of Terry Batts. I am going to ask him to lean on Adam Leighton a bit and find out what he has been up to with our friend Simon Pargeter.'

'In that case I think I will go for a walk round the Città Alta on my own while you make your call. I need to think,' Kate said grumpily, frustrated by the lack of progress.

She got up from the table and went through one of the archways under Palazzo della Ragione. The flautist was playing a beautiful melody that she had heard before somewhere. Of course! It was Una Furtiva Lacrima from L'elisir d'amore. The title translated into English meant 'A secret tear'. It was ironic, she thought, as she listened to the flute's haunting notes, that with the exception of herself and Ernesto, no one was bothering to shed any tears about the deaths of Sophie and Jean. And no one apart from herself and Steve seemed interested in finding out the truth about what had happened to them.

Once again she dropped a coin in the basket in front of the musician before wandering aimlessly into the church of Santa Maria Maggiore.

She walked slowly down the side aisle and found herself in front of Donizetti's white marble tomb for the second time. The base of the tomb was decorated with carvings of cherubs holding musical instruments. Even they appeared to be crying.

Then she noticed a similar, equally impressive, white marble monument and went across to the next aisle to have a look at it. It was the tomb of Simone Mayr, Donizetti's teacher and mentor, who Edgar had told her had been the person credited with fostering the genius of the composer when he was a young boy. He had founded the musical institute where students were still being taught today in the Palazzo della Misericordia Maggiore, the same building where the museum dedicated to Donizetti was housed.

As if drawn by some invisible force, Kate wandered out of the church by the west door and found herself walking along the tranquil and deserted Via Arena in the direction of the museum.

The narrow cobbled street was lined on each side with old houses with ornate portals and frescoed walls and she enjoyed being sheltered from the sun by them. Eventually she came to the plaque in the wall that marked the building housing the museum.

She tried to imagine Sophie coming here each day to work inside the museum, carrying out her research surrounded by the composer's piano, furniture and personal effects.

But had she really been all that dedicated? Steve had pointed out that with the many parties and concerts she had attended and the various romantic relationships she had become involved in, Sophie may have been distracted from her work. She might not have found much time for the research that she had actually come out to Bergamo to do.

Then she remembered something Marge had said to her about Sophie, which Kate thought had revealed a lot about the American's deep resentment of her cousin.

She had said Sophie had kept talking about a letter written by Donizetti that she had come across while doing her research, mentioning an Italian woman with an unpronounceable name. It had obviously really irritated Marge, who had been convinced that Sophie was just showing off her Italian by constantly saying the woman's name.

But surely it proved that Sophie had been working on her book for some of the time and must have spent a few hours, at least, here in the museum carrying out her research.

On an impulse, Kate climbed the stairs to the museum, paid her entrance fee and started to walk round slowly looking at all the exhibits again. She gave particular attention to the books, musical scores and handwritten letters that she was able to read through the glass fronts of the wooden display cases lining the walls. She slowly worked her way through the exhibits and her patience was rewarded when she found what she was looking for. Rather than translate the letter laboriously line by line while reading it through the glass, she took a leaflet in English from one of the plastic holders next to the display, which described the contents of the documents being exhibited nearest to it.

She found what she was looking for about half way down the page and read the summary in English of what the letter was about.

As she read, she began to feel uncomfortably hot and started breathing hard because a terrible idea had come into her mind.

She thought of how happy Jean had seemed when she first met her, even though Sophie had just died. Then she thought of how sad and depressed she had seemed the last time she had seen her. She could hear the melody of Una Furtiva Lacrima in her head as it had been played so poignantly by the flautist and it made her think of Ernesto and his hopeless love for Sophie. He had probably shed more than a few tears after her cousin had left him. Then she thought of all the other men in Bergamo who had been interested in Sophie.

Sophie had been beautiful and clever and had never been short of male attention during her life. But she had also been single minded and ruthless and determined to get her own way and as a result she had always seemed to end up on her own.

Kate's right hand, which was clutching the leaflet with the English translation of the letter, started to tremble as she finally began to understand what had been going on in Bergamo.

Later that evening, after Kate and Steve had spent the whole afternoon thoroughly discussing her ideas, they went to meet Aldo for a drink at the bar in Via Colleoni where he was obviously well-known to the woman proprietor.

Over a bottle of Valcalepio Bianco, in the seclusion of one of the velvet-upholstered alcoves, Kate outlined her theory to him.

He nodded in agreement occasionally and sometimes stopped her to put a specific question to her.

At the end he said: 'It all makes perfect sense and you have managed to convince me that your deductions are correct, but I am afraid that we would find it very difficult to prove and, therefore, there might be some reluctance by the prosecution to bring the case to court if there was no guarantee that we would win it.'

'I'm sorry to have to say that it would be exactly the same in the UK with the Crown Prosecution Service. They only ever want cases to go ahead if they are confident they will win them,' Steve said to Kate.

'Of course, if we could get a confession it would be an entirely different matter…' Aldo said and then paused while he thought about it.

After a while, Kate broke the silence and said resolutely 'First thing tomorrow I will go to La Torre and talk to Ernesto.'

'Is that wise?' Aldo asked anxiously.

'Yes, I am sure that he will want to help me when I tell him what I have decided to do for Sophie. I have been thinking for a while that before I return to England I would like to host a meal here in the Città Alta in memory of my cousin and invite everyone from her circle of friends to attend. It would be a sort of send-off for her.

'I will tell Ernesto that I would like to arrange the meal for tomorrow night at his restaurant so that we can all drink a toast to Sophie's memory. It will also give me the chance to say goodbye to everyone I have met out here. I am sure he will think it is a good idea and during the course of the evening, who knows what might come up in the conversation?'

'How can you be sure that everyone from Sophie's circle of friends will come?' Aldo asked.

'I will just have to be very persuasive,' Kate said. 'I'll make them feel it would look bad for them if they didn't come.'

'I have no doubt that you can be very persuasive,' Aldo said, smiling at Kate. 'But I will take the precaution of going round myself to invite Signora Mattozzi and Luisa to make it clear to them that refusing to attend would not be a sensible option for them.'

'Ask Luisa to be sure to bring Massimo with her because he is crucial to all this,' Steve said.

Aldo frowned and said: 'We are very close now to making arrests in connection with the other matter I told you that we are working on. We will just have to hope that nothing happens to alert him to the fact, or take him out of circulation before tomorrow night.'

24

It could all have been predicted, Kate thought to herself. She was at a table outside a bar with a glass of wine in front of her, watching a young girl dance around the fountain in the middle of Piazza Vecchia.

There was only ever one way it was going to turn out, she realised, as her eyes followed the small, slim girl in her simple, white cotton sun dress twirling round and round. She was dancing in time to the melody of Una Furtiva Lacrima being played by the flautist standing under the archways of Palazzo della Ragione.

The girl had blonde, wavy hair just like Sophie. She was too pretty and there would be too many men in love with her, Kate imagined. She felt certain that she knew how it was all going to end.

Her train of thought was interrupted when she saw Roberto appear at the corner of Via Colleoni, with a red rose in his hand. She watched his tall, distinguished figure as he walked slowly over to the fountain. He presented the rose to the girl, took her in his arms and they waltzed gracefully around the fountain together in perfect time to the music.

Ernesto appeared on the other side of the square, also with a red rose in his hand and walked past the covered staircase by the side of the palazzo and over to the fountain. He tapped Roberto on the shoulder and he let go of the girl and reluctantly backed away a few feet. Ernesto presented his rose to the girl and then took her in his arms and waltzed around the fountain with her. Again they were keeping perfect time with the music, Kate thought to herself as she sipped her wine while watching them.

Now Edgar appeared, from under the archways of

the palazzo, and walked towards the fountain carrying a red rose. He bowed to Ernesto, who obediently let go of the girl and turned and walked away. Edgar presented his rose to the girl and waltzed with her round the fountain. He was surprisingly graceful, thought Kate, as she watched them dancing together.

Then it was the turn of Simon Pargeter to appear at the top of Via Gombito, carrying a red rose. He walked towards the fountain with a charming smile, showing his perfect white teeth. The girl immediately let go of Edgar and allowed herself to be swept off her feet by the tall, handsome Englishman. He waltzed round in perfect time with the music, carrying the girl tenderly in his arms. But when he put her down gently on to the ground again, she collapsed and fell on to the stone slabs in front of the fountain. Kate started up from the table because she suddenly realised with shock that it wasn't a young girl at all, it was a middle aged woman. She rushed to the fountain to look at the woman more closely and discovered that the person lying on her back on the ground was Sophie and that the front of her dress had a red stain on it. It must have been caused by the roses, she thought, but then to her horror she saw that the stain on Sophie's white dress was bright red and it was spreading across the whole of the front of the skimpy, little garment.

'What has happened to the flowers?' she asked her cousin, who still lay on the ground. Then she saw the roses, strewn on a stone slab in front of the fountain, wilting and already starting to look past their best.

'You are too old to be playing these kind of games with people, it was always going to turn out this way,' she said sternly to her cousin. But then she realised that Sophie was dead. She opened her mouth to scream and was bewildered when no sound came out.

Kate became aware then that she was sitting bolt upright in bed, breathing heavily. She could feel the sweat pouring down her face. Slowly she became aware of her surroundings. It came as a relief to realise that she was in her room at the hotel and that she had just been dreaming.

Steve lay next to her, still fast asleep. She gently stroked his tanned arm, comforted by his presence, glad that for the second night in a row he had stayed in her room.

Yet she was still breathing fast and she could feel her heart pounding despite the fact that it had only been a dream because she was terrified of what was going to happen later.

In just a few hours time, after dinner, at a table in a restaurant in the Città Alta in front of a large group of people, she was going to try to trap Sophie's killer.

She sipped some water from the glass on her bedside table and then picked up her wristwatch to look at it. It was still only five thirty am and it would be several hours before she could go to La Torre to see Ernesto.

She groaned and sank back on to her pillows. She knew that it was going to be a long day.

Later that evening, after Kate had showered and dressed in her smartest clothes, she carefully made up her face and put on her best jewellery.

She stood in front of the mirror in her room at the Albergo Milano and brushed her long, dark hair over and over again, looking at her reflection, frowning.

Steve appeared behind her neatly dressed in a pair of dark navy trousers and a pale blue cotton shirt. He gently kissed her on the neck and put his arms around her. He smelt wonderful. 'It's all going to turn out well,' he said.

'But you don't know that!'

'You are bound to be worried, but I promise you, one way or another it is all going to turn out fine.'

'We are trying to get someone to admit that they killed my cousin. It is not like hosting an ordinary dinner party.'

'Yes, but we think we know who did it, we think we know how they did it and we think we know why they did it. We will have the Commissario with us and he will have men stationed near the building.'

'But supposing it turns out that we are completely wrong,' Kate said hopelessly.

'If we are wrong, we use the opportunity to try to find out more information that will help us get to the truth. We know that someone killed Sophie. That's why you and I have come out here, to find out who was responsible for her death and to stop them from getting away with it. So we must be determined that we get the right result. Tonight we will confront the person we believe was responsible and make them admit it in front of everyone else at the table. Then we will finally get some justice for your cousin.'

Kate had asked Ernesto to serve platters of antipasto, followed by a selection of pasta and risotto dishes and other local specialities so that the dinner party for Sophie could be an informal affair with plenty of opportunity for conversation.

Later that evening when they arrived at La Torre, a young waiter showed them up to the private dining room high in the tower where Kate had dined alone with Ernesto only a few nights before. It was a hot night and the windows on all four sides of the tower were wide open to let in any available cool air. Two tables for six had been put together in the middle of the room to make one long table, covered with immaculate white cloths and set with gleaming cutlery and elegantly-shaped wine glasses.

There were platters of olives, artichokes, marinated vegetables, salami and prosciutto already out on the table ready for the guests when they arrived.

Steve and Kate sat on opposite sides of the table, a few seats away from each other and the young waiter poured them both a glass of Valcalepio Bianco from one of the bottles in wine coolers that had been put out ready on the table.

The first person to arrive was Ernesto himself. He walked over to Kate and kissed her on both cheeks and then shook hands with Steve.

Kate thought how handsome he looked in his cream linen jacket, blue and white striped shirt and jeans.

'Is everything okay?' he asked Kate nervously. 'I wanted everything to be perfect for Sophie's sake.'

'It's great, just what I wanted,' Kate reassured him. He took a seat next to her and she said: 'Did you ask Anton to join us, as I asked?'

'Yes. He said he had one or two things still to do in the kitchen and then he will leave everything in the hands of his assistants and come up here.'

The young waiter then showed Aldo into the room with Signora Mattozzi, Luisa and Massimo.

Signora Mattozzi was dressed no differently from any other occasion Kate had seen her, in one of her shapeless black dresses. But Luisa looked very pretty in a tight-fitting pink, sleeveless dress with her long, dark hair flowing loose. Massimo was smartly turned out in grey trousers and a short sleeved black shirt and looked completely different without his baseball cap, although his sullen, resentful expression suggested he didn't want to be there at all.

Aldo showed them into seats opposite Steve and then came and sat down opposite Kate. He smiled at her and she immediately felt herself flush. Keep calm, she told herself, there's a long way to go and you can't let anything distract you.

Within a few seconds Marge arrived with Edgar following behind her. 'Kate, darling,' she exclaimed and kissed her on both cheeks. Kate was overwhelmed by a waft of her heavy, musky perfume. She suddenly remembered where and when she had smelt it last and another piece of the jigsaw puzzle clicked into place.

Edgar and Marge sat down on the other side of Aldo and the waiter poured them both a glass of wine.

Roberto Mariotto was the next guest to arrive and after shaking hands formally with Kate, Steve and Aldo he took the spare seat opposite Signora Mattozzi, who turned her head away from him and stared at the bare stone wall of the tower with a look of contempt on her face.

Then Anton appeared in the doorway, still in his chef's whites and bandana, and looked round the room nervously.

Aldo ushered him towards the vacant seat next to Ernesto, which was opposite Edgar. Marge immediately turned to her left to get Edgar's attention and Kate saw her look at him significantly and raise her eyebrows at him.

Simon Pargeter was the last to arrive. He came straight over to Kate, kissed her on the cheek and said, smiling at her: 'Thanks for inviting me. You're looking gorgeous, by the way.' He then sat down in the last available seat on the opposite side of the table from her between Steve and Aldo.

Two waiters started to go round the table offering to serve the guests from platters of different types of antipasto.

For the first time in my life, I can't wait for a meal to be over, Kate thought to herself.

25

About an hour later, after the pasta and risotto dishes had been cleared away and a selection of desserts and platters of fruit and cheese had been placed on the table, the waiters brought in bottles of chilled Prosecco.

They went round filling the tall, flute-shaped glass in front of each place setting and Kate took that as her cue to stand up and welcome everyone by saying a few words in Italian first.

Then she reverted to English and said: 'Thank you, for all agreeing to come here tonight at such short notice. Before I returned to England I wanted to have the chance to remember Sophie and share a meal and a few glasses of wine with her friends and the people she got to know well while she was living here in Bergamo.

'I would like to thank Ernesto and his staff for serving us this lovely, informal meal, which has given us the chance to talk freely and be able to share our memories of Sophie in a relaxed way.

'For those of you who don't know him, I would like to introduce Commissario Aldo Esposito. I have invited him to join us tonight so that he can give us an update on how the investigations are progressing into both Sophie's death and Jean's.'

Marge turned in her seat abruptly and looked at Aldo to the right of her with new interest.

Kate continued: 'But first I would ask you all to raise your glasses and drink a toast to Sophie Westmullen.'

Everyone rose to their feet, raising their glasses. 'To Sophie Westmullen!' they repeated, making a strange cacophony of noise with their different accents.

When they had all sat down again, Kate invited Aldo to say a few words.

While the waiters went round offering desserts, Aldo got to his feet, put on a pair of reading glasses and seemed to consult some notes in a serious way. Kate knew him well enough by now to guess that this was merely theatre, for the benefit of the people sitting round the table.

He started off by turning to his left and addressing Edgar and Marge next to him directly. 'Please forgive me if I speak in Italian for most of the time. Signor Bartorelli has kindly agreed to provide you with a translation to clarify anything you don't understand after I have finished speaking.'

'That's absolutely fine,' Edgar said, but Marge fixed Aldo with an intense stare and concentrated nervously on what he had to say when he began to speak in Italian. At one point as he spoke there was a gasp of surprise from most people round the table and Marge looked round even more anxiously.

Afterwards she looked at Steve inquiringly, who said: 'The Commissario has now had the results of the post mortem examination on Sophie and is sorry to have to tell us that they prove to the police that she did not die of natural causes. They show that she had been sedated and later smothered, probably with one of her own pillows as she lay unconscious in her bed.'

'Oh my God,' gasped Marge putting her hands to her mouth in shock.

Kate looked at each of the other people round the table in turn and only Signora Mattozzi's lined face showed no sign of emotion.

Aldo continued to speak for a while and then Steve provided another translation.

'The police have also had preliminary indications as to the cause of Jean's death. It would appear that her neck was broken and her other injuries were consistent with having fallen from a high place, presumably from one of the towers in the city walls that look out on to the piece of land where her body was found.

'He said he realises that there has been a general assumption that Jean was responsible for Sophie's death and had flung herself from one of the towers in order to kill herself out of remorse because of what she had done. But he has said that the police are now no longer labouring under that assumption because a trace of a sedative was found in her blood stream which indicates that she may have been drugged some time before her fall. This obviously casts doubt upon the idea that she may have committed suicide.

'The police are therefore having to consider the possibility that both women were murdered and that their deaths may in some way be connected. They would greatly appreciate hearing from anyone who has any new information that will shed any light on the case.'

There was silence from everyone at the table and then the clatter of Signora Mattozzi putting her fork down on her plate. She picked up her glass and took a sip of her wine and then glanced round at everyone else sitting round the table, her face suggesting she was enjoying a kind of ghoulish satisfaction.

Massimo, who was sitting next to her, speared a piece of water melon with his fork and ate it, staring ahead of himself defiantly.

Kate took control again, saying: 'I am sure you are all as shocked as I am to hear what the police have concluded. I know that Jean and Sophie were not particularly close so it is strange to think that their deaths may in some way be linked.

'When I first met Jean she was very friendly, kind and helpful towards me. She was completely open and honest with me and always seemed cheerful, even though her neighbour had just died rather suddenly.

'But the last time I saw her, which was the night before she was found dead, she looked upset and worried and made it clear that she did not want to spend any time at all in my company. And the next day, as you all now know, her body was discovered on the grass in front of the walls.'

'There has to be a reason for the change in her behaviour and I would be grateful for anything you can tell me that might shed some light on things.'

After another long pause when no one spoke, she said: 'Edgar and Marge, you both knew Jean and Sophie. Isn't there anything you can tell me that could explain Jean's change in behaviour?'

There was a brief silence and then Marge said: 'I'm sorry Kate, but I am afraid that you are barking up the wrong tree. I could always tell that Jean resented Sophie. She was extremely jealous of her because of all the interest she was shown by the men around here. She lived in the same building as Sophie and could easily get in and out of her apartment. I am convinced she was responsible for Sophie's death but then she must have regretted her actions and been so full of guilt and remorse that she decided to kill herself.'

'Well, how do you explain the traces of the sedative found in her blood stream?'

'How the hell would I know? Maybe she took a drug to calm herself before she jumped.'

Kate decided to try another approach.

'Edgar, you knew Jean, do you think she was capable of killing Sophie?'

The handsome American seemed to consider the question carefully for a few seconds.

Then he said: 'Well no, it would seem unlikely. But then she was very quiet and you couldn't really tell what she was thinking a lot of the time. Who of us really knew her…?' His voice trailed off and he took a sip of his wine.

Then with a smile, he gestured towards Marge and said: 'And as my friend has just pointed out she lived in the same building as Sophie and must have been able to get into her apartment easily. Apart from the domestic staff, who else would have had that kind of access?'

'Signora Mattozzi, you had a pass key to Sophie's flat, I believe,' Kate said in Italian, turning her attention to the group from the palazzo.

'Yes, what of it?'

'You were also very angry with her because of her decision to send the furniture to San Pellegrino Terme to be stored.'

'I couldn't have cared less about what she did.'

'If that is true, why did you put yourself to the trouble of travelling all the way out to San Pellegrino Terme to visit the warehouse?'

'How do you know that I did?' Signora Mattozzi said, but she had started to sound less defiant and sure of herself.

'A member of staff at the warehouse identified you from a photograph I showed him. He said he had seen you in the warehouse looking at the furniture about two days after it arrived.'

The woman's face flushed and a pattern of hideous purple blotches appeared on her neck.

She said, almost spitting with anger: 'Those pieces of furniture are extremely valuable. They have been owned by my husband's family for several generations. I didn't want them to be thrown in with a load of rubbish taken from house clearances. I wanted to be sure that they were being stored properly and so I decided to go and see for myself where they had been placed.

'There's nothing wrong with that. I wanted to be sure that they wouldn't be left in bad conditions or have something happen to damage them. How did I know that I would ever get them back? What was to stop them selling them for a lot of money and then sending inferior pieces of furniture back to me in their place? How would I have been able to prove that they had sold the original pieces? I just wanted to reassure myself that my furniture was still in the warehouse and had been put somewhere safe.'

Luisa flushed with embarrassment and Massimo turned and glared at Signora Mattozzi, but she continued. 'It doesn't mean that I harmed the Englishwoman and I certainly never let myself into her apartment at any time, whether she was in or she was out.

'In actual fact I detested her and I wanted to have as little contact with her as possible,' she said venomously.

Kate turned her attention to the young woman sitting next to her and said: 'All right then, Luisa, what about you? Sophie had treated you badly, you have already told me that. She had started to ask you to do all sorts of extra things for her that were not really part of your job. She had asked you to arrange to have the furniture stored for her and to organise replacement items for the apartment that were more to her taste.

'And she had recently threatened to report you for stealing, after she thought a tiny amount of cheese had gone missing.

'On the morning she was found dead you told me that you let yourself into her apartment early.

'You could have taken her some coffee with a sedative in it and then when she was safely asleep, either you or Massimo could have gone into the bedroom and smothered her with her own pillow.'

Luisa gasped in horror and Massimo, who was sitting next to her, stood up angrily. 'How dare you make these kind of accusations? All Luisa did was to try to help the Signorina, but as soon as she met me and we started going out together, the woman just seemed to want to turn her against me. She said terrible things about me to try to split us up. But it doesn't mean that Luisa and I wanted to kill her. That is just crazy!'

Aldo said: 'Sit down Massimo and be quiet. We are trying to get explanations for a few things here. You and Luisa are not being victimised.'

Kate turned to the man sitting next to Signora Mattozzi and said: 'Roberto, you have been very quiet but I know that you had plenty of reasons to be angry with Sophie. You could have let yourself into the courtyard of Palazzo Mattozzi at any time of the day or night and gained admittance both to the building and to Sophie's apartment.'

'But why would I have wished to?' the hotel manager asked nervously

'To put a stop to the claims Sophie had been making about you that you told me about privately,' Kate said.

'I didn't do any such thing,' Roberto said angrily. 'I never once let myself into her apartment while she was living in it.'

'It seems to me that you haven't just invited us here for a pleasant dinner, you have got us here so that you can throw random accusations about,' Marge said to her angrily.

Kate could not think of a suitable reply immediately and so Steve stepped in.

He said: 'I am sure we all feel sorry for Sophie and Jean and have welcomed the chance to remember them tonight. But the police are very keen to get new information about their deaths and I would have thought everyone would have wanted to help. The only reason anyone could have for not helping the police tonight is if they have something to hide. But I am confident that everyone here who has a clear conscience will want to volunteer any information that they might have.

'For instance, Signora Mattozzi, can you tell me anything that you think might help us?'

The woman hesitated for a moment and then said reluctantly: 'I have already told you that Jean did not like Sophie nearly as much as she pretended to. She was jealous of her because of all the men she seemed to attract. None of them ever took any notice of poor Jean.'

'That is exactly right. What did I tell you?' Marge said banging her fist on the table triumphantly.

Signora Mattozzi turned to her right and looked directly across at Kate. She said: 'I have also been honest with you and admitted that I did not like your cousin. But I was waiting for her to get bored with Bergamo and go back to England. Then I would have been able to bring the furniture back and put it out again in the room where it belonged. I did not need to kill her. I was just going to wait until she went home and I could get Palazzo Mattozzi back to how I wanted it.

'I don't know who has been telling stories about me, but why shouldn't I go and check that my husband's furniture was being looked after properly? Who would have had the right to prevent me?' She looked defiantly around the room at the other people sitting at the table and then picked up her wine glass and drank from it.

Steve said: 'Luisa, you were probably the person who had the most to do with Sophie. Can you add anything at all to what you have already told us?'

The maid looked nervous and said: 'I have already explained, she used to be kind to me but then she seemed to turn against me when I met Massimo.

'At first she often used to give me things as little presents, but then one day she shouted at me for taking some cheese from the fridge and called me a thief. I don't really know why she changed towards me. I was desperate to keep my job. I couldn't afford to be out of work because I have my little boy to support. I was afraid she would tell people that I was untrustworthy so I did everything I could to try to please her and, I promise you, I would never have done anything to harm her.

'The day I found her dead in her bed, I honestly thought she had already gone out when I let myself into her apartment and so I drank the rest of the coffee that she had made for her breakfast, although I suppose that I shouldn't really have done that,' she said with a scared look in the direction of Signora Mattozzi sitting next to her.

'I was busy supervising Massimo and Raz to make sure they took away the right pieces of furniture and so it never occurred to me to go into the bedroom.

'When I did go in, after they had gone, I had the most terrible shock when I saw her lying there dead…' Luisa put a hand to her mouth and tried to suppress the tears.

Massimo said angrily: 'What is the point of all this? You are only upsetting her again. Luisa never did anything to harm Sophie. I only met her once and I only agreed to store the furniture for her as a favour to Luisa. She was supposed to be paying me a few lousy euros a month but because of what has happened to her I have received nothing, despite all the inconvenience I have had.

'Raz and I did not go into the bedroom. We had no idea she was in there. We never saw or heard anything of her the whole time we were in the apartment, so I am afraid we can't help you.'

He stood up and said: 'Come on Luisa, I have had enough of this, we are going.'

'Wait!' Aldo shouted starting up from his seat, but Massimo and Luisa were already walking towards the door.

Suddenly two officers wearing the smart dark blue and red uniform of the Carabinieri appeared in the doorway. Kate was stunned when she heard them say in Italian to Massimo: 'Massimo Rovigo, we are here to arrest you.'

'Madre di Dio!' yelled Aldo and he ran across the room towards Massimo.

Everyone at the table gasped. Aldo turned in the doorway and looked at Kate. He said: 'I will sort this out, I promise you. Please carry on without me.' He then hustled Massimo, Luisa and the two Carabinieri officers out of the room.

26

Kate decided it was time to try another approach.
'Edgar and Marge, you have said that you never went inside Palazzo Mattozzi.'
'That's right,' Marge said at once. 'We always used to meet Sophie and Jean in the bars and restaurants around the main square up here.'
'You would probably say you had never been inside my hotel room as well, wouldn't you?'
'Well, we haven't been inside your hotel room,' Edgar said, looking puzzled.
'I'm sorry, Marge, but your perfume is very distinctive. The one you are wearing tonight is exactly the same as the one I could smell in my hotel room last Friday when I returned from the day in Sarnico and found that someone had been in there looking at Sophie's laptop.'
Kate noticed Roberto look down at his plate uncomfortably but the others were all staring at Marge, who pulled a face and said finally: 'OK, so you got me.' She took a large gulp of her wine and then said: 'I went to the hotel hoping to see you to ask if I could take a look at Sophie's laptop, but there was no one on reception and the guest book was open on the counter so it was easy to see what the number of your room was. I realised that your key was hanging up on its hook behind the desk so that you must be out.
'All the staff seemed to be busy in the restaurant so I seized my chance, helped myself to your key and went up to your room to take a sneaky peek at Sophie's laptop.'
Kate said: 'But what exactly were you expecting to find on it?'

Marge shifted uncomfortably in her seat and said: 'If you don't mind, I would prefer not to discuss it in front of all these people.'

Steve said: 'Well, I'm afraid that this poses a bit of a dilemma for us because you have to agree your behaviour looks very suspicious. If you don't tell us what you were looking for on the laptop we won't be able to think of any reason why you couldn't also have gained admittance to Sophie's apartment at Palazzo Mattozzi in the same cunning way and drugged her and killed her.'

Marge reacted with horror: 'Of course I didn't do that! That is something completely different.'

'Let us be the judges of that.'

Marge drank deeply from her glass while she considered his words.

'OK, I will try to explain it all to you.'

She looked across at Kate and then said: 'But first I am afraid that you are going to have to accept that your cousin was a Grade A bitch. I mean, you seem like a perfectly nice woman, but your cousin was pure poison, I can tell you.'

'Marge, that is completely uncalled for,' Edgar protested.

'Oh, for God's sake, Edgar, open your eyes for once. I know you bought her little miss inncocent act but believe you me she was a manipulative, controlling little cow.'

'That may be your opinion, but can you give us some evidence for this. Sophie isn't here to defend herself, is she?' Steve said sharply.

Marge considered her words carefully. 'Well, for a start, she loved to show off her Italian and exclude those of us who were not so linguistically gifted.'

While everyone digested this, she took another deep sip of her wine.

'And then she prided herself on her knowledge of music and art. I mean, she was always arguing with you about stuff, wasn't she?' she appealed to Edgar sitting next to her.

He just shook his head in exasperation as though he wanted nothing to do with it and leaned forward to spear a piece of fruit with his fork.

'Then she started making little jokes at my expense in front of other people.'

'What sort of little jokes?' Kate asked.

'They were generally on the theme of my lack of knowledge about Italian culture. But this soon escalated and she started telling people I was only here for the shopping. She used to speak about me in a very patronising way right in front of me when we were both having a conversation with someone. She used to think it was terribly funny. Then she started dropping little hints about her journalistic contacts back in England.'

'What journalistic contacts?' Kate asked in amazement.

'She said she wrote for one of your British highbrow newspapers under a pen name,' Marge said.

'Well, that's the first I've heard about it!'

'Yes, she said she actually contributed to a column about social stereotypes run by a national newspaper and that she was planning to send in a piece about me. She said she was going to feature me as the archetypal American woman in Italy, completely ignorant about what she is looking at most of the time and only interested in the designer shops.

'I have loads of friends in London and it would have been humiliating if any of them had recognised me from what she wrote about me. I was worried that she might even have named me in her article.

So you can surely understand why I was anxious to see what she had written about me, despite what has happened. For all I know she might already have submitted it.'

'Were you anxious enough to have gone up the stairs to her apartment, persuaded her to let you in and then drugged and smothered her to shut her up once and for all?' Steve asked.

'No, of course not! But once I knew Kate had been given the laptop I was just curious to see what she had written about me. And the irony was that there was nothing on it about me, not one word. So, the whole thing must just have been to wind me up,' Marge concluded.

She took another sip of her drink and then said: 'But it must show you the type of woman that Sophie was.'

Ernesto banged his fist down on the table and exclaimed: 'Don't speak ill of her now that she is dead. She was beautiful and intelligent and completely amazing.'

Keen not to lose the impetus of the conversation, Kate turned to Roberto and said: 'You must have some sympathy with what Marge experienced. Did you never contemplate letting yourself into her apartment to have a look at what she may have written about you on the laptop. In fact, did you never get desperate enough to think about trying to silence her completely?'

'No, I did not! I just decided to keep away from her and hoped that she would forget all about me,' Roberto said emphatically.

Ernesto glared at him and so Kate said: 'Ernesto at this point I would like to thank you for this lovely meal. I know you cared about Sophie a great deal and I think this is a wonderful tribute to her.'

'Thank you, Signora,' the restaurant owner said, bowing his head in appreciation.

'You know that you were seen by Jean watching the apartment the night before Sophie died. You have already told me that you don't know what time you walked home. No one can vouch for your whereabouts later that night. How do we know that you didn't somehow manage to persuade Sophie to let you into the apartment? And how do we know that you didn't have an argument with her about the new man she had met? Maybe that argument turned into a struggle that resulted in her death?'

'I would never have harmed her because I loved her,' Ernesto said simply.

'Yes, but we all know that there can be a thin line between passionate love and uncontrollable rage. She had fallen for someone else. She had told you that she didn't want you because she had met someone new. That could have pushed you over the edge couldn't it?' Steve suggested.

Ernesto glared across at Simon Pargeter before turning to Kate and saying: 'I just remember how miserable I felt that night. All I wanted to do was to somehow catch a glimpse of her with her new man. I never ever considered hurting her, I swear.'

Anton said: 'That's absolutely right. I remember him coming back to the restaurant and he looked terrible. I felt so sorry for him. I saw him take a bottle of wine from the fridge to take up to his apartment with him.'

'What time did you see him take the wine from the restaurant,' Steve asked.

Anton said: 'It was quite a long while before we closed. It was probably between about nine and nine thirty pm.'

'That's interesting, because Sophie spoke to her

mother on the telephone at about nine thirty pm Italian time and told her she was planning to stay in for the rest of the evening to get on with her book. Her mother said that she sounded happy and positive,' Kate said.

'I have told you that I never saw anyone arrive to visit her while I was out in the street,' Ernesto said. 'Afterwards I went for a walk to clear my head and when I got back to the restaurant I took some wine up to my apartment. When I had drunk it all I went to bed.'

Kate turned to Marge and said to her: 'Don't you recognise Anton?'

'Recognise him from where?' Marge asked looking across the table at the chef curiously.

'I think Anton is the man you saw Sophie talking to at the railway station the evening you arrived back from your shopping trip in Milan together.'

'But there are loads of young men of all nationalities hanging around the station. I can't really be expected to identify him now, can I?'

'Anton was born in Milan and trained as a chef at a Michelin-starred restaurant. He became such an expert in Lombardian cuisine that I head hunted him to come and work for me here in Bergamo,' Ernesto said stiffly.

He looked straight at Marge and said pointedly: 'He now works long hours at La Torre and does not have time to hang around the station.'

Anton said: 'I remember bumping into Sophie on the steps one evening when I was going down to the platform to get the train back to Milan. I seem to remember there was another woman with her.'

Marge raised her eyebrows again but Kate ignored her and asked: 'Can you remember what you talked to Sophie about?'

Anton groaned and put his head in his hands. 'I'd really rather not repeat it,' he said.

Steve said: 'Sorry, but this is no time to be shy. What was your conversation about?'

Anton said: 'I was just trying to persuade her to give Ernesto another chance. I told her about how badly he was coping with the break up. It was affecting his work. He was making expensive mistakes because he was so distracted. We had just started doing well, business had really picked up, and so it couldn't have come at a worse time. It was so frustrating.'

Steve said: 'Of course, you were employed on the basis of getting a share of the profits. So if the restaurant didn't do well, you were going to suffer financially, weren't you?'

Anton said: 'Yes, but it wasn't just because of the money that I wanted to speak to Sophie. I felt really sorry for Ernesto.'

The restaurant owner sighed with exasperation and snatched up his wine glass to take a drink from it.

'What was her reaction to what you said?' Kate asked curiously.

'Well, she listened to me but she said she thought that the break up was going to be for the best. She said she thought Ernesto would meet someone else who would be more suitable for him. But she was perfectly polite to me and prepared to listen to my point of view. I always thought she was a very nice lady,' Anton said sadly.

Kate turned to Simon and said: 'We haven't heard from you yet. Is there anything you want to add?'

The property developer gave a rather forced smile and said in his husky voice: 'I've just been interested hearing what everyone else has had to say. You already know that the night Sophie died I was in Sarnico at a business dinner with a lot of other people. I can hardly believe that she was murdered. I think I am still in shock. I wish there had been something I could have done to save her, but I was miles away when it must have happened.'

Kate said: 'But after the meal there is no one to vouch for your whereabouts, is there? You could have got into your car and driven to Bergamo. You could have rung her on her mobile and asked her to let you into the apartment even though it was after the ten o'clock chimes and once you were inside you could have killed her.'

'And how would I have got out again without that old woman downstairs hearing me?' Simon demanded. 'In any case, it is ridiculous. You know how much I cared about Sophie. I was as shocked and upset as everyone else when I heard that she had died.' Signora Mattozzi glowered across the table at him but said nothing.

Kate turned to Marge again. 'Speaking of Simon's car, reminds me of something else I wanted to ask you. The night I had dinner with you at your hotel someone in a car tried to run me over when I was walking back up to the Città Alta. Do you know anything about that?'

'No, of course I don't. It's the first I have heard about it. And in any case, I can assure you, that I don't have a car!'

'Not many people knew that I was going to be down in the Città Bassa that night and that I would be walking back up on my own.'

'Well, I can tell you that I know nothing about it,' Marge said raising her voice and starting to look flustered.

Kate turned back to the other people sitting round the table and said: 'I think someone tried to run me down deliberately to stop me asking more questions about Sophie's life out here in Bergamo because they were afraid that I would uncover the truth about what happened to her. Someone wanted to kill me as well as my cousin and I think that the same person then went on to kill Jean!'

27

Through the open windows of the tower Kate could see it was beginning to get dark outside. Everyone was silent while the waiters cleared away the dessert plates. Then Aldo came back in and showed Massimo and Luisa to their seats again.

While Aldo had a few quiet words with Steve, Kate looked at Massimo and saw the defiant expression on his face, but when she glanced at Luisa sitting next to her she could see how shocked and scared the young woman appeared to be.

Kate started the conversation going again by saying: 'I take the points made by Marge and Signora Mattozzi about the relationship between Sophie and Jean. I accept that Jean probably was jealous of Sophie. Although Sophie was older than her she still had plenty of men interested in her. Also, she had independent wealth and could go anywhere and do anything she liked. If her book took six months or six years to complete it was no one's business but her own. However Jean had to work hard in order to make a living out here. She had to teach a lot of English classes and spend many of her evenings marking her students' work.

'I have already said that when I first met Jean she seemed happy, positive and optimistic, despite the fact that her neighbour had just been found dead. But I still believe that Jean was initially shocked by Sophie's death and was decent enough to feel sorry about it.

'However, I suppose that in the end there might have been a small part of her that felt relieved. Because Sophie dying when she did meant that at last there was no one standing in her way.

'I realise now that when I first met Jean I was

meeting a woman who had fallen in love. She was a woman right at the beginning of a relationship who thinks she has found the man of her dreams and has started to see the world in a whole different light.

'And although in the past she had been worried about Sophie taking his attention away from her, it all seemed much simpler now that Sophie was dead.

'The first time I met Jean she had invited me round to visit her in her apartment. I saw that the roses were already beginning to wilt in the vase but she had kept them, along with an empty champagne bottle, as souvenirs of the night that she had finally entertained the man she was in love with at her apartment in Palazzo Mattozzi.'

There was a murmur from some of the people round the table but Kate continued: 'However, in the days that followed my first meeting with her, I'm afraid that her hopes died off along with the flowers in the vase.'

She paused and looked round to make sure that she had everyone's attention.

'It could all have been so perfect. She now knew that the man she loved was interested in her and he had actually begun some kind of a relationship with her. But I think as the days went by after Sophie's death, she began to feel less and less sure of him.'

Simon Pargeter cleared his throat and said: 'Look, I'm sorry Kate, but do I need to stay and hear all this? I can't see that it has anything to do with me.'

'It has something to do with you if you want to help establish what happened to Sophie,' Kate said sharply.

'You see Jean's death and Sophie's death are definitely linked, as the Commissario has said.'

'First let me take you back to Marge and Signora Mattozzi's point about Jean's jealousy of Sophie.

'Yes, my cousin had wealth, freedom and looks. And poor Jean had to work hard for everything and in some people's opinion may not have been quite so attractive.

'And she also had to stand by and watch after one man after another out here in Bergamo fell for Sophie and took no notice of her.

'Yes, you can understand why resentment might have eaten away at Jean and finally made her want to kill Sophie.

'But I can tell you emphatically that she didn't kill Sophie. The night before my cousin died, Jean was busy doing something else entirely.

'We have talked about who would have found it easy to get in and out of Sophie's apartment in addition to Jean.

'Signora Mattozzi, Luisa and Roberto all had keys to her apartment and Massimo and his assistant, Raz, were let in to collect the furniture.

'But having been to see the furniture where it is being stored at San Pellegrino Terme, I think there is another solution to the mystery.

'Let's just imagine for a moment that Signora Mattozzi is telling the truth and that she did not set foot in Sophie's apartment until she heard Luisa's screams on the Monday morning.

'And let's just imagine that Luisa's version of events is true and that Massimo and Raz did exactly what they had been asked to do, removing the furniture from the living room and not setting foot in the bedroom. Luisa says that when she went into the bedroom later to start cleaning she was shocked to find Sophie lying dead in her bed.'

Aldo interrupted at this point and said: 'When I first looked into Signorina Westmullen's death I was convinced that no one could have got into

Palazzo Mattozzi from outside, or got out again, without Signora Mattozzi seeing or hearing them.

'After interviewing Signora Mattozzi, Signorina Anderson and Luisa, I was satisfied that none of them would have wanted to harm Sophie and I concluded that her death must have been as a result of natural causes. But now I realise that I was wrong and that right from the start I should have treated her death as suspicious because there is, in fact, another explanation.'

He then looked in Kate's direction again and gave her an encouraging nod to signal to her that she should continue.

She said: 'We know that there was only a small amount of time for someone to arrive to see Sophie and gain legitimate access to the apartment after she made the telephone call to her mother in England and before the ten o'clock chimes prompted Signora Mattozzi to lock up for the night.'

'But something Jean said to me the night we came here for a meal together has been at the back of my mind for a few days, although I couldn't really understand why it was so important.

'She was telling me about the Campanone sounding the chimes 100 times at ten pm to mark the ancient curfew that used to exist in Bergamo.

'And then she mentioned the house rules at Palazzo Mattozzi. She said that Signora Mattozzi always locked up at night after the ten o'clock bell and that anyone who had not returned to the palazzo was locked out for the night.

'She also said that anyone inside the palazzo was in for the night. That was the significant part of what she said that I have been trying to remember.

'Steve actually commented to me that Sophie and Jean were living like Victorian spinsters because

they were not allowed to have a man in their rooms.
'And I think that this is the key to the mystery surrounding Sophie's death. The killer was already inside Palazzo Mattozzi when Signora Mattozzi locked up for the night. They were inside Jean's apartment having dinner with her, a meal she had made from the food that she had bought from the supermarket opposite the funicular station in the Città Bassa.
'The killer had arrived bringing roses and champagne and Jean was in no hurry to see him off the premises before ten pm as she had high hopes for the way the evening might progress.
'So the question is now, which of the men in Sophie's circle was Jean's secret lover?'
People looked at each other across the table nervously but no one said a word as they waited for Kate to continue.
'Roberto, you had good reason to want to silence Sophie and put a stop to the threats she had been making. You could have gone round with roses and champagne and set out to seduce Jean. Then in the middle of the night you could have slipped out of her bed, gone up the stairs, put your pass key in the lock, let yourself into Sophie's apartment and then killed her.'
There was a stunned silence and then the hotel manager said, looking red in the face: 'But my relationship with Jean has always been entirely professional. She was a tenant of mine and nothing improper ever took place between us. I'm appalled that you could even suggest something like that. I have already told you that I had been trying to keep my distance from Sophie in the hope that she would forget all about me.'
Kate then turned to Ernesto and said: 'We only

have Anton's word for it that you came back to the restaurant before the ten o'clock bell that evening and that you went up to your apartment and spent the rest of the night there.

'You could have gone out and bought roses and champagne and charmed Jean into letting you into her apartment and then after seducing her you could have made your way up the stairs and tapped on Sophie's door and asked her to let you in.'

'That's outrageous, I loved Sophie. I would never have even looked at Jean. Sophie was the only woman I wanted and I would never have done anything to hurt her,' Ernesto protested, flinging his arms about dramatically.

Kate then turned to Simon Pargeter and said: 'Or it could have been you. How do we know that you didn't go round to Jean's apartment and make love to her and then stay the night with her in order to gain access to Sophie's apartment when Jean was safely asleep?'

'This is getting ridiculous,' Simon said, becoming visibly paler. 'If you recall I was having dinner with some of my business associates miles away in Sarnico.'

'They were all people that you could have paid to give you an alibi,' Steve said.

'Well I couldn't have bribed an entire restaurant full of people, could I? And anyway, why would I want to kill Sophie? I cared about her a great deal.'

Kate said: 'Yes, you always say that. You always say that you cared about her. But you never say that you loved her.'

Simon looked embarrassed and started to mutter an explanation: 'It was early days, but I was beginning to fall for her, yes. I am sure that I was. I certainly would not have wanted to kill her.'

'Not even if she had found out what you were up to with your cousin Adam Leighton at her mother's nursing home?' Steve asked and Simon's mouth fell open in astonishment and dismay.

Kate said: 'I can tell you now that my Aunt Edna makes a pretty formidable opponent.'

'I don't know what you are talking about,' Simon said stiffly, trying to recover his poise.

'Oh, don't you?' asked Steve. 'Well, fortunately your cousin Adam Leighton did know all about it when he was asked about it by a former colleague of mine. In fact he was positively forthcoming with my mate, who happens to be a Detective Chief Inspector with West Midlands Police. Mind you, people do tend to spill the beans when Terry Batts is asking the questions.'

Simon said hoarsely: 'What exactly are you talking about?'

Steve said: 'I'm talking about the contract you both signed that turned out to have a major drawback to it. Your lawyer really screwed up, didn't he?'

He turned his attention to the other people sitting round the table. 'You see, Sophie's mother Edna Westmullen has been very clever, particularly considering she has had a stroke and is not getting any younger.

'Just to put you all in the picture, one of the conditions of Simon and Adam's purchase of Hampton House, Sophie's family home, was that Mrs Westmullen could have her choice of rooms if she ever needed to move back in as a resident.

'After her stroke her doctors advised her that she needed more care and so she left the new house she had previously bought in the village and decided to move back into her former home, which had now been converted into a luxury nursing home for the elderly.

'You thought she would choose one of the stylish, ensuite bedrooms on the first floor, didn't you?

'But she insisted on taking up residence in her late husband's former study, which was on the ground floor just off reception. She said it helped her feel closer to him, didn't she?'

Simon made an attempt at a rueful smile, but his blue eyes remained cold and calculating and Kate suddenly thought he looked a lot less attractive.

'According to Adam it is a beautiful room with a lot of period features and it was going to play a big part in the plans you had drawn up to further develop the property. You must have been furious with your lawyer for leaving you with this problem.'

Simon said: 'Well, okay, I admit that we had intended to use the study as a meeting room and for welcoming the families of residents. The other two reception rooms are taken up as a day room and a dining room for the residents.

'The study would have given us additional facilities. As it is, the only office is in a tiny room just off reception, which I believe used to be a boot room. It was a big mistake by the lawyer when he drew up the contract leaving us wide open like that.

'We asked Mrs Westmullen to choose another room when she moved into the home but she was adamant that she wanted to live in her husband's former study. It wasn't really suitable, when we were trying to impress potential clients, to have her walking through reception in her dressing gown at odd times of the day, but she didn't seem to care.

'Adam seemed to think that she wanted to keep herself separate from the other residents and that while she remained on the ground floor she somehow could feel that she was still living in her own house.'

'That's actually very intuitive of him,' Kate said.

'Don't sound so surprised, he's good at what he does and he cares about all his residents, including your aunt. He's actually become particularly fond of her.

'But we have had plans drawn up for converting the room without changing its character and we have even measured up for the new furniture, so it has been extremely frustrating. Some of the other investors have been putting Adam under pressure to get the problem sorted. They have been threatening to take their money out of the nursing home, which would have been disastrous for us. It could have affected my development out here in Sarnico.'

Steve said: 'But surely you could have found another room to use as an office, or even built an extension?'

'We looked into converting an old cottage in the grounds but it would not have been so convenient and was going to cost far too much. In any case, the other investors had put their money in on the understanding that the study, with all its period features, was going to be part of the reception facilities.

'So, we knew we were completely stuck unless we could get Mrs Westmullen to change her mind. And because I was currently out in Italy for the Lago d'Iseo project, it occurred to Adam that I might be able to get to know Sophie and persuade her to talk to her mother about moving into one of the superior guest suites, where to be fair she would have been a lot more comfortable. As it is, she has to go up two flights of stairs to the second floor whenever she wants to have a bath because she doesn't have her own ensuite in the study.'

Kate said: 'So Sophie thought she had met you entirely by accident at the art exhibition launch party and had no idea you had any connection with the manager of her mother's nursing home. But all the while you had contrived to get yourself introduced to her so that you could win her confidence and work on her to try to persuade her mother to move out of her late husband's study.'

'Yes, I suppose so, but saying it like that makes it sound a lot worse than it actually was. We thought it could be useful if I got to know Sophie. We were not planning to be heavy-handed about any of it. I had no idea that I would end up in a relationship with Sophie.'

Steve said: 'Did she find out what you were up to and realise that you could not be trusted?'

'No, not at all. As far as I am aware she never found out that I had called in favours to get myself invited to that art exhibition launch party.

'Right up to me getting the news that she had been found dead, I honestly thought we might have a future together. How I met her in the first place was irrelevant really.

'And I have absolutely no reason to think that she knew anything about the clause in the contract which gave your aunt the right to that ground floor room, or that it was causing us so many problems.'

Kate said: 'Like I have said, my aunt can be very determined. She will not give up that room unless she has a good reason. And I can tell you that if Sophie had become involved she would have taken her mother's side, so you were on a hiding to nothing anyway.'

Simon said: 'I've told you, I am sure she knew nothing about the situation with the room and I think she had begun to care about me as much as I had started to care about her.'

Ernesto sighed loudly and banged his fist on the table in frustration.

Kate said: 'We only have your word for that, though, don't we? If Sophie had found out what you were up to with Adam she might have started making life very difficult for you, which would have given you a strong motive for killing her.'

'It might also explain your suspicious behaviour after her death,' Steve added.

'What do you mean?'

'You say you were miles away from Bergamo when she was killed, but even if that is true, you would have got to know about it pretty quickly. Surely your cousin Adam rang and let you know soon after the police had contacted Hampton House with the news. So why did you call on Signora Mattozzi later and say you were worried that Sophie wasn't answering your calls? You have got to admit that looks very suspicious."

Simon looked embarrassed. "I was worried about my connection with Adam coming out. I knew the police would find out about me when they looked at Sophie's phone. I thought it would be best if I just pretended I didn't know what had happened and went to see the police voluntarily. But it doesn't mean I had anything to do with her death and it doesn't change the fact that I genuinely cared for her."

28

Kate then turned to Edgar and said: 'You were also one of the men in Sophie's life. It would be remiss of me to leave you out, wouldn't it?'

Edgar shrugged and smiled and said: 'Hey, I was hardly one of the men in her life, we were just friends.'

'Yes, of course, I now realise that there was never any romance between you and Sophie. It was another lady who was lucky enough to receive your attentions, wasn't it?'

'I beg your pardon?' Edgar said in surprise.

'Jean was clearly besotted with you. I realised that during the first conversation that I ever had with her.'

'I'm not going to listen to any more of this rubbish. Marge, I think it is time that we were going,' the American said angrily.

'Are you kidding? I wouldn't miss this for the world. I can't wait to hear what her next crazy accusation is going to be!'

'Oh, don't worry I'm not accusing anyone of anything yet. I just want to try to establish a few facts. Rather than call it a crazy accusation let's just say I'm putting a scenario to you. Where's the harm in that? Please, everyone, stay a little while longer and have something more to drink.'

Edgar hesitated for a second but then allowed the waiter to refill his wine glass.

Kate said: 'Just answer me one question. Were you attracted to Sophie when you first met her?'

Edgar took a sip of his wine while he thought about it. He said: 'She was very pretty and I suppose right at the start I thought that there could perhaps be something between us. But then I thought that it might be a mistake for two writers to get together. It probably wouldn't have worked. But then she began a relationship with Ernesto here anyway, so that was that. I can assure you, there was never any hint of a romance between us.'

'And how did you feel about Jean?'

'I thought she was a nice lady, that's all. She was interested in music and the theatre and that's how we became friends because we used to meet up at events at Teatro Donizetti and talk to each other. But we were never anything more than just friends.'

'Well, I am convinced that Jean was in love with you and that she had been for a long time. Didn't you ever give her any encouragement?'

'Never,' Edgar said with certainty.

'That was probably true right up to that Sunday evening when you went round to see her carrying champagne and roses, having previously suggested that Jean invite you round to her apartment for dinner.

'It must have been after Ernesto had given up his vigil and left the street. Jean would have let you into her apartment while Signora Mattozzi was in her sitting room watching television, so she wouldn't have known anything about it. Jean herself told me that the apartments were as good as soundproof. You enjoyed a romantic dinner with Jean and stayed in the apartment after the ten o'clock chimes and after Palazzo Mattozzi had been locked up for the night.

'I think that you spent the night with Jean in her bed, but then got up early the next morning while she was still sleeping soundly and crept up the stairs to Sophie's apartment.'

'Why would I have wanted to do any of that? I

wasn't in the least bit attracted to Jean.'

'Yes, but you were prepared to use her in order to gain access to Sophie's apartment.'

'But I have never been in Sophie's apartment.'

'Again, that was probably true right up to early that Monday morning when you were determined to get inside there because she had something that you desperately wanted to get your hands on.'

Kate turned to Marge and said: 'Do you remember the name Marianna Pezzoli-Grattaroli?'

'Who?'

'You told me that Sophie was constantly going on about a letter written by Donizetti mentioning a woman with an unpronounceable Italian name. You were convinced that Sophie just kept saying it to show off her Italian.

'But I know now that her real interest in this letter was because it completely contradicted something Edgar had written in his book about Donizetti.'

'This is all news to me,' Edgar said to the others round the table with his usual good-natured smile.

'Well it shouldn't be unless you have completely forgotten what you wrote in your book about Donizetti.'

'I happen to have read it only recently and I remember that when you were writing about Donizetti's early life you mentioned that he avoided military service because an Austrian army officer was so impressed with one of his operas that he arranged to have him summarily released from the service so that he could pursue his career as a composer.'

'Well that's true.'

'No it isn't. There is a letter written by Donizetti that says this lady, Marianna Pezzoli-Grattaroli, paid for him to be excused from military service.

The letter is in the museum for everyone to see.

'The story about the Austrian army officer is just one of these myths that get handed down over the years that aren't actually true. You just repeated a mistake made by someone else in their writing without checking your facts. For all I know, there could have been other inaccuracies in your book. I wouldn't be able to spot them, most people wouldn't. But Sophie was another expert in the subject. And she would not have hesitated to tackle you about them.'

Edgar just shook his head but he had gone noticeably redder in the face.

'I can just imagine Sophie arguing about it with you, going on and on about it to the extent that it really began to irritate Marge. Sophie would have been like a dog with a bone, never prepared to let it go. Knowing Sophie as I do, I am sure that she would have taken great delight in telling you that she was planning to put the record straight in her own book.

'She was going to discredit you and you couldn't cope with that. Not you, Bergamo's Donizetti expert. I think you were really worried about what she was going to write. So you concocted a plan to get into her apartment so that you could get your hands on her manuscript and read what she had written about it and find out how badly it was going to affect your reputation.

'You tapped on her door. Thinking it was either Jean or Signora Mattozzi, she opened it and you were able to push your way in.

'She was just wearing her grey silk dressing gown, drinking coffee and working on her book, wasn't she?'

'You tell me. You're just making this up as you go

along, aren't you? Edgar said hoarsely. He took a sip of his wine but it made him start to cough, Ernesto signalled to the waiter who quickly went and refilled Edgar's water glass.

While he drank some of his water, Kate continued: 'You dropped a sedative into her cup of coffee while she wasn't looking and then sat talking to her about her book until it started to work. Then you carried her into the bedroom and laid her on the bed and smothered her with one of her own pillows. You put her body back in the bed and straightened the covers over her to make it look as though she had died in her sleep.

'But that is where you made your first big mistake. It was far too hot for Sophie to have been wearing her dressing gown in bed all night. That is what made me suspect that she had already been up and about that morning.'

Edgar just shook his head but didn't say anything. There was a deadly silence in the room while everyone waited to hear what Kate had to say next.

'Your next step was to look on the laptop, find what you were looking for and delete it.

'But you went too far. You deleted everything relating to Bergamo, all her notes for the book, everything. You probably deleted a whole file of information relevant to her time here, which was stupid really as the absence of any work connected with Bergamo made me suspicious.

'You washed both coffee cups so that no trace of the sedative could be found in hers, then, rather than leave them on the drainer you put them with the other items in the kitchen sink so they would not attract attention. I would imagine that you then looked for the manuscript or any of her notes for the book.

'The manuscript could have been out in full view if Sophie had been working on it when you knocked on the door and you could have just helped yourself to it. But you obviously felt that you wanted to find everything relating to the book, which is why you went through her drawers.

'However a lot of the furniture was empty because it was going to be taken away to be put in store. Luisa noticed one of the drawers was half open when she arrived for work. She was puzzled because, as she said, Sophie would have known that it was empty and would not have been looking for anything in it.'

By now Edgar had recovered from his coughing bout and asked: 'How on earth would I have managed to get out with these items without disturbing the lady on the ground floor?' He gestured in the direction of Signora Mattozzi, whose face remained impassive as always.

'I think you were planning to creep back down to Jean's apartment and you hoped she would still be asleep,' Kate said.

'Then, once the gates were unlocked you could have asked her to find out when the coast was clear and you could have left Palazzo Mattozzi without anyone ever knowing you had spent the night in there.

'My guess is that you had already persuaded Jean to tell no one about your relationship, which is why she never mentioned it to me, even though it was clear that she was infatuated with you. You could have told her that you just wanted to be discreet and keep quiet about things to begin with. She was so crazy about you, she would have probably agreed to anything you asked.

'But you didn't get chance to get safely back down

to Jean's apartment because all of a sudden you heard Luisa letting herself into Sophie's apartment with her key. She was starting work early that morning because she wanted to make sure she was there before Massimo and Raz arrived to collect the furniture in their truck.

'I believe that you panicked. You looked for somewhere to hide and the most obvious place was the huge wardrobe in the living room. Luckily for you it was completely empty because Luisa had already packed all Sophie's clothes away in suitcases. And so you climbed inside it.'

'Ridiculous!' Edgar said. He gave an amused smile, looking round at the others again as if to gauge their reactions.

But Kate stuck to her task. 'Once inside the wardrobe you tried to stay calm and wait for your chance to escape from the apartment. You couldn't possibly have known what was going to happen next. You would have had no idea how quickly you were going to be leaving the apartment. It came much sooner than you expected.

'You suddenly felt the wardrobe being moved. Luisa told me that Massimo and Raz manoeuvred it out on to the balcony. They placed it on a small platform that they had raised to the window with a ladder from the truck parked below. Then they carefully lowered it so that it could be positioned on the truck. Luckily for you they had been warned by Luisa that it would be heavy and that it was an extremely valuable piece of furniture so they took great care with it.'

Massimo, who had been frowning with concentration as he followed Kate's version of events, stood up. 'I knew there was something strange about that wardrobe,' he shouted. 'It felt far too heavy. I could not believe how heavy it was. Now I understand why it was so difficult for us to move it out on to the balcony.'

Kate looked at Edgar and said: 'It probably wasn't the most comfortable experience for you but, nevertheless, you kept quiet inside the wardrobe during the journey to San Pellegrino Terme and waited patiently until you were sure there was no one around. Then you opened the wardrobe door, looked round and climbed out of it.

'We wouldn't have known anything about it at all. But at that moment Raz came back into the room where the furniture was being stored and found you in there. You told him that you were interested in buying the furniture and he told you that it wasn't for sale, I believe. He was able to point you out to me when I showed him the pictures I have stored on my digital camera.'

Edgar coughed again. 'I was genuinely interested in buying some pieces of furniture. I had gone out to the warehouse to see what I could find to furnish my house in the Città Bassa. I had no idea that I was actually looking at Sophie's old furniture. It was just a coincidence'

'Do you really expect us to believe that?' Steve asked.

Marge turned her head to look at Edgar thoughtfully but she made no comment and Kate could not tell what she was thinking from the expression on her face.

She continued: 'In the days that followed Sophie's death, Jean became increasingly anxious and depressed. When I first visited her in her apartment she was still on cloud nine because of her new romance with you and she obviously didn't connect you in any way with Sophie's death.

'She was delighted to be able to arrange for me to meet up with you and Marge for a drink in Piazza Vecchia.

'But as the days went by and you showed no particular interest in her, or any inclination to want to stay the night with her again, I would imagine she became increasingly disappointed.

'And it must have occurred to her to wonder why you weren't there the next morning when she was woken from a deep sleep by Luisa's screams. She might have started to ask herself whether you had anything to do with Sophie's death and whether you had just been using her in order to get into Sophie's apartment.

'She may well have tried to talk to you about it on the phone. She was certainly anxiously waiting for a call from someone when I saw her on Thursday evening.

'I think on the Friday night, the night before she was found dead, when I met her on her way to the funicular station, she was coming to meet you to have it out with you once and for all. And once you realised that she suspected you, I believe you regarded her as a liability and decided that she had to go as well.

'So you gave her a drink laced with a sedative, took her to the top of one of the look-out towers and pushed her unconscious body off, knowing the fall would kill her and rid you of your problem.'

29

There was a stunned silence in the dining room high up in the tower and then Edgar cleared his throat and said: 'Well, it's a great story but I think you know that you can't prove any of it. There is absolutely nothing to link me with Sophie's apartment. I was never in there.'

'I bet you wore surgical gloves to make sure you didn't leave any finger prints, didn't you?' Steve said, looking sideways down the table at him.

'That's just a product of your imagination,' Edgar said dismissively with a contemptuous wave of his hand.

Aldo also turned to look at him intently and said: 'But I think those gloves became hot and uncomfortable when you were inside the wardrobe on your way to San Pellegrino Terme on the truck. They really made your hands sweat, didn't they? So you took them off and slipped them into one of your pockets.

'And I wouldn't mind betting that when we take your finger prints we will find that they are a perfect match with the ones we have found on the inside of the wardrobe doors,' he said, continuing to stare directly at Edgar.

Kate, who had never taken her eyes off Edgar, saw a muscle twitch in his cheek. She joined in, saying: 'If you continue to stick to the story that you were looking at the wardrobe in the furniture warehouse with the intention of buying it, you will have to eventually explain to a court why you felt you had to climb into it and close the doors from the inside. It is strange behaviour for someone browsing among antiques in a warehouse. But it is the only explanation you would be able to give for the finger prints that the police have found on the inside of the door.'

'You bitch! You think you are so clever, don't you? Just like your vile little cousin,' Edgar snarled. 'I should have run you down that night when I had the chance.'

He then started coughing again and put his handkerchief up to his mouth and left it there for a few seconds while he appeared to be composing himself. Marge pushed his water glass nearer to him with a grim expression on her face and shook her head.

Edgar finally took his handkerchief away from his mouth, swallowed hard and drank some water before mopping his perspiring brow. His face was scarlet and he looked in distress.

Kate turned to Marge and said: 'Did you ring him after I had left the hotel and tell him that I was walking back alone up to the Città Alta?'

The American woman said: 'Hey, I'm saying nothing until I have spoken to my lawyer.'

Kate turned to Edgar again and said: 'You had a baseball cap pulled down over your face and I didn't even know that you had a car, so I had no idea it was you behind the wheel.'

Edgar said hoarsely: 'It was a hire car, I hardly ever used it. Most of the time it stayed in the garage. When Marge phoned me and told me about some of the questions you had been asking, I drove up to the Città Alta, thinking that if I spotted you I could scare you off and stop you poking your nose into things. I wasn't intending to really hurt you.'

'Just tell me why you felt you had to kill Sophie,' Kate said simply.

Edgar put his hand to his mouth again and coughed

behind it. He tried to compose himself and said wearily: 'I never meant to kill her, but she had been making my life a misery with her threats. If she had shown my book about Donizetti to be flawed or inaccurate it would have ruined my reputation all over the world. I wouldn't have been able to cope with the shame.

'I bought some barbiturate on the internet. They were like sleeping pills in powder form. I thought I would get into her apartment that morning and put her out of action while I looked for the manuscript for her book. I didn't really have a clear plan.

'But as soon as I got in there she started going on about the letter again and I realised she was never going to let me off the hook. She kept ranting on about how she needed to be the one who told the truth in her book. She even told me she was going to make an announcement about it at my book signing in the Città Alta, which made me panic. 'I asked for some coffee and while she was getting me some from the pot in the kitchen, I emptied a sachet of the powder into the cup she was drinking from.

'When she came back with the coffee she made it clear that it was her intention to ruin me. There was no reasoning with her.

'I had read about this guy in the States who had put his hand over his wife's nose and mouth and suffocated her while she slept. The police thought she had died from natural causes and he would have got away with it if he hadn't been overheard bragging about it to some other guys in a bar a few months later.

'But once she had passed out and I had got her into the bedroom and laid her on the bed, I couldn't bring myself to touch her mouth even though I had put on the gloves. So I just put a pillow over her face and pressed down hard.

'I did the right thing, I am convinced. She didn't just want to expose me, she was going to ruin Donizetti's reputation as well. She was going to write about all the details of the illness that caused his death and how it marred his final years as a composer. It would have been terrible. He had a disease given to him by vile women. It was women who were his downfall when he was alive and now a woman was going to wreck things for him all over again. I couldn't let it happen. Donizetti was a genius and deserves our respect. But she just kept going on and on about needing to tell the truth.

'He was suffering and in pain near the end, but he still managed to write the beautiful music for Don Pasquale. She just wanted to smear him by telling the whole world all about the hideous symptoms of his dreadful illness. It would have been grotesque. So in the end I had no choice, I had to kill her. I did it for the great man, just as much as I did it for myself.'

Edgar paused and took another drink of water and mopped his perspiring face with his handkerchief again.

Then he smiled in a strange way as though unaware of everyone else. He said: 'If only that could have been an end to it all, everything would have been fine, but there was Jean to deal with.

'She kept ringing me and asking me questions and so I decided to invite her over to my house. This time I put a sachet of the powder into her glass of wine and when she was unconscious I carried her to the garage and put her in the back of the car. I drove her to one of the old watch towers and somehow managed to drag her heavy body up the stairs. When I was sure that there was no one around to see me, I threw her off the top.'

At this point Marge appeared to recover from her shocked state and said: 'For God's sake, Edgar, don't say any more until you have a lawyer present. Whatever you have, or haven't done, you need proper help to get you out of all this.'

Edgar had now started to breathe heavily and sweat continued to appear on his forehead but he turned to look at her with a superior smile.

'Don't worry, Marge. Nothing bad is going to happen to me. I won't be going to court or needing the help of lawyers. I couldn't risk all this becoming public knowledge. I made sure I had some insurance with me before I came here tonight.'

Kate saw that his face had started to take on a purple tinge and then he started wheezing before slumping forward in his seat.

'Oh my God!' Steve shouted, suddenly springing up from his seat and running to the end of the table.

But Aldo got to Edgar first and prised open his fingers, revealing empty sachets of sleeping powder inside the handkerchief.

'All finished now,' Edgar gasped and fell sideways off his chair on to the antique, red-patterned rug.

Aldo knelt on the floor next to him and took his pulse. After a couple of minutes he looked up at Kate and shook his head.

30

Autumn had finally arrived in Bergamo. As Kate emerged from Via Colleoni into Piazza Vecchia on the following Monday morning she could feel a distinct nip in the air. The sky was blue and cloudless and there was the promise of another beautiful day in store but it felt noticeably cooler than the temperatures she had been experiencing over the last few days.

Aldo was waiting for her on the library steps holding a large carrier bag from Intimissimi, a lingerie shop.

'Buon giorno, Kate,' he greeted her, kissing her on both cheeks. 'Shall we go for coffee?'

They crossed the square to the bar next to Palazzo della Ragione and when they were seated at one of the tables outside he held out the bag to her and said: 'I have something for you.'

She felt anxious for a few seconds, but when she looked inside the bag she saw that it contained a collection of files and notebooks. She reached inside and took one of the notebooks out to open it. When she saw Sophie's familiar handwriting her heart missed a beat.

'Aldo, how can I ever thank you for what you have done for me?' she asked, tears suddenly coming into her eyes.

'Please don't cry. I know that I was not very good at the beginning but I got there in the end, didn't I? We searched his house over the weekend and I believe that I have managed to find everything that he took from your cousin's apartment. I think he must have grabbed this carrier bag and placed the items in it.'

After the waitress had taken their order Aldo asked: 'Where is your English policeman this morning?'

'I have left him at the hotel arranging our flights back to England,' Kate said.

'Ah, so when will you be leaving?'

'Tomorrow possibly, or the day after, I'm leaving it up to him.'

'He's a good man,' Aldo said, much to her surprise.

'I know. I'm very lucky.'

'No, it is he who is lucky.'

Their coffee arrived then and after an awkward pause Aldo said: 'Marge Ransom is also preparing to depart from Bergamo. She has arranged to join up with some American friends in Florence. I called in at the Majestic earlier this morning just to see how she was doing.'

'Is she terribly upset about Edgar?'

'She seems to be a remarkably resilient woman. She told me that she thinks things have probably turned out for the best. She said he would have hated going on trial and having all the media attention. She even said that being shamed in the newspapers would probably have killed him anyway.'

'He was a wicked and dangerous man,' Kate said fiercely.

'And he may also have been mentally unhinged, because to murder two women to save himself from professional embarrassment isn't the work of a sane person, is it?' Aldo observed.

Kate sipped some of her coffee and then put her cup down on its saucer again. She said: 'Right from the start I could tell that he was vain. Marge told me that he loved people to recognise him from his very flattering publicity photographs and to talk to him about his books.

'Like Sophie, he did not need to make any money from his writing because he was from a wealthy family back in the States, but he liked to be admired and looked up to by people. If Sophie had gone on to publish her book and discredited his poor research he would have felt humiliated.'

'Do you feel at all cheated by him because you won't see him go on trial for what he has done?'

Kate considered this and then said: 'I don't know really. I think it would have been an anxious time for myself and my aunt, waiting for the trial to start and hoping for the right verdict. And even if he had been found guilty he might have appealed against his conviction. It could have dragged on and ruined the last years of my aunt's life. At least this way we have the chance to put it behind us and try to rebuild our lives.

'I'm going to finish Sophie's book and have it published. That's the only thing I can do for her now. There will be no need to refer to Edgar or his book. I will just present the facts about Donizetti as Sophie saw them and make sure that the book puts the record straight once and for all.'

They were silent for a moment and then Aldo said: 'I am sorry to have to tell you that we now have Massimo Rovigo in custody. He was arrested late on Friday night in connection with a big, multi-agency operation to round up some of the gangs responsible for bringing in *clandestini*.'

Seeing Kate's bewildered expression, he said: 'Illegal immigrants. He is only a small part of a big people-trafficking operation. But he has been discovered to have been employing some of them at his furniture warehouse. While we were having dinner at La Torre, the Carabinieri were searching his premises at San Pellegrino Terme. They discovered some rather primitive living accommodation in a building behind the warehouse where people were staying. One of his assistants told the Carabinieri where he had gone for the evening, which is why they suddenly appeared in the doorway of the room at the restaurant.'

'Poor Luisa!'

'Yes, I am sorry for her. Basically she is a decent girl.'

'Thank goodness he turned up at the dinner, because his evidence about the weight of the wardrobe was crucial.'

'Well, I had called in a few favours to get his arrest delayed until later that night. Luckily it all worked out well.'

With a little smile he said: 'Sorry about the slight confusion with the Carabinieri, they obviously hadn't read the email, but fortunately I was able to get them to back off for a while.'

'Thank you for sending your officers to look for finger prints on the inside of the wardrobe doors. I hadn't thought of that.'

Aldo coughed and gave an embarrassed smile. 'I would love to be able to take the credit for painstaking forensic work, but I am afraid that I have to admit that I never actually sent anyone out to the warehouse to dust the wardrobe for finger prints. It was just a shot in the dark.'

'Well you certainly had me convinced!'

'It was Steve who gave me the idea when he suggested to Edgar that he deliberately wore surgical gloves in the apartment. It was just a lucky guess that he might have taken them off while he was still in the wardrobe and left finger prints on the doors.'

'Thank you for everything you did to make him confess,' Kate said.

'I wanted to be able to put right what I had done wrong in the first place, that was all. You did most of the work. You have been very courageous and determined. You never gave up and you always believed in your instincts. After all, you knew your cousin better than anyone.'

Aldo then took some euros out of his wallet and put them down on the table.

'I'm sorry, but I am going to have to get back to the office. I have a mountain of paperwork waiting for me. It never stops, I'm afraid.'

They got up from the table and walked across the square to the covered staircase. Then he turned to face her and said: 'Arrividerci, Signora Kate, I am going to miss you.' He gently kissed her on both cheeks and then they found themselves hugging each other emotionally. A few seconds later he turned and walked away under the archways into Piazza Duomo to go back through the Città Alta to the Commissariato. He never looked back.

She watched his retreating figure, wondering why she had ever thought of him as small. What might have happened between them if Steve had not come out to join her in Bergamo?

Aldo was now out of sight but she remained by the staircase, lost in thought, staring unseeingly at the façade of the Colleoni Chapel, thinking about how different things might have been.

Suddenly she felt a hand on her shoulder. She turned and saw Steve's smiling face.

'Have you been crying?' he asked anxiously.

'No, it's okay, I'm fine,' she reassured him.

'What have you got there, some shopping?' he

asked, pointing to the carrier bag.
'No, it's the files and notebooks for Sophie's book. Aldo has just given them to me. He searched Edgar's house over the weekend and thinks he has got them all back for me. I'm going to finish Sophie's book and get it published. At least it is one thing I can do for her.'
'And, of course you will be able to include the letter from Donizetti.'
'Of course! I want to put the record straight just as Sophie did.'
'Three deaths because of one letter written by a 19th century composer. It could have been a plot for one of his operas. But at the end of the day, was it really worth it, do you think?'
'Yes, for once I'm on Sophie's side. Whatever else you might say about her she stuck to her principles. People should check and double check their facts if they are going to be writers. If everyone was as sloppy as Edgar, the world would be full of false information. She wanted to write the complete truth, even down to giving details about Donizetti's illness and death. He had a degenerative illness caused by syphilis so, apparently, it wouldn't have been pleasant. Edgar must have felt in some kind of weird way that it was his duty to protect Donizetti's reputation.'
'All the same, for Sophie to lose her life over it….' Steve said, shaking his head.
'I know what you mean, but she would never have expected it to come to that. She was used to always getting her own way. She had never come up against someone completely deranged like Edgar before.'
'Let's go and have a last glass of wine in Piazza Vecchia,' Steve suggested. 'I've got something to

tell you.'

They went back to the bar and sat at their favourite table next to the statue of Torquato Tasso.

When Steve had ordered their drinks he said: 'I have been having a chat with your friend Roberto this morning. He is very relieved that the investigations into Sophie and Jean's deaths are complete and he says he thinks he has now managed to make some kind of peace with Signora Mattozzi.'

'That's good,' Kate said.

'Apparently he has already arranged for the furniture to be brought back by a reliable removal firm and he has told her she can put it wherever she likes. He says he is going to look out for her in the future and make sure she isn't short of anything. He thinks that is what his late father would have wanted.'

'I'm pleased about that,' Kate said.

'He has also helped me to arrange a little surprise for you. Through his contacts he has managed to get us a room for three nights at a hotel overlooking Lago d'Iseo. I thought we could go back to the hotel now and pack our things and then go there by train this afternoon.'

'Is the hotel at Sarnico?'

'No, it is on the other side of the lake at Sulzano, a resort directly opposite the island in the middle of the lake, which is called Monte Isola.

'I thought you might like to go to the island. Apparently our room looks out over the water and has a lovely view and there are regular boats going backwards and forwards to the island.'

'It sounds wonderful, but what about Aunt Edna? I ought to get back to England to make sure she is all right and talk to her about all that has happened.'

Steve said: 'I've spoken to her just now and she

thinks it is a wonderful idea and that you deserve a little break. After you rang and broke the news to her about Edgar's confession, I asked Terry Batts to go and see her. I wanted him to make sure she was all right and to try to explain everything to her. From what he has told me, it sounds as though she is coming to terms with what has happened. She told me she was very sorry for Jean as well as for Sophie.'

'That is so typical of Aunt Edna.'

'She said she was glad Edgar killed himself because it showed remorse.'

'Well, I'm not too sure about that,' Kate said.

'But mainly I think she is glad that there isn't going to be a long trial and a harrowing wait for a verdict. If Edgar had pleaded not guilty, with all the money he had available to spend on lawyers, I wouldn't have liked to predict how it would have gone. He might even have been able to persuade them to let him go back to America and then they would never have managed to get him back to serve his sentence.

'Edna has said she will never get over losing Sophie but she is going to try hard to adapt to life without her.

'Amazingly, it sounds as though Adam Leighton has come up with a good idea. He has offered her the cottage in the grounds and suggested that she has it converted to suit her needs. She will have all the facilities that the home has to offer, available literally on her doorstep, but she will be able to live independently. I think she said it was the cottage that the gardener used to live in.'

Kate smiled: 'No, she will mean the cottage that the housekeeper, Mrs Gardiner, used to live in years ago with her husband, who did odd jobs for my aunt and uncle. It is a nice house.'

'Anyway, Edna sounded excited about the idea. Apparently Terry Batts has a brother who is an architect and he is already drawing up plans for it. She says it will be good to have a new project to get her teeth into.'

'So, Simon and Adam will finally be able to get their hands on my uncle's study,' Kate said thoughtfully.

'Yes, things have worked out well for them as well,' Steve said.

'Simon will forget Sophie quickly now, I think. But what about poor Ernesto, how will he ever get over it?'

'Oh, he'll bounce back,' Steve said. 'Another attractive woman will come into the restaurant one day and be charmed when she is given a free jug of Valcalepio Bianco and soon enough she will start accepting other complimentary extras.' He gave her a mischievous smile.

'At least he's got Anton to look out for him. He seems to be a decent chap,' Kate said thoughtfully.

'And you've got me to look out for you.'

'Have I?'

'Yes, of course you have. I've got over my resentment about the whole redundancy thing now and I think I could take to this kind of life, travelling around with you and taking photographs for your feature articles and books. And I want to be there for you from now on, watching your back. When I think about that lunatic and how he could have killed you in his car, it terrifies me.'

'And I thought he was so charming when he took me out for lunch at the funicular bar. Yet he could have dropped one of his little sachets of powder into my drink and I could have become another victim.'

'He was probably a man who enjoyed sedating women so that he had power over them. He may not have felt able to cope with women when they were conscious. It occurred to me that he may have even sedated Jean before he spent the night with her. That could be why she was sleeping so soundly when Luisa screamed after the shock of finding poor Sophie dead in bed the next morning.'

Kate thought about this for a moment while the waitress put their drinks down in front of them and then asked: 'Do you really not mind having to give up being a policeman?'

'I don't suppose you ever really give up being a policeman, just like you will never really give up being a writer. There will always be some little problem to look into, some wrong to be put right, somewhere, I'm sure. But that is what you and I seem to be good at, isn't it?'

They raised their glasses and as they clinked them together they heard the sound of breaking glass. Kate turned and saw that a plump pigeon had swooped on to the crumbs on the next table, sending all the wine glasses flying in different directions, before they shattered into pieces after landing on the ancient paving stones of Piazza Vecchia.

ABOUT THE AUTHOR

Val Culley was a journalist for more than 30 years, working in newspapers, television and PR, until her love of Italy started her writing about her favourite locations as a freelance travel writer. Val has combined her interest in Italy with her fascination for detective fiction in her first novel, **Death in the High City**. Set in one of Val's favourite places, Bergamo in Lombardia, the novel introduces detective duo Kate Butler, a freelance journalist, and Steve Bartorelli, a retired Detective Chief Inspector.

Val lives in Leicestershire with her husband, Jon Culley, a national newspaper sports writer. They have two grown up children.

She is now looking forward to Butler and Bartorelli visiting another beautiful part of Italy….

If you would like to find out more about Bergamo visit www.bestofbergamo.com.